DATE DUE

COCOON

COCOON

DAVID SAPERSTEIN

THORNDIKE PRESS • THORNDIKE, MAINE

Library of Congress Cataloging in Publication Data:

Saperstein, David.
  Cocoon.

  1. Large type books. I. Title.
  [PS3569.A584C6 1986]   813'.54   86-22970
  ISBN 0-89621-755-8 (lg. print : alk. paper)

Large Print edition available in North America by arrangement with Susan Schulman Literary Agency, Inc.

Cover design by Jonathan Graves.

*The quote that appears on p. 366 is from an article by Robert Jastrow which appeared in *Natural History* magazine, and is used by permission.

To

Ellen-Mae, Ivan and Ilena,
for their love and patience . . .

and

To my dear brother Bert, who
always encouraged and believed.

● **1** ●

The large cruiser moved slowly down the canal past the sleeping residents of Coral Gables. Schools of leaping mullet made the only sound other than the chug of the powerful twin inboard diesels of the *Manta III*. The houses along the canal were sparkling shades of pastel pink, blue, and green, and the lawns were perfectly manicured. The docks were immaculate with at least two boats moored alongside each one. It was very quiet and very early.

The *Manta III* turned into the main channel and left the tranquil, misty scene behind. The engines responded as Jack Fischer urged them up to six knots. He stood on the flying bridge, spun the wheel hard to the right, and then positioned the *Manta III* to the left of the channel markers. It was a mile run to the sea wall and then out into the open ocean.

Jack sipped his coffee and breathed in deeply. This was the best time of day for him. The rim of a red sun rose in front of him, and there was peace and quiet. All was well this morning, and if those folks below were a little strange and secretive, well, that wasn't any of his business. The short bald guy was obviously in charge, even though he never spoke.

A pelican flew across the path of the boat in search of breakfast, which reminded Jack of the buttered roll he had not eaten. He found it and took a healthy bite. Yes, it was going to be a good week. These folks were paying top dollar for the *Manta III*.

He glanced back toward the stern and eyed their equipment. He counted ten scuba tanks. There was an assortment of flippers, weights, masks, and markers. The large suction pump and hose were off to the left. A vacuum cleaner of sorts. The other cases were unopened so he could only speculate as to what they held.

This was not the first diving expedition he had chartered. There were always treasure hunters, although it was rare that they didn't have their own boats. Actually, these people had never said they were after treasure. In fact, they hadn't really told him the purpose of the trip.

He glanced over to the map and the overlay they had supplied. It marked an area that he had fished many times. It was just to the southeast edge of the reef. In season, that was a good spot for trolling for barracuda. He took another bite of his roll and a sip of the coffee.

There was a noise on the deck and he turned to see one of the three divers moving a crate to the center of the deck. Jack watched as he opened the crate and lifted out what appeared to be a small transmitter. There were two coils of silver wire that he placed on the deck. He then turned and began to climb up to the flying bridge.

Jack kept his eyes on the channel markers and then judged that they were about five minutes from the open sea. The young man, was his name Hal or Hank, came onto the bridge and smiled.

"How's it going, Captain?"

"Fine . . . we'll be out in a few minutes and I can open this tub up. Then we can make some time. It's going to be a great day."

The young man looked at the rising sun and smiled. "Can I use the outriggers? I want to string an antenna like this." He outlined the shape of a triangle with his fingers, indicating that he would use the tips of the outriggers as the base and vortex would be attached to the stern. Jack could find no reason to say no, and he was curious to know why they needed a transmitter.

"What kind of radio is that?" he asked.

"Oh, well, it's not really a radio . . . just sort of a direction finder for working under the sea. Actually, it's a new piece of equipment that we designed and were going to test out today." The young man seemed uneasy, but Jack dismissed that as he gave permission.

"You're Hal?" Jack asked.

The man looked up as he was leaving the bridge. "No, Harry. Hal is the guy with the blond hair." He disappeared from view as he went down the ladder to the deck.

Jack heard the squeak of the pulley attached to the outrigger. His thoughts then quickly turned to the sound of a motor ahead of him.

The sleek bow of a Hatteras emerged from the canal that led to the site of the new condominium dock. That was some place . . . brand new and built in record time. It was the talk of the Gables. And what a name . . . Antares. It took the newspaper two weeks to track down the owners and another week to confirm that Antares was an obscure star in the constellation of Scorpius. Why in God's name they called the place Antares was a mystery to everyone.

The Hatteras was out into the channel now and in front of him by about fifty yards. As the bow swung around he could read the name – *Terra Time*. He observed that her outriggers were spread and that thin silver wires were attached to the tips and joined on the bow. There was a young blond man attaching the lead to a double of the transmitter on his own deck. They were passing the sea wall now and the sleek Hatteras was opening up. Her heading was due east into the rising sun. Jack opened up his engines and turned toward the southeast and the reef. Behind him other charters were emerging from the main channel and he had to pay attention to the traffic. He reminded himself to ask about that antenna setup later. Now he had to get down to the lower bridge and get on the radio to check the weather. His customers had also asked him to check to see if there would be many boats in their area today. Jack took a quick look around and then set the auto pilot down to the lower controls. He gathered up his coffee and roll and left the chart and overlay in place. One of these days he would run a mike connection and speaker up to the flying bridge on a permanent basis, but for now he would have to go below.

Harry had finished attaching the antenna setup and was opening another crate as Jack negotiated the last rung of the ladder and dropped to the main deck. The crate contained a gas cylinder and what appeared to be a shiny metallic cloth. Jack felt that this was going to be a different kind of treasure hunt. As he turned to enter the bridge, the bald man emerged from below decks.

The man nodded. He was short, perhaps five feet, two inches, but extremely well built. He appeared to be in his early forties. He had stripped off his clothes and was wearing only a pale green bikini bathing suit. Jack nodded back and walked into the cabin as the man passed him and knelt next to Harry.

There was something strange about that guy, Jack thought. He seemed to glow, yet he wasn't sweating. As a matter of fact, he was as dry as a bone . . . Then it hit Jack. The man had no hair. Not just on his head, but on any part of his body. Jack glanced back to confirm his thought. Yes, no hair. Probably a result of a severe case of scarlet fever . . . too bad.

The radio crackled as he turned the "On" switch and moved the squelch knob. He punched in channel 27.55 and keyed the mike. "This is KAAL-9911 . . . *Manta Three* — Phil, you out yet? Over."

A voice came back immediately. "Hey, Jack, how are you this morning? Yeah, we're out about five miles . . . gonna take a shot at some sails over in the Stream. Picked up two yesterday . . . What are you up to? Over."

Jack keyed again. "I got a party for the week

here . . . gonna do some diving over by the south reef. Anyone say they were heading that way? Over."

"No . . . no way. That's been real dead over there for the past two weeks. Not even a stray cuda. Strange, because it was really hot, and then . . . nothing. Let me know if you see anything over there . . . I'll give you a call around noon . . . over."

"Roger, Phil – what the hell!" Jack was startled as a huge shadow nearly blocked his view. He saw a flash of silver then realized that Harry and baldy had launched an enormous silver balloon. "Sorry, Phil, I got to go . . . no problem, just have to talk to these folks about rules and regulations . . . okay . . . I'll look for your call around noon. Over and out."

He placed the mike on its hook and pulled the accelerator back to slow. The engines responded immediately and their forward motion slowed. The swells caught the bow and the boat began to roll. Jack spun around and found the bald man standing directly behind him. For a moment he was startled and then realized that he was looking into the coldest eyes he had ever seen. It was as though he was looking at them for the first time. They were ice blue (hadn't they been brown before?), and the man did not blink.

"What did you guys do with that balloon? I don't think we're allowed to let things like that go without the proper permission."

The man's expression didn't change. "We are," he said. Then he asked, "How long before we reach the reef?"

"About an hour, if the sea stays this way . . . Wait a minute . . . What do you mean *we* are? I mean, I think I ought to know if there are any more surprises."

A voice emerged from below, then the body of the man who had originally made the charter arrangements. His name was Bright – Amos Bright. When he came aboard in the dark that morning he had been wearing jeans and sneakers and a sweat shirt. Now, as he came up onto the bridge he was wearing a metallic diving suit. It was copper-colored and had wires hanging from the shoulders and knees. Mr. Bright was finishing his apology. " . . . really sorry, Captain. I should have told you . . . it's my fault. That's a high-altitude marker to test some new equipment . . . that stuff out on the deck. We're going to bounce an underwater signal off it and make some calculations. There won't be any more surprises, and I'm truly sorry." He had stepped between Baldy and the captain. Harry followed behind Amos and placed his hand on Baldy's shoulder. The shiny little man turned and they both walked to the stern of the boat.

The moment of silence was now interrupted by a toot from the horn of an approaching charter boat. Jack realized that he had better get under way. The traffic was getting heavy and he was an obstruction. "Okay . . . okay . . . I was just startled . . . didn't mean to yell. Please tell him I'm sorry."

Bright answered, "No harm done." Then he turned to join the two men at the stern.

Jack was about to ask him about the Hatteras and the antenna, but Amos was moving away. *None of my business; besides, the money is good,* he thought. He pushed the throttle. Once again the diesels responded and soon they were quickly making twenty five knots. The skyline of Miami Beach was visible off the stern, but the near shore was dominated by the new Antares complex.

Now, nearly thirty minutes had passed since he went back up to the flying bridge. They would be at the reef site in another fifteen minutes. It had been a while since he had seen another boat. The party seemed to sense that they were nearing their destination because they had all assembled on deck. The only one missing was the bald man.

There were a total of six men on deck. Mr.

Bright, Harry, Hal the blond, two other men dressed in the copper suits, and another short, hairless man who could have been Baldy's brother. The only difference was that this man was jet-black. It was as though he had been sprayed with a shiny black enamel paint. He stood apart from the others and looked up toward the sky. Jack's eyes followed his line of sight and saw the large silver balloon hovering over the boat. He couldn't tell how far above it was because he hadn't really had a chance to see how big it was close up. Now it seemed about five hundred yards away and slightly off to port. For a moment Jack thought he saw two balloons. He rubbed his eyes and looked again, but there was only one.

The sonar pings off the ocean floor came quicker and he knew he was nearing the reef. He eased the engines back and checked the overlay on his chart. Jack figured that he was about a half mile west of the site and slightly to the north. He turned the wheel and peered out for the marker, which was the reef buoy number forty three Green. It lay off the starboard, about one hundred fifty yards. He swung the wheel so that they would pass to the south of the buoy. That would bring them straight to the site.

As Jack reached for the ice chest on the flying bridge, the white bald man came on deck. He was carrying a black rod. Attached to the rod were two wires. One wire ran to a silver disk that was stuck to the center of his bald head. The other wire was held in his hand and had a disk at the end of it.

Jack looked down and pulled a cold beer out of the ice and closed the Styrofoam chest. He opened the can and looked up. The second wire was now attached to the black man's head. Both knelt at the bow and placed a hand on the antenna wire that ran from the outriggers. The black rod was being lowered into the water by Mr. Bright. As the rod sank into the greenish water above the outer reef, Mr. Bright stepped back below the bridge. All the others followed except Hal, who knelt and moved some switches on the equipment.

A faint humming sound reached Jack's ears just as the antenna wire began to glow. It was a sunny morning, yet the light from the wire was brighter than sunlight. It was almost as though a triangular welding machine was in operation. Suddenly, a bright red glow appeared beneath the water off to starboard. Jack estimated that was the position of the black rod. The glow broke the surface and a red beam of light flashed directly up to the silver balloon hovering above the boat. The humming increased. Jack didn't realize that Harry had come up onto the bridge, but he felt his presence and turned to him. "What the hell is going on here?"

Harry put his finger up to his lips to silence Jack and whispered, "Just watch . . . we'll explain shortly."

There was yelling from below as Mr. Bright and the two other copper-clothed men were pointing off to the starboard beyond the red beam. Entering the water was a blue beam. Jack glanced up to see the source of the blue beam was a second balloon. So he had seen it, after all. Mr. Bright shouted up to him, "Captain . . . over there! That's the place we want to anchor. Right at that spot. Quickly. Please." Mr. Bright turned and signaled to Hal, who immediately turned off the transmitter device. One of the copper men reeled in the black rod and the bald twins let go of the antenna. The beams stopped, but Jack had already marked the spot by triangulating it with the buoy and reef edge.

Jack looked at Harry. "Now, what the hell is this all about?" Harry, who was obviously excited, assured Jack that Mr. Bright would explain it a lot better than he could. The important thing was to get to the spot quickly. He then scampered down the ladder to the deck below.

Jack started the engines and eased the *Manta III* toward starboard and the indicated area. He took a sip of beer but it had a metallic taste and he set it down on the compass. He looked up and then his eyes went quickly back to the compass. It was spinning wildly and undulating so that the needle was hitting the glass covering the face of the compass. It made a clicking sound against the glass. The closer he got to their destination, the faster the needle spun, and when they were directly over the spot, the glass popped off the compass, spilling his beer. He moved back as this happened, which was fortunate because the needle flew out of the compass, missing him by inches and whizzing off into the air. *What the hell is going on here?* he thought. Then, angered to his boiling point, he stopped the engines and rushed down the ladder to the deck below. But there was no deck, only a bright flash, and then a blue black void as his body seemed to melt,

• 2 •

If death had a smell, then that was the first sensation Jack was aware of as he awoke. The second feeling was that his feet had been on a vibrator for twenty years. As he opened his eyes, the pleasant face of Mr. Bright came into focus. Harry was there, too, removing a sticky white substance from Jack's neck.

Mr. Bright spoke first. "Captain, please . . . I want you to collect yourself and try not to be angry. Relax if you can, but please just listen to me. I am going to tell you a story that you may not believe, but you will certainly come to believe it. Let me also say that we need you, and that we hope you will come to understand our requirements, and you will continue to help us. We thought that what we had to do here, we could do ourselves, without . . . shall we say . . . outside help . . . but we know that this is impossible now. Please listen, and try to understand."

20

Jack settled back on the bunk and felt calmed by Mr. Bright's voice. Harry set the white goo aside and smiled reassuringly. The deathly smell seemed almost pleasant and his body stopped vibrating. He became aware of activity on the deck above as he turned his attention to Mr. Bright. "What happened to me? Did I fall . . . and what the hell are you guys doing up there?" Then he remembered the compass needle and he felt frightened. "What are you going to do to me. . . . to my boat?"

Mr. Bright began to speak calmly and quietly. "Jack — may I call you Jack? — do you know exactly where you are? I mean, do you know what this place is called . . . I mean, this reef?"

"Yes," Jack answered. "It's called The Stones. I fish out here all the time."

"Good," said Bright. "And do you know why it's called The Stones?"

"Yes . . . because of those slabs below. Some people say they are from a lost city or continent . . . "

Bright smiled and continued. "Fine. Now let me tell you what this place really is . . . what those slabs really are . . . and who we are . . . and . . . " — he sighed — " . . . why we are here."

Bright spoke for almost an hour. Jack

interrupted three times — once to get a beer because fear had made his mouth go bone dry, once to play spy, and once to ask the black bald man to take his face off again.

Actually, the story was simple. Believing it was difficult. He could understand the words, but not the concept. He was just not prepared. Now he was on deck, and, by his own oath, he was a part of the team. Three of the party were on deck with him: Harry, Mr. Bright, and Hal. The shiny black, whose name was Bill, was in a small yellow rubber raft about ten yards off the stern. The white bald man and the two others in copper suits were working underwater on the reef. Amos Bright had removed his copper suit and was dressed again.

The balloons were still overhead, but now he knew only one was a balloon, and the other was a spacecraft. What was it they had told him? Yes, it was not really a spacecraft, but a guide ship. Their mother ship was a spacecraft from Antares and was moored on the far side of the Moon. This balloonlike vehicle was expendable and would self-destruct after it served its purpose.

Now there was some excitement on the deck and Bill was shouting in a shrill voice, "It's coming . . . it's coming!"

Off to the left of the raft, the surface filled

with bubbles and two copper-suited divers popped up. They were followed by a canister . . . no . . . more like a large white roll-on deodorant container. It was covered with a white gooey substance. Its presence filled the air with the same smell that Jack had experienced earlier.

The copper divers guided the canister toward the *Manta III*. It took ten minutes and a great effort to lift it aboard. Five minutes after it was on deck a second canister popped up. Within two hours there were six more, and the *Manta III* resembled a World War II P.T. boat with torpedo tubes on bow and stern. It was only after the seventh canister was aboard that the bald white man came to the surface. Jack had forgotten about him, but at this point it did not surprise Jack that the man was able to stay below for such a long period of time. It didn't even seem strange that he wore no scuba tanks.

Mr. Bright had a few words with baldy white and then turned to Jack. "This is the final member of our unit, Jack. I'd like to introduce you." He gestured toward the shiny white figure who now moved toward Jack. The eyes were no longer icy and menacing. They were brown and friendly. "This is James . . . uh . . . Jim, yes, Jim is better."

Jack extended his hand, and Jim did likewise.

The vibration went through Jack like a shot and he pulled back. "Sorry," said Jim. "I have to control that better."

Jack said it was okay. Mr. Bright suggested that it was getting late and that they should head back to the dock. That would be the dock at the Antares condominium complex.

As the rest of the group packed their crate and removed their suits, Jack climbed to the flying bridge. Hal was on the bow pulling up the anchor, and he waved an okay to the bridge. Jack started the engines and glanced at the compass. It was repaired and working perfectly. He turned the bow toward Miami and reached for another beer. He also decided to stay up on the flying bridge by himself. There was much to think about and only one hour to make a decision that might affect the world . . . his world, and his race – the ones they called "dwellers." He definitely belonged to the "dwellers."

• 3 •

Atlantis was a misnomer. Actually, the island had been named Antares Quad Three by the visitors. It had been a thriving Antarean colony for almost five hundred Earth years. It was a large island, stretching from the islands commonly known as the Azores westward to the islands of the Bahamas. Its northern shore extended nearly to Greenland, and to the southernmost point of the island was a mere two hundred miles from what is now Brazil.

Antares Quad Three was a trading post, and in its final days, it was a miliary base and the site of the signing of the Quad Three Peace Pact that settled the space wars in this quadrant of our galaxy. That happened seventy Earth years before the colony was destroyed. Antares Quad Three had been wiped off the face of the Earth five thousand Earth years ago when a section of the planet Saturn, having torn away from its orbit, passed close to Earth. The inhabitants of Antares had ample warning about the impending disaster and were able to evacuate their colony. At that time they chose to leave a portion of their army behind.

Jack's mind raced. The idea was overwhelming, but he realized that he had to understand. He forced himself to organize his thoughts and go over the story from the beginning, just as Mr. Amos Bright, Antarean force leader, had related to him.

He began with The Stones. "Yes," Jack had said. "I know this place . . . we call it The Stones because of the slabs that are beneath the water around the reef." Then Bright had said, "I want you to picture a large island filling most of what you now call the Atlantic Ocean. There was an island here once. You actually suspect that, and you call it Atlantis. Well, the name was Antares Quad Three. It was our colony . . . here, on this planet, in this place. We were thousands there because we were settling this quadrant, the third quadrant, of the galaxy our planets share. You call it the Milky Way.

"In the beginning we avoided contact with the 'dwellers' here because they were quite primitive, and we did not want to interfere. Besides, we had our hands full with some rather aggressive and advanced beings on a planet near the red star you call Rigel. In any case, we

26

finally had a minor space war on our hands. It lasted sixty-one earth years and ended with Rigel's joining in a pact of peace that is in effect to this day.

"After the treaty, this colony became a thriving center of interplanetary trade and government. I wish it were here today so that you could see it. Beings from all over our galaxy gathered . . . different languages . . . customs . . . evolutions. So much was happening everywhere you looked. Once we had a governmental meeting that lasted three years here, and important ambassadors were in residence here. At one time we maintained forty-seven different atmospheres for the conference . . . "

At that point, Bright had a faraway look in his eyes and Jack had asked for a beer, which Harry brought to him. The group leader continued. "I speak of those times because I was here. Believe me. We have death in our system, but it is at our choosing."

"Then interest in this place started to wane as we opened exploration beyond our galaxy. Ships had been developed that enabled us to enter the black holes in space and explore other galaxies. The first galaxy we explored was in Andromeda. Ah . . . those were times. We were like children again with a new toy. Our efforts had diminished, but our leaders saw fit to leave a modest army behind in case our newfound allies had second thoughts about the pact. That is why we are here now."

Jack had interrupted again and asked about the army. He had been in the American Army in Vietnam ten years earlier. He had been an artillery spotter. Somehow, he felt he was in the enemy camp and he wanted to know about their strength. He was sure Bright knew why he was asking, but still he believed that Bright told him the truth.

"An army is an army," Bright had said. "Ours numbered nine hundred forty-one, and they were some of the best combat soldiers we have. They fought in units of ten, with each unit possessing a unit leader, and nine specialties. There were ninety such units. Every ten units had a group leader." Bright had been a group leader at one time and, in fact, still carried that title. "Then there were thirty transport beings, again in units of ten with a unit leader. They had a group leader. Their responsibility was, of course, transportation and logistics for the fighting units. Finally, there was what you would call a commander. The hairless ones who are with us . . . the light and the dark ones . . . they are commanders. They are special beings and we must honor them with great respect."

Bill had just smiled and then reached under

his chin and peeled off his shiny black face. Behind it was another face. There were eyes that were slits and they wrapped around both sides of the head. Through the slits Jack could see a glow, but no more. There was no nose . . . no mouth . . . no ears . . . no hair. Then Jack heard words inside his brain. The words were not coming through his ears . . . but were just present in his brain. The voice was Bill's voice, and it told him that he was telepathing to Jack. He then told Jack he could read his mind and control his body if he chose to. He could do this to all beings that were carbon-based. That is why he was a commander. He then put his face back on and left the room. At that point Jack didn't want to know any more. He believed.

Bright continued the story of Antares Quad Three "About five thousand years ago they became aware of a celestial accident that was going to affect their colony. A comet had passed close to the planet Saturn and had torn off a rather large chunk of matter. It had also affected the orbit of the planet and caused debris to be scattered out into space. Thus, the rings of Saturn. The large piece of the planet broke out of the planet's orbit and was pulled along by the comet for one hundred years. Then it broke free and by pure luck . . . bad luck . . . headed for Earth. The inhabitants of the colony had sixty-three years' warning, so it was not a disaster as far as life was concerned. In fact, the decision was made to alter the orbit of the earth as much as possible so that there would not be a direct collision, but rather a glancing blow, at the worst. In order to accomplish this, a thruster was set on a predetermined spot on the Earth and ignited. Of course, the dwellers in the area were evacuated, but they were unable to understand what was happening. The effect worked and, with some minor disturbances to life here, the planet was saved. Our calculations showed that the chunk of matter would pass directly over our colony and destroy it. So we evacuated. However, just as a precaution it was decided that the army was to be left behind. They were put into a form of life that you would understand as suspended animation and sealed deep in the rock of the island. They were left behind. The disaster happened and the colony – in fact, the entire island – was destroyed. Eventually, that piece of Saturn became the planet you call Venus.

"We have passed this way many times since that destruction and you have seen us from time to time. You have advanced and perhaps you are ready to understand more about our Universe. We shall see. Right now we have a need for our army in a place far from here. So, to put it as simply as possible, we have returned to get our soldiers. They are sealed in containers . . . like cocoons . . . under the slabs that you call The Stones. We have to get them out, and we need your help. We mean no harm, and when we have our soldiers we will go. The cocoons must be opened and the soldiers reprogrammed at our base in Miami. Will you help?"

Those words rang in his ears. Why in the name of what-ever did these advanced space travelers need him – Jack Fischer – and his boat to raise nine hundred forty one cocoons from under the sea floor? Why not just buy a boat – or build one – and get the army out? And why was he believing all this fantastic mumbo-jumbo, anyway?

He had answered, "Yes, what do you want me to do?"

Bright had said, "Just help us . . . do what we ask, and stay with us until we are finished."

"How long?" Jack had asked.

"Three months. It will take three months to raise all and bring them up to date," answered Bright. "We will pay you well and we will make you a very important man on this planet."

Now Jack sat on the flying bridge and once again steered toward the sun, although this time it was setting in the west. He was still in shock and undecided as to what to do. Those commanders frightened him. They could probably will him dead or, at the very least, fry his brain. He was also dying to have a look inside one of those cocoons, and the idea of living five thousand years hadn't exactly been lost on him, either. Neither had the promise of money and importance.

The skyline of Miami was on the horizon, silhouetted by the setting sun. He swung the bow toward the channel outside Coral Gables. Off to the left he saw the Hatteras wending its way home, too. He had forgotten about that boat. What was it called . . . *Terra Time?* Then he remembered that he had asked Phil to call at noon. The radio had been off, and Phil would have the Coast Guard alerted. But there had been no Coast Guard. More mysteries. He wished he had the mike up on the bridge again. Once again he reflected back on the story that Bright had told. The clincher had been the part about their base. That was something he had to see.

• 4 •

Bernard Lewis was once known as Bernie Lefkowitz. His wife, Rose, was always Rose, except at their wedding, when the rabbi had called her Rifka. Their red Buick was a gift from their son, Craig, which made it a business expense because Bernie was still listed as the Florida representative of Bernal Woolens, and that meant that it wasn't really a gift at all. Bernie understood that . . . Rose thought it was a marvelous thing for her son to do.

When Bernie was active with the company in New York, few people ever asked him twice about the Al in Bernal Woolens. The first time one asked, he answered, "I don't talk about Al anymore." And one knew he didn't.

This morning Bernie and Rose were driving, in their new red Buick, to look at the Antares condominium complex. They were in the market for larger quarters. Bernie wanted to move because in the past eight months more than fifteen people had passed away at their present condominium complex, Sunset Village. The more he lived there, the more Bernie felt that it should have been called End of the Trail. He was depressed. Rose had explained, "Sweetheart, old people die, and Miami is full of old people."

Bernie answered in a tone that was similar to his answer about Al: "I don't want to talk about old." So they were looking.

After turning into the driveway of Antares, the Buick moved along a dirt road edged with palm trees that were still unplanted. The roots were wrapped in burlap balls and the trees were dying.

Bernie puffed on his cigar and tapped his diamond pinky ring on the red steering wheel. He pointed to the trees and said to Rose, "Well, so far, at least here only trees are dying. . . ."

"I don't want to talk about it," she said.

He grunted and swerved to hit a pothole. "Got it." He smiled.

But Rose was not responsive this morning. Looking for a new place meant leaving her bridge ladies. That was unthinkable, but deep down she knew it was going to happen. Kismet, she thought, and she began to hum "Stranger in Paradise" as the car pulled up to the unfinished entrance of Antares Building A.

Tony Stranger sat behind his desk and stared in disbelief at the couple seated across from him. They were on the verge of killing each other. He had learned a half hour ago that to interfere with these people was to risk his life. At the moment they were discussing the wedding of a niece – his brother's daughter who had been married six years ago. She was reminding him that they served chicken and no hors d'oeuvres and that they were "cheap, no good, I-don't-know-whats", and that she would never have them as house guests after the way they treated their son Harold with such a cheap "I-don't-know-what" gift for his wedding five years ago after they had given such a generous gift to that cheap "I-don't-know-what" daughter and the bum she married, so they didn't need a larger apartment because they didn't need an extra guest room . . . and that was the final word.

"So, Arthur, what will it be?" she asked, pointing to the floor plan laid out on the desk. "This apartment, with one guest room for fifty thousand? Or the one with two guest rooms for fifty-seven that I won't live in?"

Arthur Perlman blew his nose and studied the plans. He smiled at Tony and then leaned closer to the floor plans. He then turned his face toward his wife so that Tony could not see him mouth the words, *Bess, I'm going to kill you.* He sat up and said to Tony, "Does the condo with one guest room have a patio on the corner?"

Tony checked his available list and found a corner apartment on the fifth floor of Building A. "Yes, Mr. Perlman, we have one left."

"Sure, they always have just one left." He looked at Bess and said, "Okay, love of my life, you have it. You'll pay it off with the insurance, because in this place I'll be dead in two months."

Arthur Perlman was saying those words as Bernie and Rose walked into the salesroom. Bernie stopped dead in his tracks. Rose smiled and said, "See, people are dying all over Miami. You can't get away from it by moving, unless you want to move to Alaska, and even in Alaska people die, but from the cold."

Bernie walked over to the wall and studied a floor plan. Tony said, "I'll be a few minutes, folks. There are brochures and more floor plans on that table and some coffee, if you'd like."

Tony then turned back to the Perlmans and handed them an application form, credit form, and insurance form. "You folks can fill these out and bring them back, or mail them in.

They take about two weeks to process. We will need a deposit when you return the forms. It's all spelled out there in plain English." He chuckled a little and added, "That's the law these days . . . it has to be in English so you can understand. I'm sure you'll be very happy here just as soon as we finish the construction. But Building A is ready for occupancy immediately, and as I told you, it's almost full. You were fortunate to come in when you did." His voice was louder than it had been, and it was not lost on Bernie, who was at this time pouring coffee into a plastic cup. He didn't notice that the coffee machine had not yet filled the glass coffeepot he now held in his hand, and that hot coffee was spilling down onto the hot plate and the brochures.

Rose shouted, "Bernie, put back the coffee!" He muttered something about stupid machines and placed the carafe back on the hot plate with such force that the puddle of coffee that had collected there splashed onto his oyster-colored slacks and white cane shoes.

Tony made no move to help, and he was amused by the whole scene. He had his orders: discourage everyone he could from buying an apartment. He was one of the worst salesmen in Miami, so this job was perfect for him. But in spite of his efforts, he had accepted twenty-seven couples who wouldn't be dissuaded. These people would live in the middle of a battlefield if they thought that they were exclusive, or getting a bargain. He had made the mistake of trying to discourage them up front. They took that to mean they weren't wanted, or that the builder had made a mistake and underpriced the apartments, or something was going to raise the value of the apartments soon and the owner wanted to hold on to them.

• 5 •

Terra Time was already at the dock as Jack eased *Manta III* toward the Antares complex. He could make out three people on the deck in the late-afternoon light. The sun was setting behind the two buildings that made up the complex. The dock was in shadow.

Harry had been riding with him on the flying bridge, but they had not spoken to each other. He had come up as they entered the channel, and Jack knew he was there to keep an eye on him. Harry motioned for Jack to dock the boat in the righthand slip. Jack eased back on the throttle and then shifted into neutral. The boat edged toward the slip and just before entering he reversed the engines and came to a stop.

Hal and Mr. Bright jumped onto the dock and secured the bow and stern lines. They had even remembered to put the bumpers over the side. The thought occurred to Jack that this slip was built for his boat. They must have scouted him for some time, and they knew he would agree to take on the job they had offered.

The commanders were directing the two other men, whom he had not met yet, to begin unloading the cocoons onto the dock. Two more men from the *Terra Time* had come over to help. Hal and Harry were heading up the path from the docks that led to Building B. Hal stopped within sight of the dock and Harry continued on ahead to the door of the building. Jack was able to see the activity from his vantage point on the flying bridge. The men continued to load the cocoons onto a flatbed that was pulled by a small tractor. Jack counted ten cocoons. He did not hear Mr. Bright call him at first because he was fascinated by the activity. The second time he not only heard his name, but he felt it, as though someone had poked him in the ribs.

These boys can play rough, Jack thought. He waved okay and took the ignition key and put it in his pocket. He quickly checked around as he descended to the main deck. Things were reasonably shipshape and buttoned down. There was no food to clean up because these people had not eaten, and there was no mess because they had not been fishing.

Mr. Bright was waiting for him on the dock and extended a hand. "Welcome to Antares . . .

40

our home away from home. It will be your home for the next few months, too, I trust?"

Jack just smiled, shook Mr. Bright's hand, and said, "If you say so, boss."

"Good," said Mr. Bright. "Now, let me show you our lab and equipment and what is actually inside these cocoons. Just come this way." They both headed toward Building B. Behind them the tractor started up. The cocoons made the trip to Building B, too.

• 6 •

It had taken two weeks to get the swimming pool filled. Ben Green had taken it upon himself to accomplish the feat. He met daily with the manager and the maintenance chief. With the morning meeting finished, Ben made his way toward the pool. It was time for the daily gin game to begin, and his three cronies were waiting as usual. Bernie Lewis and Art Perlman were setting up the chairs. Joe Finley was shuffling the two decks. The score pads were neatly placed on the table next to Ben's chair.

A meeting of the bored, Ben thought as he approached his buddies. Life had become a bore for them, and without each other's friendship they would have been committed to the funny farm long ago. Four healthy, educated, and bright men. Together they had almost two hundred years of business experience. The reward for this was to be retired and cast into a role of slow decay and boredom.

Ben thought back on this morning's meeting with the manager and maintenance chief. He had handled them well, just like the old days at the agency, when he was an account supervisor in charge of the big oil account. He could really throw the bullshit at a meeting and terrorize those creepy creative people. Just do your homework, cover all the bases, and then sit back and wait for them to put their foot in their mouth. Then attack . . . attack . . . attack until they were so confused that they would agree with anything just to get back to the safety of their own offices. Ben was physically a big man. He was gaining too much weight these days and felt it in the hot Florida sun. He stood over six feet, three inches and weighed two hundred thirty pounds. His height had also been helpful in business, especially when he would storm into the art department and throw layouts onto the art V.P.'s desk. The head art director was a little man, just about five-foot-five, and even when he stood up to argue with Ben he still had to look up. It was a child-parent scene, carefully orchestrated by Ben with a devastating effect on the little man. Those days were gone now and there had been little fun of that sort until Ben met the manager and maintenance chief. It was like the old days again.

Ben planned each step of his campaign against them.

The first time he had tried to speak to the manager, he was told he would have to make an appointment because the manager, Mr. Shields, was a very busy man. The secretary had been curt. Ben had asked for an appointment, but the girl told him that Mr. Shields' appointment book was in his office and that was locked. Ben would have to call or come by later. She suggested he call first. Ben did, but of course Mr. Shields was out. The game went on for over a week. At first Ben was annoyed. The feeling was familiar and he realized that it was the same feeling he used to have at the agency. With that realization joy filled his life. He was reborn and fulfilled with a sense of worth that he had not felt for many years.

The next day he stopped into Mr. Shields' office and, of course, the manager was out. The secretary's manners had not changed, either. Ben approached her desk slowly. His walk had a slight shuffle to it and he forced his hands to shake a bit, too. He tried to look as old as he could. It worked, because the young snotty secretary began to speak slowly to him and explain things as though he were a child. He listened as she told him that the pool was not quite finished yet. They were waiting for delivery of a special paint to seal the lining. The paint had been ordered from the manufacturer, in Ohio, but it would be several weeks until the order could be filled. Her final words were, "Do you understand that, Mr. Green?"

Ben had tried to look as confused and beaten as possible. He smiled and started to turn away from her desk. Then he stopped and turned back to his original position. The girl had gone back to her typing. She stopped typing and was about to speak when Ben, in a clear deep voice, spoke to her. (It was the same voice he had used once to tell the executive vice president of the agency that he was about to take the three biggest clients to another agency if the stupid son-of-a-bitch creative director was not fired.) "There is just one other thing, young lady. You tell Mr. Shields for me that if his ass is not in this office at two-thirty this afternoon to discuss the swimming pool, I will personally find him and kick the living shit out of him. Good morning."

Mr. Shields had greeted Ben at the door at precisely two-thirty. He was a little man. Although he had the title of manager, it was obvious to Ben that this man was not calling the shots. He was a front for someone else. Shields had given Ben the same story about the

45

special paint, and Ben had answered, "Bullshit." When the manager had tried to explain, Ben asked him if he had been out to the pool. The man said yes, and Ben then told him to try to remember what kind of lining the pool had. Shields couldn't, so Ben reminded him that it was plastic and it was a stupid ploy to tell him they were going to paint a plastic pool.

"That's what they tell me, Mr. Green," the manager said.

"Who tells you?" asked Ben.

"Well, the maintenance chief. Perhaps you would like to hear it from his lips?"

Ben smiled and said politely, "Yes, by all means, let's meet the expert."

Shields buzzed the secretary and asked her to get Wally Parker on the radio. Ben could hear the girl calling, "Wally . . . come in, Wally," for a minute or so. She then came into Mr. Shields' office and told her boss that Wally must be off the grounds because she couldn't raise him.

Ben muttered "She couldn't raise anything" to himself just loud enough for everyone to hear. Mr. Shields suggested that they would contact Ben and arrange a meeting with Wally Parker as soon as possible.

As he left the office, Ben told Mr. Shields that he expected to hear from him within twenty-four hours. He did not say good-bye this time.

It took three days before they met. Friday Ben had been told that Wally Parker had to go up to Fort Lauderdale because they thought that a wholesaler up there might have some of the special paint. Saturday Wally was in for only half a day and he had several emergency repairs to supervise as a result of the storm Friday night. Sunday was Wally's day off.

Monday found Ben greeting the secretary as she opened the office at nine A.M. She was very polite to him now and told him that Mr. Shields would not be in until after lunch. Ben told her, "Fine. I'll be back at two, and have Wally the Wonderful here, too."

He left, but instead of going to his apartment, he went over to Joe Finley's place. Joe's second bedroom overlooked the entrance to the office. Joe made some coffee and his wife, Alma, went over to the Greens' apartment for the morning coffee klatch with Mary Green, Rose Lewis, and Bess Perlman. Ben and Joe kept a vigil and they were rewarded by the appearance of Mr. Shields slinking along the edge of the building toward his office. He stopped at the door and waved toward the parking lot. A blue Chevy door opened and a very fat man in overalls slid out of the driver's seat and made a beeline toward the manager's office. "Wally the Wonderful, we have you now," Ben muttered, and he motioned for Joe to get to the phone.

Joe dialed the manager's office and identified himself to the secretary as Mr. Bonser, of the Florida Attorney General's office. He asked to speak to Mr. Shields on official business. The girl put him on hold and then Mr. Shields got on the line. He nodded to Ben, and Ben left the apartment on the run.

"Mr. Shields, this is Mr. Bonser, of the Attorney General's office. I'm calling about a complaint we received from a Mr. Green, who says that services . . . let me see, I'll read the complaint to you . . . that services herein described and duly paid for have been withheld without cause justified *en corporatum per legalum*. . . . What that means is that this Mr. Green is charging you with . . . let's see . . . ah, yes . . . not fulfilling a contract to provide a swimming pool according to contract. Now, Mr. Shields, I know what a pain some of these old people can be, but they are citizens of this state and we have to follow up on these things. What seems to be the problem?"

Just as Shields was about to answer, he heard a ruckus outside his office and then Ben burst through the door into the room. Shields asked Mr. Bonser if he could call him back, and Bonser agreed. The manager hung up just as Ben reached across the gray metal desk and grabbed him by the lapels of his blue Antares jacket.

Wally Parker started to get up, but Ben glanced over at him and suggested that Wally remain in his chair. He turned back to Shields and let him down into his chair. "Good morning, Mr. Shields. Good morning, Mr. Parker. I'm really glad you could both make our meeting this morning. Tell me, Mr. Parker, were you able to locate that paint in Fort Lauderdale on Friday?"

Parker looked at Shields with an expression that told Ben he knew nothing about the trip to Fort Lauderdale.

Ben pulled out a piece of paper from his pocket. It was a score sheet from yesterday's gin game. He studied it for a moment, then put it back. "Now, Mr. Parker, I would appreciate it if you would explain this special paint to me. I had a pool in Connecticut, where I come from, and the lining was quite similar to the pool *we* have here. I don't recall ever having to paint it, because it was a special substance that sealed the pool. But I'm an old man and tend to forget things from time to time. Perhaps we did paint it." Ben slid into his old-man act again, realizing that Wally had just met him and that Shields hadn't told Wally too much about the situation.

Before Shields could say anything, Wally proceeded to patronize Ben, explaining slowly that this lining required painting. He said, "You know, Mr. Green, here at Antares we pride ourselves on having a facility that is not just beautiful, but durable, too. We expect our tenants to be with us a long time and we want things to be right for them. We want things to last. This special paint will add years to the life of the pool, and that means years of enjoyment for you and Mrs. Green. I'm sure you understand." He smiled at Ben, secure in the feeling that he had set this old buzzard straight.

Ben smiled back and put up his hand just as Shields began to speak. "No, Mr. Shields, allow me to speak first." His voice was still that of an old man.

"Wally, may I call you Wally?" Wally nodded and smiled again. "Wally, you are a fat, stupid asshole." Ben's voice was that of Ben the adman again. "I will tell you three things. One, I am not a tenant here; I own the goddamned place. Two, that is a fucking plastic pool liner out there, and any kind of paint would peel in one day. Three, we will meet here at ten tomorrow morning and you will have a schedule for me of when the pool will be filled. This meeting is over."

• 7 •

Amos Bright had been amused when he telepathed Jack Fischer from the dock. The first time he had summoned him by voice only. This time he sent an electric impulse to the charter captain's brain and the effect moved Fischer physically. Amos made a mental storage memo to cut his telepathing to the Earth dwellers several millivolts.

Jack Fischer caught up to Amos at the end of the Antares dock and they walked silently toward the Building B complex. The sun had nearly set, and the lights along the path were on. They were mercury vapor lamps and gave off an eerie greenish light. The only sound was from the small tractor behind them as it made its way along the service path to the back of Building B and the loading dock. Jack glanced back to the tractor one more time and noticed that the cocoons, now dimly lit, had a faint glow coming from within them. He had not

51

seen that in the daylight.

Amos read his thoughts and quickly recalled the reason for the glow. It was the power system installed in each cocoon to maintain life-force electronics. The glow was caused by the fuel cell, a small piece of the mother planet core. A piece of home to keep one warm.

Home for Amos Bright was Antares. It was a planet in the constellation the Earth dwellers called Scorpius. By all reason it should have been abandoned millennia ago, but the Antareans were an old race and had learned to deal with their ice planet quite well. Their world was physically a cold place. From the surface it appeared desolate. Ice covered the entire planet and the poles had more than fifty miles of ice through which one had to travel before reaching the surface of the planet.

It was another eighty miles below the surface that water could exist without freezing. That point was the beginning of the temperate zone of the planet. It was, in fact, very much like Earth, except Earth zones were on the surface in a lateral dimension and the temperature was dependent on the distance from the sun and the altitude of the surface terrain. On Antares it was just a matter of depth. Heat was determined by the vertical plane. The closer one got to the core of the planet, the warmer it was. So

Antarean heat and energy came from within. Most other planetary life depended upon energy from without, usually a nearby star.

It was this fact that formed the basis of Antarean thought, inner philosophy. Examination of the inner self had rapidly brought the Antareans to develop their energy and life centers, the things the Earth dwellers called brains. Telepathic communication was simple. But a well-developed Antarean brain could move mountains and navigate spacecraft. It could also melt ice and refreeze it in milliseconds.

Amos let his mind wander with thoughts of home and he grew slightly taller. Jack Fischer though Amos had just straightened up, or stretched. They had reached the outside back door to the B complex. It opened without Amos touching the knob.

It was cool inside. They walked down an unfinished corridor. Jack thought it was a bit strange that the building was air-conditioned at this stage of construction. Then he noticed that the air-conditioning duct work was not complete, and he realized that it was cooler on his left side, the side closer to Amos Bright. As he moved a bit closer to the alien, it became even cooler. Amos was putting out his own air conditioning.

They turned a corner and stopped at a stair-well. Again the door opened, and they walked up the stairs to the second-floor landing. When they entered the corridor, Jack saw that it, too, was unfinished. He also noticed that the coolness emanating from Amos had stopped and that they were now in an air-conditioned area. They came to a door painted blue and Amos stopped. "We will go in here for a while. The others have preparations to make before we open the first cocoon. Are you hungry?"

Jack answered, "Yes, and I'm also a bit cold."

"Yes, of course," Amos said. "You will get used to that soon, I promise. This room will be comfortable for you." He opened the door with his hand this time and motioned for Jack to enter. He did and Amos followed him into the room.

• 8 •

"Four, bam . . . two, crack . . . soap . . ." Then silence. Rose Lewis and Bess Perlman looked across the table at each other. It was Mary Green's turn and she was staring down at her rack, deep in thought.

Alma Finley spoke first. "Come on, Mary, you've been playing for two months now. You should know the card by now." Mary looked up with a hurt expression on her face. "I'm trying to play a hand I never played before, and I think I just went dead."

Bess leaned over and looked at Mary's rack. She thought for a moment and then suggested that Mary call the soap and plan an exposed hand.

Mary looked at the mah-jongg card in front of her and then smiled as she realized that she could do what Bess suggested. "Thanks, Bess. I guess you have to be Jewish to be really good at this game."

Alma laughed. She was the best player of the foursome, and she was as un-Jewish as one could be. Bess and Rose had made her an honorary Jew the day she cleaned them all out after only three lessons in mah-jongg. Actually, she was a terrific card player and she approached mah-jongg the same way. She could count tiles the way she counted cards and therefore knew the odds at any given time. She played the percentages. Before Joe had been forced to retire they made a few trips to Las Vegas. She always won at the blackjack table because of her counting ability. Joe admired her for it, but he always believed that the next time it wouldn't work. He never allowed her to gamble with more than a few hundred dollars. Even so, she had managed to stash away over ten thousand dollars from her winnings in a bank account that Joe didn't know about.

Mary called the soap tile and the game progressed.

"West," Bess said.

"Take for mah-jongg," Alma called, and she exposed her winning wind hand.

Rose looked at her with disbelief and said, "Somewhere in your WASP past a Jew must have snuck in . . . Either that, or you cheat."

Alma laughed again. "Actually, it might have been an Oriental."

That started the laughter again and Bess Perlman made a mental note to have a talk with Mary regarding exactly what a Jew was, and was not. Now was not the time or place.

They dumped the tiles into the center of the table and began turning and mixing them for the next game.

Alma spoke again. "Joe told me that the pool was going to be filled soon."

"Today," Bess said. Bess was a women of few words. "My Arthur said that Ben told him today."

Rose looked at Mary and asked, "So, is it today?"

Mary answered, "Yes. Ben told me that he was having a meeting with the manager this morning and that the pool was going to be filled today. It's a crusade with him, but when he says something will be done, usually it's done."

That was the way with Ben Green. He was a man of action, not reaction. He was a leader, and until Mary had realized that she was a person unto herself, she had been a follower of Ben Green. Sometimes that was a royal pain in the ass. But it wasn't Ben's fault. In fact, he had pointed that out to her on a day she would never forget. They had been married twenty-two years and their three children were out of the house. The youngest was nineteen and she was a student at Cornell studying marine biology. The middle one was a permanent resident at Arlington National Cemetery. He had been drafted and given the honor of serving his country in Vietnam. Whenever Mary saw a golf bag being shipped on the plane to Florida, it reminded her of Jimmy, because she had seen pictures of body bags being shipped back from Vietnam and, although they had received his body in a casket, she knew that at one time it had been in a bag like that. Her third and oldest child was married and was about to make Mary and Ben grandparents. She was in her sixth month and lived in Chicago. Her name was Patricia and she was married to Michael Keane, an up-and-coming product manager for General Foods.

On a particular day in May 1965, Mary had followed her usual routine. Ben had been up and out of the house by seven A.M. It was eleven A.M. and she was still in bed. She heard the key in the front door and then Ben's voice calling to her. "I'm up here," she said. He came into the room and looked at her. Then he shook his head and went to the large walk-in closet and took out his double-suiter suitcase.

She had asked "Where are you going? It's Friday."

"I have to go to Los Angeles this afternoon.

I'll be gone all of next week. We have to rush through a pool of commercials on that new oil account." While he spoke he continued to pack.

Suddenly she felt very depressed and alone. Then she got an idea. "How about my coming with you?" she asked.

He had stopped packing for a moment and just stared at her. He knew then that what he was about to do was cruel but necessary. He truly loved his wife, but in his mind she had become a vegetable. Her life had always been the children and the house and taking care of Ben. Now that was over. The kids were gone. One of them was already buried. Mary had become a slug . . . a sloth, and she was going to seed. Ben knew women older than Mary who worked at the agency. They were vital and exciting. Mary was a disaster, and if this way of life continued for her, he knew that it was just a matter of time before he would drift away from the smothering experience of being with his wife. He decided that now was the time to speak out directly to the problem. He loved her, but he was a coward when it came to fighting with her. Years of living a relatively easy life around children and other homemakers had dulled Mary's fighting spirit. She was a push-over in a logical argument and her perception of the world was twenty years old.

Ben sat down on the side of the bed. "Mary," he said, "I want you to listen to what I'm going to say. Please listen carefully. I love you very much. I think you are a good woman. I think you are a beautiful woman. I think you are an intelligent woman. But I also think you are becoming a pain in the ass and a bore. You can't come with me because I have a long hard week of work in front of me. It's my work, which is a part of my life. It is what I do, and I do it well. It really has nothing to do with you other than that it provides money for our standard of living. I happen to love what I do and I find it stimulating and exciting. But that's for me. I think that you should take a good hard look at yourself in the mirror, and a good look at this house, and then sit down and find out who you are and what you want to do and be in this world. You can do what you want, you know. I'll be back next Friday or Saturday and we should talk about it then. Now, please don't say anything. Just let me finish packing and get the hell out of here."

He had stood up and quickly finished packing. He left without saying anything else. He slammed the door and she heard the tires of his MG squeal as he drove out of the driveway onto quiet Westport Lane.

Ten minutes later, with tears drying on her

cheeks, she screamed, "Fuck you, Ben Green!" Then she poured herself a glass of bourbon.

The next four days were spent in and out of a hazy drunken stupor. She wandered through the house spending time in each room. She had emptied drawers, folded their contents neatly, then refilled them. She had thrown out a stack of *Good Housekeeping*, *Redbook*, and *McCall's* magazines that dated back fifteen years. She had stripped naked and stood in front of a full-length mirror in their bedroom and examined her body. She began to see flab and the flattened breasts. She studied the slight bulging varicose veins on her legs. She gentle touched the wrinkles around her eyes and mouth. She had let strings of four-letter words fly out of her mouth on a regular basis. Some of them surprised her because she didn't think she knew such words. In the beginning they had been directed toward Ben, but as time passed they just came out in a general undirected way.

The morning of the fifth day she woke up with a start. She had slept for only three hours. It was seven in the morning. She was naked. There was a sound coming from the kitchen and she realized that Betty, her cleaning lady, was in the house. It must be Tuesday. Mary Green got out of bed and walked slowly to the bathroom. She realized that she hadn't bathed since Ben left. She smelled her breath. It was foul. She smelled her body and the odor was unpleasant.

The she recalled the punch line of a joke that her son, Jimmy, had told about a hermit who had a long beard. He fell asleep one day in his cabin and some young boys crept in and rubbed Limburger cheese into his beard. When he awoke he sniffed a rotton odor. He went outside his cabin and sniffed again. It was a clear, bright day and his cabin was in the mountains. Still he smelled the cheese. Finally, he muttered to himself. "The whole world stinks."

Mary said it out loud. "The whole world stinks." Then she thought: *No, it's only me and my body. I can brush my teeth, and wash my body, and perfume myself. Then what?* The answer to that question had to be found, and she had three days to find it.

Betty was washing the kitchen counter when Mary came into the room. "Miss Green," Betty said. "What's been going on here? This house is a mess." Betty had been working for the Greens for seven years and took a proprietary interest in the comings and the goings of the family. She had been the only person who had been with Mary when news of Jimmy came to the front door in the person of a marine captain. She had cried like a baby with Mary. She had hovered over the family and cared for them all. She was a Catholic, just as they were. She was black and they were white and that made a difference, but only outside of the house. She truly loved these people and felt their love for her in return. Now, as she looked at Mary Green, she realized that a very troubled woman had entered the room.

Mary stopped near the kitchen table and sat down. "Is there any coffee, dear?" she asked. Betty poured her a cup and brought it to the table.

"You want some breakfast? You're up kinda early." Mary didn't answer. She just looked down into the coffee. Betty saw a tear drip into the coffee and Mary's hands started to shake. She sobbed. Betty sat next to her and put her arm around Mary, who leaned over to the big black woman and cried.

Betty just held her. "Okay, honey. I'm here. Let it out."

It was ten minutes before Mary could talk. She sipped her coffee and told Betty what had happened. At first it came slowly and with difficulty. Betty listened patiently. She liked Ben Green. He was a fair man, a bit pushy, perhaps, but nevertheless fair. She knew the truth of what he had told his wife. It was the method that she didn't approve of, but what was done was done, and now her concern was for Mary.

"What have I done wrong?" Mary asked Betty. "You're married, Betty. Does your husband think you're a vegetable or a slug? What does he want, Betty?"

Betty was slow to answer. She wasn't sure this problem was in her domain, yet she did love this woman. "Well, Miss Green," she said, "I don't know exactly what is on Mr. Green's mind, but I can understand how he might be feeling. You know folks get on, we all do, and the years seem to go by, and suddenly we get to the forty and then fifty and the kids leave and being a mother and father isn't there anymore like it was. Mr. Green he has his work. He likes that and it keeps him feeling . . . well . . . alive. It's a reason to get up in the morning and to be tired at night. Me and George, we have that, too, both of us. We have a nice small house and a good car and we travel a bit and go out a lot. But we have a life of our own, too. I have my friends and he has his. Sometimes I go back to North Carolina to visit my sister and he doesn't come. I come here three days a week and go to Miss Kramer two days and at night I sleep real good. You get what I'm saying?"

"I know you work hard, Betty, and I know it isn't easy for you and George. But we have money. I mean we're comfortable."

Betty shook her head. "You miss the point, Miss Green. Honey, look at yourself. Are you comfortable?"

Mary stared at Betty for a moment and then said, "I'm about as uncomfortable as I can be right now. Help me. Please."

Betty spoke again. "What the man was saying, honey, is to make something for yourself in this world. Do your thing, like the kids say. Let it hang out, Mary Green. You're a good-looking woman with a brain and an education. You don't need money, that's true, but you do need to find something to do. Something that will make you feel good and important. Honey, there's not too much we can do about getting older, but we sure don't have to get dumber at the same time."

"You mean get a job?" Mary questioned.

"Right on," Betty replied. "Get a job and get your ass out of this house. Next time you'll be the one packing for a business trip."

They had talked for the rest of the day and then cleaned the house together. Betty had called her husband and told him that she was going to sleep over that night. Betty and Mary talked into the night exploring the possibilities for a fifty-two-year-old woman. By morning Mary was as excited as the day she had graduated from college.

By the time Ben came home from Los Angeles, she had written out a program for herself. They had sat together all day Saturday and discussed the plan. Mary would enroll in summer school at the University of Bridgeport and take a few refresher courses. She had been a business major. She would also take a steno and bookkeeping course in a night-school program at the local high school. In the fall she would look for a job in the area and continue taking courses at the university at night for as long as she felt it necessary.

That was fifteen years ago. In the time since that fateful week Mary had changed her life. She was still shy and a woman of few words, but she had confidence and a good feeling about herself. Her life with Ben had been wonderful since that week.

The business with the pool had brought back the memory, and as she built her wall of mah-jongg tiles for the next game she wondered about her new friends around the table and hoped that someday soon they might discuss their feelings the way she and Betty had so long ago.

• 9 •

The light kept changing in the room. It was a subtle change and Jack hardly noticed it at first. Now it was blue again. A pale blue, like the dresses the bridesmaids had worn at his brother's wedding last week. That thought shook him a bit because he remembered that Judy would be coming home to the apartment in an hour and wonder where he was.

As the blue faded to yellow he spoke to Amos Bright. "I have a girl living with me. She is going to wonder where I am."

Amos thought for a moment and replied, "You will have to call her. Tell her you are on the radio phone. Yes, call her from the boat. Then you will be on the radio phone. Tell her that the charter will be out for a week. That will give us time to think of how we can deal with her."

Jack thought: *You're a clever spaceman.* And he agreed to the plan. They had been in the room for a half hour. The food had been more than he had expected. Steak, French-fried potatoes, salad, wine, and coffee. If that was a sample of the treatment he would receive, Jack felt better about his situation.

The room moved to a pale orange as Amos stood up and said, "I think we can get to work now. The processing area is prepared." He motioned Jack to precede him through the door and, without thinking why, Jack turned left and walked down the hall to an orange door. He could hear a faint hum coming from behind the door. Amos was behind him and they were joined by the two men who had been wearing the copper suits earlier in the day. They were still wearing the suits, and on close inspection Jack saw that the fabric was made of tiny hexagons fitted together without any obvious stitching. The fabric was a deeper red than copper, but definitely metallic.

The four men entered through the orange door into a large room that resembled a very modern health club. Along the left wall were metal cabinets roughly the shape of the cocoons. There were twelve of them. They looked like steam cabinets. A misty vapor rose from ten of the cabinets. The smell was sweet and pleasant, like a mild perfume that Judy had worn at the wedding. He put her out of his thoughts again and concentrated on the rest of the room.

There was a table in the center that was at least eight feet by eight feet. Overhead there was a large conical lamp. Harry and Hal were standing at the table. They looked up at Jack as he entered the room, smiled, then moved toward the first metal cabinet. The far wall was partially hidden from view by the center table, but Jack could make out what appeared to be a row of cots with blankets and pillows. Above the cots were smaller versions of the large center lamp. On the right side of the room was a screen. It took up the entire wall and Jack judged that was at least forty feet. The screen ran from floor to ceiling, wall to wall. Cinemascope, Jack thought, but his thoughts were again distracted by a noise from the back lefthand corner of the room. Through the mist he saw that two commanders, James and Bill — Shiny White and Shiny Black — had entered the room. They were met at the center table by the copper men. Although there were no words, Jack knew they were communicating rapidly. Amos touched Jack on the shoulder and then pointed to a raised chair halfway between the wall screen and the center table. Jack walked over to the chair and climbed into it. Amos said, "Good. Just watch and please don't interrupt."

The silent conversation continued at the center table. Hal and Harry were in the mist near the first metal cabinet. They were intent on whatever they were doing and seemingly oblivious to the others in the room.

Amos Bright had joined the others in the center. Jack felt as though he was on a movie set, sitting in the director's chair. The only problem was that he had no idea of the script or what the actors were going to do.

He had been on a movie set before. Judy was an actress and lately there had been a few movies shot in Florida. She had had a minor role in a low-budget film last month. Jack had come to the location to pick her up one day. They were working late and he was allowed to hang around in the background until they were finished. He had been fascinated at first and then realized how boring the process really was. They were doing a scene in a bar and Judy was playing the part of a hooker. Two men were jockeying for her attention and the director wanted to play the scene in one long take from the time the second man walked into the bar until the fight between the two men broke out. It was about five minutes of dialogue and required a tough bit of acting by Judy. She was very good and he was proud of her and her talent. But they had done the scene seven times and Jack could see the actors were getting tired. The last two takes had been lost because the camera had bumped into a table once and into a wall the second time. That seemed to have spoiled the take and the cameraman had yelled "Cut!" The director went through the roof and chewed out the man who was pulling the camera dolly. The cameraman had interceded on behalf of the dolly man and told the director to shove it up his ass because it was an almost impossible shot and move and they were doing their best. The dolly man was forgotten as it became a confrontation between the director and the cameraman and grew into a screaming match. Suddenly, the director spun away from his adversary, yelled, "Wrap it for the day!" and walked off the set.

There was a moment of silence and then the assistant director had yelled, "Wrap! Seven tomorrow. We are in the right place." The lights started to go out and as he left with Judy they passed the assistant director talking to the bar owner about what it would cost to close the bar for the night so that they wouldn't have to move the equipment and lights. All Jack heard was the assistant director saying, "Five hundred bucks? Shit! You don't do five hundred bucks a week here . . ."

Judy was a pretty girl. She was not beautiful,

but she was sweet and pretty. She was a child of the seventies, which meant she was serious about her career and herself. The only vestige of the sixties that she carried was a mild interest in rock music. She dressed fifties and her hair and makeup were forties. These days she had a permanent and wore deep red lipstick.

It was the thought of the lipstick color that jolted Jack back to reality, if it could be called that. He was suddenly aware that the screen behind him had turned a deep penetrating red color. It bathed the room in red light. The conical light above the large center table was also glowing red.

From the corner where Jack had seen Hal and Harry working, there came a screech like the sound of chalk on a blackboard, then a loud hiss. Red steamlike mist shot out of the first metal cabinet and two blond men rolled a jitney with a cocoon on it toward the center table.

· 10 ·

The applause was for Ben Green. Art Perlman and Bernie Lewis stood clapping as Ben approached. Joe Finley continued shuffling the cards. He had been at the meeting that morning when the final confrontation took place in the manager's office.

In a few moments they would all sit under the gold-and-white umbrella with the Antares logo shading them from the bright Florida sunlight. They would play their ritual gin game until lunch. Today would be different, however, because the gurgling sound of the pool filling would serenade them while they played. *Yes,* Joe thought, *it is a sweet sound.* He knew what it represented was winning. In a very real sense, both he and Ben felt as good as they might have if they had closed a big advertising account and for Joe it was as if he had landed a juicy part in a Broadway show. For each of the retired men this morning had been a real triumph.

Joe Finley had been an actor, a bartender, a salesman, a taxi driver, and an elevator repairman. He had done many other odd jobs. Too many to remember. He had done eight years in the army, too, from 1941 to 1949. But he thought of himself only as an actor. That was a love and the only joy he could remember besides being married to Alma. His first wife, Dotty, had walked out on him after sixteen years of marriage and two kids. They had lived in Boston and, although they hadn't been poor, life had been without many of the luxuries that Dotty saw on television every day. It had finally become too much for her and she succumbed to what Joe liked to call "Her American Dream." She met a widower who fell in love with her. He had money and he was willing to support the kids and send them to college. Most important, he was eager to give Dotty all the things in life that she hungered for.

Joe and Dotty had had so many fights about money that when she came to him and told him she wanted a divorce, he just said okay. Of course, that wasn't enough for Dotty, so she proceeded to tell him every detail of her recent adulterous life with Mr. Moneybags and outlined every detail of her future life with him and the kids. Joe just didn't care anymore. Their life had been a struggle and an argument about money from day one. All Joe could think of was Martin Luther King's epitaph. "Free at last . . . free at last . . . oh, my God, I'm free at last." He had no remorse about his two daughters, either. They were both carbon copies of their mother. Someday they would make their husbands miserable as they harped on them for material possessions and luxuries. They would drive the poor slobs to an early grave.

After the divorce Joe moved to New York and got a small apartment on the West Side. He drove a cab during the day and joined a small off-off Broadway group at night. He was forty at the time. A very handsome man with dark hair, graying slightly at the temples, and steel-gray eyes. He was in good shape physically, and at the age of sixty he used to jog five miles every morning. Now he couldn't even walk one mile without tiring.

Alma came along when he was fifty-one. He had a supporting part in a long-running off-Broadway show. In the eleven years that Joe had been in New York he had made a living. He even managed to save a few thousand dollars and had built a pension plan in the Screen Actors Guild and AFTRA. He was an actor and his future was always going to be in acting.

Then, suddenly, he was sixty. He had been

married to Alma for four years, and he wasn't thinking of retirement. He was making plans to go to Hollywood and try for some television parts. His hair was gray and his face chiseled. His eyes were penetrating, and he had developed his craft to an extremely professional level. He had become a good type now. He was starting to get some TV commercial work, too.

Alma, dear Alma, had noticed it first. "Are you feeling all right, Joe?" she would ask. "You seem tired." Joe would tell her that it was just her imagination, but she bothered him and loved him to the doctor's office for a checkup. The words had fallen on him like a lead weight.

"Mr. Finley, you said you wanted it straight. Okay. You have leukemia." Joe felt as though someone had punched him in the stomach.

"I thought that was a kids' disease," Joe had said.

"Not so, Mr. Finley. However, when we find it in people of your age we are able to treat it quite well. I can assure you that you have many, many good years ahead of you. As a matter of fact, I believe we can keep you going indefinitely." He wondered what that meant. Was it like living at all?

He didn't tell Alma for two weeks. He waited because the doctor was going to try a new medication. If it worked, he said he was sure things would be all right. But there were qualifications, as he had known there would be. "You can't push yourself. You should think about retiring to a quieter life, if possible," the doctor had said. Then the tests had come back. The new medication had had some effect. The doctor had been optimistic, so Joe had met Alma after the show and they had gone to a quiet French restaurant on Forty-ninth Street. They ordered mussels and a good white wine and he told her.

She reached across the table and touched his hand. "I love you," she said. From that day on she was all that mattered to Joe Finley.

Watching Ben Green approach to the sound of applause brought back to him his own performance this morning, and he felt proud.

They had met early at Ben's apartment. Mary made breakfast for them and she sat at the table while they went over their plan. Joe brought all the props. He was wearing the pinstriped suit and the white shirt and rep tie. His wing tip shoes were polished to a dull buff. His hair was trimmed and he had even trimmed the hair in his nose and ears. His nails were also buffed.

Ben had the attaché case, the I.D., and the papers. It was amazing that Ben was able to get it all done in one afternoon, but there it was.

Ben had told Joe that he had a friend who owned an ad agency in Miami. The guy owed Ben a favor. Ben never said what the favor was, but it must have been a biggie because there was a messenger at Ben's door at six A.M. that morning with the papers.

They rehearsed one more time, finished their coffee, and shook hands. Ben left the attaché case on the breakfast table and headed for Mr. Shields' office. Joe waited five minutes and followed. When Joe arrived at the office, he found Ben waiting in the reception area.

Joe ignored Ben, and spoke to the secretary. "Good morning, I'm Mr. Bonser, from the Attorney General's office. Is Mr. Shields in?" He flashed the I.D. that Ben had given him earlier. The girl was very nervous now.

"Well, sir, uh, Mr. Bonser, uh, let me just check. Uh, will you have a seat?"

Joe started to sit and then said, "In case he forgot, we have an appointment."

She smiled and made her way to the back office. Ben Green leaned forward to peer into the office as she opened the door a crack and slithered inside. Both men had trouble controlling their laughter.

When the girl returned, Joe got up and went over to the desk. "Can he see me now? I'm in a terrible hurry."

She spoke to Joe, but she was looking at Ben Green. Her voice was only a whisper. "Mr. Shields says he doesn't recall having an appointment with you. Could you make it another time?"

Joe's voice boomed. "You tell Mr. Shields that either he sees me now, or he sees me in federal court."

With that, Ben Green jumped up and rushed to the desk, yelling, "He's in there, isn't he? Goddamned son-of-a-bitch! I'll kick his ass all over this goddamned office!" Before the girl could stop him, Ben rushed into Shields' office. Joe followed and stood in the doorway. Shields was backed against the wall of his office under a large mounted tarpon. Ben loomed over him and threatened to stuff Shields down the mouth of the fish.

Joe moved toward the desk and took out the I.D. card again. "Mr. Shields, I'm Mr. Bonser, from the Attorney General's office. We spoke the other day regarding a complaint from a Mr. Green."

With that, Ben spun around and said, "I'm Ben Green. Goddamn, I'm glad to see you. Now we can put this rat in the slammer." He loosened his grip on Shields and moved over to shake Joe's hand.

"I'm glad to meet you, Mr. Green," Joe said.

"We don't want our new Florida residents to think that, just because they are new to the state, we don't pay attention to their complaints. A senior citizen is still a citizen, and a voter." Joe smiled the politician's smile that he had used in *The Last Hurrah*, when he had played the mayor of Boston in an off-Broadway production. He then sat down and opened his attaché case and took out the papers they had prepared.

"Please, Mr. Shields, I'm sure we can settle this matter amicably." Shields moved slowly back to his desk and sat down as Joe handed him the papers. He wore a defeated look on his face, and Ben and Joe knew they had won.

What they didn't know was that he was under strict orders from the "owners" to keep the people in Building A happy. They didn't want any publicity and they certainly didn't want to go to court. *Hell,* Shields thought to himself. *I'd take this old fart to the Supreme Court before I'd fill the pool.* He put the papers down on his desk and looked up at Bonser. He saw that Bonser wasn't a young man and that he would get no sympathy from him. He decided to make it short and sweet. "Mr. Bonser, I'm sorry for the confusion. I'm sure Mr. Green here just misunderstood. Actually, we are filling the pool today . . . yes, today." He buzzed the girl on the intercom and told her to find Wally Parker immediately and have him come to the office.

A few moments later Wally walked into the office and moved to the opposite side of the room from Ben.

"Wally, you know Mr. Green, and this is Mr. Bonser, from the Attorney General's office. I want you to begin filling the swimming pool right now."

Wally looked confused. Then he said, "Okay." He turned to leave, but Joe Finley stopped him.

"Mr. Shields, I'm sure you don't mind if I go with Mr. Parker and watch him. I'm sure Mr. Green would like to come along, too."

Ben Green looked at Joe Finley, then at Shields, then at Wally, and said. "You people all give me a pain in my ass. Don't patronize me, Bonser. Just get out there and do your job. I have to take my nap, but when I get up, that goddamned swimming pool had better goddamned be filled or I'll blow the fucking thing up!"

Then Ben had left the office.

• ∎∎ •

Rose could see the four men from her terrace. Bernie and Arthur were applauding Ben Green as he approached their table. Joe Finley didn't applaud. Seeing the card table brought back a vision of her daily bridge game at Sunset Village and thoughts of the friends she left there. She would adjust. She always had. Early in her marriage she had been unhappy, and her mother had had a heart-to-heart talk with her. Her mother, who had come from Russia, told her daughter that happiness was not a right in a marriage. If one had it, then one was lucky. A woman had to adjust to a man's ways. *Well,* she thought, *mother was certainly right. My marriage to Bernie Lewis has been just that, a series of adjustments.*

Her thoughts were interrupted by the ringing phone. She left the terrace and took the call in the kitchen. "Hello?"

"Hi, Mom, it's Craig. How are you?"

"Wonderful, darling. And how are you and Beth and the children. How *are* the children?"

"Just great, Mom."

"That's wonderful."

"How's Dad?"

"He's just fine, dear. He's out by the pool playing cards with his cronies."

"Great. It sounds like you really are settled in there. I can't wait to see the place."

"Yes, dear, and we can't wait to see you. Just two more weeks and three days."

There was a pause on the phone and then Craig spoke again. "That's why I called, Mom. There's a problem. I won't be able to get down this time. It's business. I won't bore you, but we have to redo some of the fall line, and then I'll be at the factory after that . . . to set up the run . . . you know . . ." His voice trailed off.

Rose was crying.

"I'm really sorry, Mom. We were looking forward to the trip. The kids are really disappointed. I'm tempted to send them without me, but I know after a day or so they would drive Dad crazy."

And that bitch you call a wife would put me in the hospital, she thought. Then Rose composed herself, but she didn't dry her tears. They just dripped slowly down her face. As she spoke again, she tasted their salt. *These are the tears of affliction*, she thought, recalling the story of Moses and the Exodus. "Listen, darling, business is business. We understand. When do you think you can get down?"

"Well, Mom," Craig answered, "you know the problem is the kids and school. The next vacation they get is in four months. We'll plan for that, but it's right in the middle of our busiest season. We'll talk, though."

Rose listened and took a deep breath. "Fine, darling. Let us know. I'll call you on Sunday."

"Okay, Mom. Love to Dad. Be well."

He hung up, and she slowly replaced the phone. She reached toward the roll of paper towels, pulled off a piece, and dried her tears. She put her foot on the garbage-can lever, opened the top of the can, and dropped the towel with a flourish. *Adjust*, she thought, *then readjust. Is that a life?*

When Rose Charnofsky met Bernard Lefkowitz, she was seventeen years old and beautiful. Her eyes were brown and large and innocent. Her long dark hair reached to her waist. Her figure was slender but carefully hidden. The Charnofsky family was a very proper family that prided itself on high morality. They were Orthodox Jews, and her father was an extremely religious man. After all these years it was hard for her to remember him. Once when she had gone to visit an aunt in Miami Beach she had vividly remembered her father.

Rose's aunt was over eighty and lived in a small apartment hotel on Third Street, off Collins Avenue. It was a neighborhood filled with old people, old houses, and old hotels. She found it extremely depressing. Yet, to those people it was part of the good life they had found in America. They were all immigrants from worlds Rose could not imagine. She had, as a child, heard all the stories about the Czar and the anti-Semitism and the pogroms, but it seemed so far away and foreign to her that she never believed it was really true. When the atrocities of the Nazis were revealed after World War II, she watched the old people nod their heads and understand. She had been horrified and furious. They had been complacent and accepting. To them it had seemed only natural that Jews should be murdered.

This old aunt, Aunt Ruth, had been one of those who accepted it all. As Rose climbed the stairs to her aunt's efficiency apartment, she experienced a memory. The odor of heavy cooking was in the hallway, and suddenly it was the odor of Friday night at home — the three-room apartment in Brooklyn was spotless. Her mother had spent the entire day cleaning and cooking. Her father was home early. Dinner was early. Conversation was sparse. Then he was off to synagogue, but the smell of Sabbath stayed behind.

This hallway was filled with the same smell, and for a moment Rose expected her father to open the apartment door. When Aunt Ruth opened it, Rose was startled, but then she reached out and embraced her aunt and drank in the smell of her. Then, uncontrollably, Rose began to dry. The tears were not for Aunt Ruth, nor for her father. They were tears for the pain that her people had endured . . . for the courage they had to leave their homes and to find a new life in a foreign land. They were tears of understanding, because no matter how poor they were, Rose realized they were safe. They had been delivered. They, too, had adjusted. The fact that Rose couldn't quite face was that the tears were also for herself. She had also spent her life adjusting, but to things that were unimportant. Her affliction was self-imposed. Perhaps it was the times; perhaps it was the burden of being first generation in the promised land; perhaps it was because her suffering was so small compared to what the old people had experienced. In any case, the tears flowed and a part of her opened to let out love that she had not felt before.

• **12** •

The cocoon had no cover or hinge or door. Instead, it was peeled away by the two copper men. The room remained flooded with red light. As the layers were peeled from the cocoon, they disintegrated. This happened at the instant they were no longer attached to the cocoon. It happened in a flash, and there was no apparent trace of the material after that. For a moment, Jack had the feeling he was in a massive dark room watching technicians develop a huge photograph.

Amos Bright telepathed to Shiny Black, *It goes well. The first is an expendable, but I think we will have it.*

Shiny Black answered aloud. "No reason to doubt. The process had proven itself before in the Cenedar Quadrant."

Hal interrupted. "True, Commander of No Light, but Cenedar is an ammonia ice planet. I recall no time test of cocoon in an oxygen-hydrogen medium."

The conversation was terminated by Commander Shiny White, known as Commander of All Light. "Your kindness, please! It is peeled, and to my sensors it seems wet. Some condensation, I believe. Check me, No Light."

The Shiny Black turned his face toward the cocoon on the table. It was now almost the shape of a man. He telepathed, *I concur. Some moisture has entered. But it is not harmful and the soldier is not spoiled. We will require more time for the drying than anticipated.*

The copper men were removing the last of the covering. In the red light Jack could see a man, or at least the shape of a man, lying on the table. It did not move as Commanders Shiny Black and Shiny White moved around the table examining the body. Finally, Jack was able to see the full figure. It was a male human, with a few variations.

Oddly enough, Jack did not notice the lack of genitals at first. The initial shock was that the body had no eyes. There were sealed slits that wrapped around the face to where two ears should have been. He remembered Shiny Black's face when he had taken his human face off on the boat. This man also had no nose or mouth. And there was no hair. Then Jack noticed the lack of penis and testicles. At that point the room began to hum and pulsate.

Before Jack could react, Amos was at his side, helping him down from the high chair. "It's getting late and we have some work to do. I think it might get uncomfortable for you here. Let's go out."

Jack followed him to the door. Just as the door was closing behind them, Jack heard a shrill piercing sound coming from the room. Then it was gone. "Part of the process," Amos said. "I promise that you will see it all very soon. This is the first and we must test it very carefully before we release the others. They have been here for a long time."

He took Jack to another room with a blue door and opened it with a key. "This is your room. I will come for you in the morning. Please rest and don't worry, but by all means contemplate what you have seen and learned today. There is much more to come."

He closed the door behind Jack and locked it. The room was not unlike a Holiday Inn or Howard Johnson's motel room, except that Jack was locked in for the night.

Amos Bright returned to the processing room after stopping just once more. That was to get a silver case from another room with a red door. He took the case into the processing room. By now the heat had dissipated and the group was huddled around the center table. Amos knew their disappointment immediately. As he approached the table the others were silent. *How bad?* he telepathed.

"Recoverable, but damaged," Hal answered. "I don't think we can revise the programs to overcome the damage."

"We can try," Shiny Black interrupted.

"We must," Shiny White said.

Amos set down the silver case at the head of the table. He quickly scanned the body and saw the spots. "Did the moisture do this?" he asked.

"Perhaps," said copper man one, "but it may also be from the electrical input. I will have to send the scout probe back to the base tonight and bring down more instruments. I think we will lose this soldier. In any case, it is no good for this mission." He turned and left the room.

Amos opened the silver case. In it there were two teardrop-shaped glasslike bulbs. Copper man two came over and touched them. They began to glow. The copper man then slid his forefinger along the eye slit of the body on the table.

"You will do an insertion, anyway?" Shiny Black asked.

"We must," Amos answered. "This is procedure, even with damage."

Copper man then inserted one teardrop into the slit. The opposite side of the man's body quivered. He then inserted the other teardrop and the other side of the body quivered. "Good tone," copper man said. They all agreed. He then removed a small red glowing rock from under the head of the soldier and passed it to Amos.

Hal and Harry rolled a narrow table next to the center table and slid the body onto it. They then wheeled the body to the back of the room and placed it onto one of the cots. The cone-shaped light above the cot switched on and a white beam came from the light, then split into two beams and entered the eye slits. Another beam, blue in color, came from the light and widened to cover the upper torso of the man on the cot. Finally, a third beam, deep green in color and shimmering, came from the light and spread out to encompass the entire body.

Back at the table Amos Bright was placing the small glowing red rock, the size of a golf ball, into the silver case. Copper man two, Shiny White, and Shiny Black gathered around the case and each reached a hand into the case and touched the rock. They all telepathed the same thought: home.

• 13 •

The water gurgled into the pool as Joe Finley dealt the cards. Today he was partners with Art Perlman. He liked playing with Art because Art was not only a shrewd card player, but a quiet man who didn't jump on anyone if he made a mistake. That was important to Joe. He had always been sensitive to criticism. As an actor he had taken it very personally.

As the others arranged their hands, Joe poured a cup of lemonade from his Thermos and popped a pill into his mouth. He washed it down with one gulp and then returned to his hand and the game.

Art Perlman watched from across the table. *That is a brave man*, he thought. *I don't know how I would react to having leukemia.* Art chuckled to himself at the thought because death was not a stranger to him. He had lived with it all his adult life. However, that kind of death was quick and always for a reason one could understand.

It began on the streets of downtown Brooklyn. Arthur Perlman was the third son of Abraham Perlman, mattress maker. His oldest brother had died in World War I on some godforsaken battlefield in France. He was buried there, and no one from the family had ever seen the grave. Art's second oldest brother had gone to City College and was going on to medical school. It was 1923 and Art was sixteen and a creature of the streets. The roaring twenties were roaring and Prohibition was in its third year. His parents had withdrawn from him and from life in general after the death of his older brother, Sam. They had spent most of their money on his brother Harry's education. They had written Art off as a wild son. They were simply too tired to control him.

First generation, third born was the way Art looked back on his childhood and his eventual chosen profession. *I was just there at the wrong place at the right time,* he thought.

The wrong place was the Brownsville section of Brooklyn. The right time was Prohibition. His first job was unloading booze from Canada in the middle of the night after it had made the run from Long Island to Brooklyn. The bootleg whiskey got to Long Island on the smugglers' boats. The pay was good and he could make in a few hours what it took his father a day to make. On good nights he might even get a bonus.

The next step was delivery to the clubs. He was doing that by the time he was eighteen. By then he was part of an organization that controlled the bootlegging and waterfront of Brooklyn. It was run by Italians and Jews. Words such as Mafia and Family came later. They were just gangs in those days.

When Arthur was eighteen his father came out of his depression long enough to take notice of his son's ways. There was a confrontation that brought his mother to tears and brought Arthur to City College as an accounting student. His father forced him to promise to finish school and keep away from the "bums." Art kept the first part of the promise, but not the latter. He was actually encouraged to go to school by the head of the gang . . . one Angelo Sorocco. Angelo was an immigrant and had been given a small section of Brooklyn by the "big boys." He was a good soldier and followed orders. As a result he was privy to the larger plans of the gang, and he was able to foresee the day when educated men, who could also be trusted, would be needed by the organization. "Go to school, Arty. Be an accountant . . . be a lawyer . . . use your Jewish brains and I promise you we will have a place for you when you finish."

Meanwhile, Arthur was given a steady night job in one of the downtown clubs at the cash register. By the time he had finished school, the Depression had begun. He was a Certified Public Accountant by day, and at night he collected the cash from fifteen different clubs in Brooklyn and Manhattan. When Prohibition was repealed in 1933, Arthur Perlman opened his own accounting firm. His only clients were the various businesses of the Brooklyn "Family." Many of the financial dealings of Brooklyn's organized crime filtered through the hands of Arthur Perlman, C.P.A.

Death entered the picture once again when, in a secret meeting in Atlantic City, a new company was formed. It was later known as Murder, Incorporated. Arthur Perlman was spared the job of handling its finances, but he was involved in setting up the fee structure and payment methodology for its services.

He took good care of his parents by buying them a home near his own in Manhattan Beach, an exclusive section of Brooklyn. He met Bess Bernstein at a neighborhood party one New Year's Eve, and they married one year later.

He loved Bess and especially loved the home she made for him. They had one child, a son, Harold. Bess had nearly died in childbirth and the doctor warned against having any more children. Harold and the house became Bess' life. Art's life was his work.

Now, as he watched Joe Finley pop the pills into his mouth, he thought back on the day that he had to tell Bess about his work. He knew he was going to be called before a grand jury and that his books were going to be subpoenaed. There might be publicity, and although the right newspapers, judges, and politicians had been taken care of, there was always the possibility that some nosy young D.A. wouldn't get the message and would begin to snoop around his home. The Organization had authorized him to reveal to Bess whatever he felt was necessary.

She had taken it well. Far better than Art had expected. But she did pop some pills into her mouth, too. "Just to relax me," she had said.

Then later, as they sat alone in the darkened living room, her voice broke the silence with a question that made Art realize how alone he was in the world outside of his business friends. "Arthur, tell me . . . did you ever kill anyone?"

"What are you asking?" he had answered. "Kill? Me kill? Are you crazy?"

"Arthur," she had replied, "I am not a stupid woman. I read the papers and from time to time I see the work you bring home. Some of the names . . . some of the clients . . . I read about them in the papers and I put two and two together. Just answer me that one question. I have to know. The rest will go to my grave with me . . . I promise."

"Never, darling . . . as God is my witness . . . never . . . " he had answered.

"What are you, a comedian today?" It was Ben Green talking to him.

Art said, "What?"

Ben answered, "I asked you to throw a card and you say never . . . "

"Sorry, Ben . . . I was daydreaming." Art threw a king of clubs and the game began.

• 14 •

The week had passed quickly for Jack Fischer. He stood on the flying bridge in the late afternoon light and watched the commanders bringing the last cocoon of the day to the surface. By his count, that made number sixty. He figured a bit more and calculated that at this rate it would take them about thirteen more weeks to raise all of the buried army of nine hundred forty one soldiers.

Jack was anxious to get back to Antares. Tonight he was going to see Judy for the first time since the adventure had begun.

He recalled how he had been locked in his room that first night and then had heard the key in the door and watched the light revealing Amos Bright. "I was so busy I almost forgot that you have to call your girl friend on the ship-to-shore radio. We'd better do that now."

Judy had been upset because she did not like to be alone. Jack suggested that she have a friend move in for the week. He even suggested a fellow actress with whom Judy took a class. "You can work with each other on that part you're going to do at the Grove Theater," he had said, and her mood had lightened.

"When will you be back?" she had asked.

Jack looked over at Amos and mouthed. "One week from now." Jack repeated those words to Judy.

There was a silence and then she said, "I'll see you here then. Don't bother to call. I may be out!" And she hung up the phone.

Amos apologized for the inconvenience and promised that if Judy was unreasonable he would do his best to explain to her. Jack told him that it would not be necessary.

The two copper men were lifting the last cocoon onto the deck. Hal and Harry were breaking down the equipment. Amos was giving All Light and No Light a hand as they climbed onto the deck.

The drill had become routine. Jack started the twin diesels and raised the anchor. Off to starboard, the *Terra Time* was already under way, heading back toward Coral Gables.

With a final check to be sure all were aboard and secure, Jack eased the powerful engines into gear and pulled back on the throttle. The twin diesels responded, cutting a neat wake through the darkening Gulf Stream. Home . . . a night off and the company of one warm, female, human being. He could imagine the taste of her and his body tingled with anticipation. The title of a recently popular song, "It Ain't Love, but Baby It Feels So Good," passed through his mind, and he began to sing the song to himself.

Below decks the scene was glum. A perfunctory inspection of the cocoons showed the same problem. There was condensation present. After the discovery of water damage in the first cocoon, they had sent their probe ship back to the mother ship, parked on the far side of the Moon. It had returned that night with special power supplies and regulators as well as a high-frequency drying unit. The new equipment made little difference. They had opened all ten of the cocoons that first night and revived them before dawn. When they were done the soldiers had been removed to another room on the upper floors to undergo intensive drying.

Both commanders agreed that the removal operation should continue, but instead of removing layers of cocoons they would penetrate the stack of cocoons vertically in order to reach those cocoons stored farthest away from the water. Today's batch was from the bottom of the sealed chamber, yet still they were damaged.

We will need nutrition from mother ship to-night, telepathed Bald White.

"Yes," they all agreed.

"I have already arranged the beaming," Amos volunteered.

Silence again. Each had closed down externals and was searching deep inside for answers. The mind was but an arrangement of atoms. With proper training and centuries of practical discipline, the Antarean beings could plunge themselves inward and reach the very centers of those atoms wherein lay all accumulated knowledge of their species. The energy controlled within the cabin of Jack Fischer's boat was immense, and now it was being directed down to the depths of the very souls of the strange visitors to Earth. They knew they had come up against a very serious problem. If they could not solve it, then their mission would end in failure and the Antarean reputation would be tarnished for millennia to come.

Oblivious to the galaxy-shaking problems below, Jack eased the *Manta III* down the canal and headed into the Antares dock. *Terra Time* was docked and deserted. Its crew was smaller than that of the *Manta III* and was made up only of aliens. There were three young men who resembled Hal and Harry and a woman who seemed to be in charge. Jack was convinced she was a commander with a female disguise. He wondered if she was bald under the beautiful head of blond hair that she wore. He thought briefly about the night three days ago when he had docked before the *Terra Time*. She had been on the flying bridge. Jack had casually sauntered over to the boat to say hello. The three boys had replied to his greeting, but the female only looked at him and then went about her business. Jack had a specific thought in mind as he bent down to tie his sneaker while she climbed down the ladder from the bridge. *I want to have a look under that dress*, he thought. *I want to see how much detail they gave you, my alien beauty.*

He still wasn't clear about telepathy and mind reading, and, of course, she knew exactly what was on his mind. Halfway down the ladder she stopped and stretched a leg for Jack over the outrigger bracket. He had a clear view under her skirt, but he was not prepared for what he saw.

Staring at him, where the flower of her femininity should be, was a duplicate of her pretty face and blond hair. The face was smiling and the lips were pursed. It blew him a kiss. He looked away quickly and the adrenaline pumped through his body.

• 15 •

As dusk came to Florida, the Antareans completed the off-loading of the day's cocoons harvest and prepared for processing. Jack Fischer showered and prepared for his night off. He always kept a clean change of clothes on board the *Manta III*. He made a mental note to remember to pack a bag for the week ahead.

Building A of the complex was alive with Friday night activity. There were sixty couples living in the building ranging in age from mid-fifties to late seventies. On Friday nights they gathered in the recreation room for dancing and general socializing. Usually at least thirty couples attended. Joe Finley brought his record player, and his collection of music from the thirties and forties.

The people gathered and the cliques formed. Tonight the Greens, Lewises, Perlmans, and Finleys were joined by two other couples they had casually befriended. They were Paul and Marie Amato, and Frank and Andrea Hankinson. The Amatos were from Boston. He was a retired stockbroker. The Hankinsons were from St. Louis. Frank Hankinson was semi-retired and still spent half the year in St. Louis tending to his interest in a radio station. They were referred to as "snowbirds" because they spent only the winters in Florida.

"Great job you guys did on the pool." Paul Amato was sincere. Ben Green told him they were only getting what they had a right to expect. The discussion drifted to the fact that Building B was still unfinished.

"You would think that they would want to get it completed as soon as possible," said Bernie Lewis.

They all agreed. Then Joe Finley asked Alma to dance. They were joined by the Hankinsons. Several couples were on the floor. They danced a fox trot to a Frank Sinatra song. It might have been a ballroom out of the forties as the couples swayed slowly to the music. These were couples who, for the most part, had spent their lives together. They knew what love and companionship were, and although society had discarded them to the Florida peninsula, they were content and at peace with each other. The active and hectic days of fighting for a living and rearing children had passed. The music was warm and slow. It reflected their lives.

Ben Green and Art Perlman sat observing the scene in silence. Their wives had gone to the kitchen to help with the coffee and cake.

Ben spoke in a sad and soft voice. "Look at us, Art." He gestured to the room of dancers. "It's not right to farm us out this way." It was a theme that Ben had brought up several times in the past few days.

Art nodded. "True, my friend, but what are you going to do? It's the way of our society . . . the old are useless, they say. Everything is young . . . young . . . young . . ." His voice trailed off.

"Bullshit!" said Ben. "I'll tell you the truth. I really felt good when we were pushing that bastard Shields to fill the pool."

"Yes, that was fun, I have to admit."

Ben continued: "I was thinking that we might speak to Shields about the mess over at Building B. I think we have a right to know when it will be finished."

"I agree," said Art. "He won't be around over the weekend, but we can see him on Monday morning before the card game."

"Good. Let's keep Joe Finley away just in case we need our Mr. Bonser from the Attorney General's office again."

Bernie, who had not commented at first, agreed.

The song ended and the two couples returned to the table. Ben and Art huddled with Joe and told him what they had planned to do. He thought it was a good idea. Bernie Lewis spoke up. "I think we ought to have a look over there tomorrow. We can get a better idea of how much work is left to do and we'll be able to confront Shields with some facts." Once again, the table agreed. The four men promised to meet at seven the next morning to have a look at Building B.

Amos Bright watched the lights go out in the recreation room of Building A. He turned to Jack Fischer. "They are going to bed. You can leave in twenty minutes. Let's be sure we understand each other, Mr. Fischer."

Jack prepared for the lecture again. "Mr. Bright, I promised to be back tomorrow morning before sunrise, and I'll be here. Judy won't know anything about this place."

"And you'll tell her that you have a treasure-diving charter for the next few months. Make sure she knows that you will be gone for a week at a time. I don't want her to be suspicious, and I certainly don't want her poking around this place."

Jack resented being treated like a child. Surely Amos knew that he was sincere. All he had to do was read Jack's mind.

"Harry has brought your car from your dock. It's parked in back. The keys are in the sun visor, and the tank is filled. Have a nice time. I will see you in the morning." Amos got up and walked to the door of Jack's room.

"Thanks," said Jack. There was no sarcasm in his voice this time. He realized the seriousness of the Antarean's problem with the cocoons. "I hope you can lick the moisture problem," he said.

Amos stopped near the door and looked at Jack. "Thank you, Jack. I'm not sure we can, but we have to continue trying every way we know. I appreciate your concern." He left the door open.

Ten minutes later Jack was driving out of the Antares complex. He drove over to U.S. Route 1 and then three miles south to his apartment near the Kenwood Shopping Center, where the neat garden apartments were set back from the street. Jack pulled into his parking space. The lights were on in his apartment and his heart skipped a beat as he thought of Judy waiting for him. He realized that he felt very deeply about her. *Easy,* he thought as he took the stairs two at a time. *That's a marrying type of lady up there, and you are not a marrying type of man right now.*

Judy was dressed to kill. She had the stereo playing a Judy Collins album. A bottle of wine was in the ice bucket. Two joints were neatly rolled. A plate of stone crabs with cold mustard sauce completed the table arrangement. Jack closed the door, and she crossed the room quickly. Her satin jumper clung to her body and shimmered in the light. Before Jack could say anything she was on him and her arms were around him and her body was tight against him. She kissed him hard and long and wet.

"Welcome home, sailor . . . welcome home from the sea." She led him to the sofa and left to pour to wine. She filled two glasses and then lit one of the joints. He watched, amazed at the care he was receiving.

A few drags and a few sips later and Jack completely forgot the world of cocoons. Judy did not speak again until they had finished their lovemaking. Jack knew they would not sleep that night. He felt the desire rising in him again. Judy brought the plate of crabs and the sauce to the sofa. They ate and sipped wine. Everything was delicious, including his beautiful girl.

"Now, lover, how was that?" Judy asked.

"I feel like I just died and went to heaven.

You are one super lady."

"Well, I knew that you would have had a long, hard week. We've never been away from each other for this long. I really missed you."

"And I missed you, Judy." Jack thought to himself that he'd better get the bad news over with quickly. "I'm afraid I have some unpleasant news, honey." Judy looked at him without any expression on her face. "I have a long charter. This could just about pay off the boat. I had to take it. I know you'll understand."

"Understand what?" she asked.

"Well" – he sipped the wine – "these folks are treasure hunters. I can't really talk about it, but . . . well . . . they are on to something and I agreed to work with them for the next few months."

"Oh, shit, Jack." Judy was furious. Right away, he could see that.

"Honey, it's over a thousand a week plus expenses. They might even cut me in on the booty. I had to take it!"

Suddenly she was crying . . . not hysterically, just softly. "Jack, your being away this week . . . it made me realize how deeply I feel about you. I think I've fallen in love with you . . . and now . . . away for two months . . . it hurts."

Jack felt suddenly smothered. Christ! The last thing he needed now was a demanding woman. The months ahead of him were going to be filled with his new space buddies. What if he told her that he couldn't spend the time with her because he had to work with creatures from another planet? That would go over big. Yet, he felt for her. He decided to ask Amos Bright whether he could bring her to the Antares complex. But right now he would have to deal with her present sorrow or he felt he would lose her forever. He reached for her and slipped her robe off, then bent and kissed her breast, and her neck, and her mouth, and her eyes, and on and on, until they were joined as one.

It was after midnight. The tenants of Building A were asleep. All except Alma Finley. She sat alone in the kitchen and sipped tea. Her thoughts were of Joe sleeping in the bedroom. There had been a definite change in him during the past few weeks. She noticed that he was walking slower and going to bed earlier. He was tired. The doctor said that this might happen from time to time. But this time it was prolonged, and he wasn't responding to the medication. Could this be the beginning of the end? Did she have the strength to face living without Joe? Did she want to?

Alma stood up and walked out onto the terrace. It was a mild night. The air was cool.

The sky above was filled with stars. As she glanced to the south her eye was stopped by a faint red line that seemed to come from the sky and pass directly onto the roof of Building B. She blinked because she thought she was seeing things. When she looked again it was gone. Then it was there again. *It looks like a laser beam,* she thought. *Maybe it's coming from the top of the building like a beacon.* Yes, that was it. It was an airplane beacon. There was probably one on top of Building A, too. Her thoughts returned to Joe.

The three commanders, Amos, the copper men, and the five crewmen were seated in a circle on the roof of Building B. In the center of the group was a glass object shaped like a bowl. Inside the bowl was a cluster of red glowing rocks. Each of the aliens had glasslike rods extending from their eyes into the bowl. Their human faces were off. As the red beam from the mother ship struck the bowl, the rocks glowed, and then the glow traveled up the rods into the eyes of the Antareans. The feeding lasted for thirty minutes. The crew sat in silence and ecstasy as they fed.

There was a large unfinished room on the roof. It was to be the solarium when Building B was completed. Now it was occupied with fifty

Antarean soldiers sitting in neat rows of ten. They were still and showed no sign of life except the glow in their wraparound eyes. In each row nine of the beings were dressed in pale blue, skintight jumpsuits. The tenth was a copper man. Each of the copper men had a device attached to his head that protruded in front of his eyes. A red beam inside the device was split three ways. Two of the beams went into the eyes of the copper men. The third beam came out of the device and passed down the row to the eyes of the other nine soldiers. The faces of the soldiers were splotchy. The stains were dark brown, as though their faces had been made of pine and the stains were knots. The first two soldiers in the first row were stained the worst. Suddenly the beam feeding the first soldier cut off abruptly in front of him. He twitched and emitted a deep humming sound. His eyes glowed bright for a moment and then went dark.

Outside, on the roof, Commander of All Light stopped feeding. He looked toward the room that housed the soldiers and then telepathed for the others to stop feeding. *We have lost the expendable. The second will go soon. I fear we will fail.*

Amos grew a bit, and silently blessed the departed soldier with the old thoughts: *Serve* the Master as you did your own. You have taken your reward. Guide us if you can as you move among the stars. We love you.

• 16 •

By the time the four men had entered Building B, the Antareans had left for the Gulf Stream. The first thing they noticed was the air conditioning.

"That's weird," Ben Green said.

"Maybe they're just testing the unit," Bernie suggested. The others made no comment.

"Where shall we start?" Art asked.

Joe Finley suggested they walk up to the second floor and then work their way higher until they were satisfied they knew enough. He hoped secretly they would be satisfied with just a few floors because he was tired this morning.

"Okay," Ben said. "Here's a stairwell . . . let's go."

Ben Green led the way from floor to floor. When they came to a new landing they would split up. Ben and Bernie would go to the south wing of the floor, and Art and Joe would go to the north side. If their search turned up nothing, then they would head back to the stairwell. If either team was not back, the other would wait five minutes and then look for the missing team.

At ten-thirty they were on the sixth floor. They had found nothing new since the second floor. Joe Finley was very tired and suggested that it was to no avail to search any farther. Ben Green disagreed but then quickly understood when Art Perlman flashed him a severe look.

"Okay," Ben said. "Let's head down. But I want to have a look at those locked doors we found on the second floor. I'm sure I heard sound coming from behind the orange one."

They walked down to the second floor and moved directly to the orange door. Ben put his ear against the door. "I hear a humming noise. How about it, Joe?"

Joe put his ear to the door. "I think you're right. Sounds like a machine of some sort." Art and Bernie leaned their ears to the door and agreed.

Ben tried the doorknob, but he couldn't budge it. "I'm going to get this door open," Ben said, "one way or the other."

"You mean break in?" Art asked.

"I said one way or the other, didn't I?" Ben answered.

Bernie and Joe looked at each other. Bernie

spoke first. "That could mean trouble, Ben . . . you know, breaking and entering."

Ben laughed. "I told you guys I was bored last night. So I spend a few days in the clink. It's better than sitting around here and vegetating. Besides, we own this place, don't we? How can you get in trouble for opening a door on your own property?"

"It's not exactly our property, friend," Art said, "not until the contractor finishes the building and turns it over to the corporation."

"A mere technicality," Ben retorted. "You guys give up too easily. I'm coming back after lunch with tools and get this lock opened!"

They left the building and went to the pool. They had worn their bathing suits on their excursion that morning, so before playing cards they all went for a swim. Ben Green was a strong swimmer and did ten laps. Bernie and Art swam a lap each and then lolled around in the Jacuzzi at the far end of the pool. Several of the Antares tenants were at the pool and they all had warms hellos for the boys.

"We're going to name this the Pool of the Fearsome Foursome!" yelled Paul Amato. Ben waved to him.

Joe was the last into the pool. He swam a few strokes, then turned and got out of the pool. *I could have swum a hundred laps a few years ago,* he thought. *Now* . . . and the expression "tired blood" crossed his mind. His blood wasn't tired. It was killing him.

They gathered at their table and played their daily gin game. As the noon hour approached they promised to meet in Building A's lobby after lunch. Joe begged off, saying he was going to nap. "If you need tools, I have some in the car," Joe volunteered. Ben told him that he had plenty of tools for the job.

They met at one-thirty without Joe, and the three men proceeded to Building B. On the way they saw Wally Parker walking in their direction. Bernie and Art suggested that they continue, but that Ben, who was carrying a toolbox and his auto jack, circle around the back of the building. They would open the back door for him.

Wally said a polite hello to the two men as they passed. He stopped and watched them walk toward Building B. "Excuse me gentlemen!" he shouted. "Where are you going?"

Bernie yelled back, "For our walk, aren't we?"

There was definite sarcasm in his voice. Wally decided that all old people were senile and those two seemed harmless enough. "Be careful of the construction equipment. We don't want any accidents," he called.

Bernie answered, "Who wants accidents? When are you going to finish this place, anyway?"

There was anger in his voice and Wally felt he had made a mistake in stopping the old codgers. The memory of Ben Green and the man from the Attorney General's office was still fresh in his mind. He didn't need more trouble. "Right," he called and continued on his way.

Art and Bernie laughed to themselves and detoured around the pool to Building B. When they arrived they found Ben waiting for them.

When the trio arrived at the orange door, Ben put his ear to it again. "Still humming," he remarked.

"How are you going to get in?" Bernie asked.

Ben answered, "I saw this in a movie once. We pry the back side of the door with the tire iron and I slip in the 'L' bracket so that it rests under the hinges on the other side. Then we slip the putty knife into the lock and it pops open."

"I don't understand," Bernie said.

"Just watch. You're never too old to learn."

He began to slip the tire iron into the slot at the rear of the door when Art Perlman spoke. "Just a minute, Ben. I think I have a better way . . . without damaging the door." He took an envelope from his pocket and removed a lock-picking set.

Ben and Bernie stared in amazement. "Where did you get that?" they both asked simultaneously.

"Arthur Perlman is a man of many accomplishments. In other words . . . don't ask!" he answered.

He slipped the lower pick into the deadbolt lock and then selected a smaller metal strip from the bottom of the lock. As he worked he thought about his youth again and the education he had received from the "Family." He could hear Angelo Sorocco explaining the art of picking a lock just as though he were standing by Art Perlman's side right now: *Be gentle and slow. Slip in the bottom probe carefully until you feel a click. If it doesn't click after two tries, then use the next smaller probe.* But that wasn't necessary because the lock popped almost immediately. Art pulled the probes out and, with a grand gesture, said, "Gentlemen . . . after you."

Although Ben was the official leader, it was Bernie Lewis who went into the room first. "What the hell is this?" he whispered. The others followed immediately. They stopped in their tracks and scanned the room.

The center table was empty. All of the cocoons that had been processed the night before had been moved to the roof. The room was glowing pale blue. The fixture over the center table was dormant. On the left there was a slight mist rising from the cabinets. The cots at the rear of the room were empty and their overhead units were also dormant. The screen on the right wall was the source of the pale blue light. On the floor in front of the screen were several pieces of apparatus that the aliens had brought recently from the mother ship in order to combat the moisture problem that was plaguing the cocoons.

Ben spoke first. "It's a health club."

"A health club?" Bernie asked. "Why a health club?"

"Well, just look. Those are steam cabinets over there and the table in the center is for massages. The cots in back are where you wait for the masseuse. Believe me, this is a health club," Ben answered.

"*Our* health club," added Art, who was walking toward the blue screen. "What the hell is this for?" he asked.

"Movies," Ben answered. Now he was sure of himself. "It's a wall TV unit. We had a smaller version at the ad agency. You can run films, or ball games, or music. We used to show pornos on it, too."

Bernie was excited. "Hey, this is great. It

looks ready to me. Those rats were going to keep it closed until they finished the building. I think we ought to go down there and chew their asses out about this." He moved toward the cabinets.

"Just a minute," Ben suggested. "Let's think about this."

Art asked, "Why? Bernie's right. The club looks okay to me. Why shouldn't we use it?"

"I'm not saying we shouldn't use it," Ben said. "I'm only saying that it seems to me that if we keep our mouths shut about this place, we can have exclusive use of it . . . and no one will be the wiser . . . for a while, anyway."

"We have to tell Joe about it," Art said.

"Sure . . . of course we tell Joe, but that's all. At least for a week or so. What do you say?" Ben asked. Both men agreed and each went off in a different direction to examine the room in detail.

Joe awoke from his nap to find Alma sitting on the edge of the bed. She was holding his hand. "Feel better?" she asked.

"Yeah, that was a good sleep," he answered, "and I'm hungry."

"Good," she said. "I'll fix you a ham-and-Swiss on rye. Want a beer?" She didn't wait for an answer. If he didn't say no, that meant yes.

Joe got out of bed and decided to shower.

When he came into the kitchen his lunch was on the table. He did feel better, but he still felt tired. "Couldn't you sleep last night?" he asked. "I heard you get out of bed after midnight."

She looked at him with some surprise because she was sure he was fast asleep when she had gotten up. "Just restless. I had too much coffee at the dance last night," she answered.

"How late were you up?" he asked.

Why is he pressing me, she thought. *Maybe he wants to talk about it.* "Not too late, dear. I think I got into bed around one."

"Oh," he answered, and went back to eating.

No, she thought, *he doesn't want to talk. I'll change the subject.* "I would have gone to bed sooner, but I saw something strange over on the roof of the other building. It took me awhile to figure it out." *Good going, Alma,* she thought.

"What did you see?" he asked.

She proceeded to tell him about the red laser light on the roof of Building B and how she had finally deduced that it was an airplane beacon.

"That's strange," he said. "These buildings aren't so tall that they would be a menace to air traffic."

"Maybe we're in a flight pattern," she said.

"I don't recall hearing planes at all," he said, then went back to his lunch.

"Well, anyway, it stopped after a few minutes. I'm sure there is some explanation," she remarked. "What do you want to do for the rest of the day?"

"Let's just take it easy, honey. How about a drive down to the beach?" he suggested.

"Love it," she said, and went to the bedroom to change into a bathing suit. She felt good that he wanted to get out, but deep inside she knew he was fighting off the desire to sleep. She promised to call the doctor Monday without his knowing and ask about these recent symptoms.

By the time Joe and Alma Finley were heading for the beach, Bernie Lewis was in a "steam cabinet" having a very good time. It had taken a few minutes to open the cabinet. Bernie had been puzzled because he was used to sitting in a steam cabinet. One had to lie down in these. He slipped his body in and called Art over to close the door. It took some time until they figured out how to turn it on. When the mist increased they knew they had hit the right button. It wasn't hot, but Bernie felt as though he was being massaged inside the cabinet. It felt great and he suggested that Art get in the next one and show Ben how to operate it. With Art encased next to Bernie, Ben went off to explore the other equipment.

He walked around the big center table twice.

The surface was smooth, but it had give to it. He could press his fingers into the material, which resembled a shiny black patent leather. Once he withdrew his finger the material immediately sprang back to its original form. Strange stuff, thought Ben. He left the table and went over to the row of cots on the back wall. He lay down on the first cot and the overhead conical light went on. It began to hum and then the white light beam came out of the cone and split into two green beams. Ben jumped off the cot just before the beam reached his eyes. The overhead light went off. He yelled over to Art and Bernie, "This is weird, guys. They really have the latest equipment here. I've never seen some of this stuff."

Bernie yelled back, "It might be weird, but it sure feels great. You ought to try this. I'm about done. Come on."

Ben went over and helped Bernie out of his cabinet. Bernie stretched and felt wonderful. "Boy, I don't know what that thing is, but it sure woke this old body up."

Ben started to get into the cabinet that Bernie had just vacated when Art suggested that Ben try the third cabinet. "Maybe they're different. Let's find out. All I know is I'm not leaving this one for a while. I feel like I'm getting laid."

Ben laughed and eagerly slipped into the

third cabinet. Art closed the door and turned it on. A smile came across Ben's face. "Holy shit . . . this is sensational! If we tell the others about this place, we won't get near it for a month."

"Roger," agreed Bernie. "I bet this place will perk Joe right up, too!"

They agreed that as soon as possible they would bring Joe to their new, and private, health club.

· **17** ·

Although Judy Simmons had reluctantly agreed to accept the fact that Jack would be away for a week at a time, she found herself depressed and lonely the next morning. It took two hours to clean the small apartment, do laundry, and make her calls. This morning she had exercise class at eleven. Otherwise, she was free for the day. By two that afternoon she had worked herself into a state of anger. She understood Jack's taking the work, but she was not convinced that she would be in the way if she came along for a week or two. He could tell the clients that she was the mate and that he needed her aboard.

Later that evening Jack's brother, Arnie, called, looking for Jack. Judy told him about the charter. Arnie thought it was great news and then put his new wife, Sandy, on the phone. She invited Judy for dinner the next night. "I'd love that," Judy responded to the invitation.

"Maybe we can call Jack on the radio phone."

Sandy said, "Fine . . . we'll see you about seven." and hung up.

Okay, Jack Fischer, thought Judy, *you're going to invite me onto that boat next week whether you know it or not.* After that she felt better. She called her friend Monica and the two actresses got stoned and listened to music until three in the morning.

At the time that Judy and Monica were crashing on the waterbed, Jack Fischer was up to his waist in cocoons. The day's harvest had been brought into the processing room. Amos Bright had been pleased with Jack's promised return and his obvious cooperation. As a reward the aliens agreed to reveal more of their operation to Jack.

After docking that evening they allowed him to off-load the cocoons with Hal and Harry. Jack was surprised by the texture and apparent lightness of the cocoons. They were not solid but pliable and pleasing to the touch. He thought of Jell-O as he lifted the first one, nearly dropping it onto the deck. The other surprising quality of the cocoons was their warmth. He was so enthralled with the sensations that he did not notice the black commander watching him. However, shortly thereafter Jack felt him.

Take care, Commander of No Light telepathed severely.

The thought ran through Jack like an electric shock. *Sorry,* thought Jack. The pain immediately stopped.

Another voice in Jack's head said, *Very good, Jack . . . you are beginning to telepath.* It was the voice of Amos Bright.

Hal and Harry both looked at Jack and smiled warmly. Jack smiled back, very proud of his accomplishment, but not quite sure how he did it.

Amos signaled again. *Don't think about how, Jack, just do it. Practice with us and you will come to know how to control. For now we will listen for your thoughts and send you ours. Later you will be able to call us at will. Your race has the ability, but you have not yet developed that ability. Perhaps you can teach the rest when we are gone.*

It was good to be able to work and communicate with aliens, but it bothered Jack that he could not have a private thought without their knowing. That was unsettling, yet there was little he could do about it. He accepted it.

After the cocoons had been delivered to the processing room and encased in the cabinets, Jack went to his room for a shower and dinner. There were fresh linens on the bed and fresh towels in the bathroom. Maid service, he thought. The warm shower felt especially good this evening. The lovemaking last night had continued through the wee hours of the morning. He was tired. Why did Amos pick this night to reveal more things to him? *Maybe I'll explain to Amos and he'll give me a rain check.* As he dried himself there was a knock at the door.

"Just a second," Jack called. By the time he opened the door his visitor was gone, but his dinner was on a tray placed neatly in front of the door. The menu tonight was red snapper in lemon-butter sauce, mashed potatoes, carrots, salad, coffee, and cake. *I've got to meet their chef one of these days,* Jack thought. The food was getting better each day, as though someone was getting attuned to his taste. Perhaps someone was. With these folks, anything was possible.

By the time Jack got to the orange door, the group was processing the third cocoon. Amos telepathed him to enter the room. Jack thought about being tired and Amos read his thoughts. Amos' voice filled his mind. *Go to the last cot and lie down for a moment. Don't be afraid of the light beams. They won't hurt you. Relax, and the tiredness will leave you.*

Jack did as he was told and felt wonderfully refreshed after a few moments. *The world could sure use this device,* thought Jack.

Amos silently agreed. *Perhaps we will leave one for you Jack,* he beamed, *but for now we could use your help.*

Jack got off the cot and the beams shut down. "How can I help tonight?" he said aloud.

Commander of All Light motioned Jack to the cabinets and telepathed for him to give Hal a hand. As they loaded the cocoons and adjusted the settings on the cabinet control panels, Hal explained that the cabinets began the process of tissue restoration as well as a complete cleaning and priming of all glandular activity. The process, like most of the technology of the Antareans, began from within the cocoon. There were chemicals and molecular constructions stored inside the cocoon and the body of the soldier. The process in the cabinet filtered through to the stored chemicals and started a chain reaction that was the first step in restoring life to the soldier. Hal showed Jack the various settings on the first five cabinets. Jack had not realized that the last five cabinets were different and that the cocoons had to spend time in one of the first five cabinets, and then a few moments in one of the last five cabinets before moving to the center table to be peeled.

"What do the second group of cabinets accomplish?" asked Jack.

Hal did not answer for a moment because he was checking with the commanders to see whether he was authorized to explain that part of the process to the Earth helper. He received an okay from both commanders in the room. "Help me with the first cocoon and I'll show you what happens next." As they slid the cocoon from the first cabinet onto the wheeled table, Hal gestured to leave it for a moment. They walked to the back of the room and wheeled a fresh cocoon to the first cabinet and inserted it for processing. Then they wheeled the other cocoon to the sixth cabinet and inserted it. Hal closed the cabinet door and beckoned Jack to the control panel. "All living matter carries some disease and decay within it, Jack. This set of cabinets cleanses the tissues, organs, and blood of all such substances. It gives the soldier a perfect start for his new life."

Jack couldn't believe what he had just heard. "That's incredible. You mean these soldiers start over with perfect health?" Jack asked.

"Absolutely," answered Hal. "It's quite necessary for a mission to another planet. We don't want them carrying diseases for which there is no immunity on other worlds. That would be disastrous."

Just like the white man did to the Hawaiians, thought Jack.

Amos' voice entered his mind. *Hawaiians?*

Yes, thought Jack. *We have a place on the Earth called Hawaii. They are islands in the middle of the Pacific Ocean. When they were discovered by the white man there were natives living on the islands. The white men brought diseases with them for which the natives had no immunity. Almost all of them were killed by illness.* Jack realized that he was telepathing once again.

Amos entered his mind, saying, *That was good, Jack, and you are correct about the purpose of the second set of cabinets. That is exactly their function.*

For the rest of the night Jack helped Hal insert and move the cocoons from cabinet to cabinet to center table. It was dawn when they finished, but Jack was not tired. Amos told him that he could sleep for an hour or two if he chose.

"But I don't feel tired," Jack answered aloud.

"Good," Amos replied. "I didn't think it would work that well with Earth beings. You can use the cots if you do not wish to sleep. It provides the same purpose as sleep."

To fortify himself in case of drowsiness, Jack walked to one of the empty cots and lay down for five minutes. When he got up he felt as though he could work twenty-four hours non-stop. The level of energy surging inside him was a sensation he had never felt before and that he could never forget.

· **18** ·

Ben Green looked as though he was covered with a fine white ash. "You look like you're covered with Shake 'n' Bake," said Bernie. "What the hell is that stuff?"

Ben Green wiped some of the ash from his forehead. It came off easily and disappeared from his finger. "Beats me," he said, "except I feel very . . ." – he hesitated – " . . . dry . . . yes . . . dry is the word. Like I've been in an oven, but there was no heat."

The ash was a result of his lying on the center table for a minute. He had decided to try the table today. This was their third day in the "health club." Ben had tried the table the day before, but when the overhead cone turned on he got scared and jumped off the table. This time he stayed there and the feeling was quite pleasant. The ash could not be explained, but it didn't seem to be harmful. He brushed if off his hands, but none of it ever reached the floor. It simply vanished in air. "I thought the damned thing burned me," said Ben, "but my hair is still here. I don't know what this lamp does, but I can recommend it highly."

Art, who was in the first cabinet, yelled that he would try the table after he finished his steam bath.

The most confused man in the room was Joe Finley. At this moment he was lying in the eighth cabinet. He had been in there for ten minutes and was experiencing a very strange feeling. He had discovered that the control panels on the last five cabinets were slightly different from the first five. The others had not noticed that before. Yesterday, when his friends had shown him the room, his thoughts were still on the effects of the disease he was experiencing. The tiredness was definitely growing. What good would a health club be to a dying man, he thought? But because of his friends' excitement, he decided to come and share their discovery. He had spent twenty minutes in the third cabinet next to Bernie Lewis. It was odd, but when he got out he felt much better. Then they all had watched Art Perlman lie down on one of the cots and allow the beams to spread over his body. He related the experience to his buddies and they all had taken a cot and shared the experience. Afterward, they went out to the pool for their swim and card game, which was when the surprises began to happen.

Ben Green hit the pool first and began to swim his normal laps. Bernie and Art dove in next and caught up with Ben. The trio swam until they realized that they were racing and that the people around the pool were cheering them on. They had done twenty laps when Bernie suggested they stop. No one was tired. They were breathing very hard and their hearts were beating rapidly. But they were definitely not tired. Then they saw that Joe Finley was nowhere to be seen. Ben yelled for him. No answer. Suddenly Joe exploded out of the water in front of them. He had swum the entire length of the pool underwater. He slid out of the pool in one graceful motion up onto the ledge. In a split-second he was standing next to his three buddies. "Guys," he said, "I don't know what kind of equipment they put in that health club, but I feel absolutely great. I can't wait to get back there tomorrow."

The four men then sat down at their table and began the card game. No one could think straight because of the new physical feelings they were having.

Finally, Ben spoke. "Let's meet in my apartment this afternoon. The girls have their mah-jongg game, so we won't be disturbed. I think we have to talk about that place."

"I agree," said Art. "I think we have stumbled on to something special. I can't explain. Just a feeling. But . . ."

Bernie Lewis interrupted. "Keep it down, guys, or we'll have the entire condominium jammed into that room."

They nodded.

They didn't notice the other phenomena that were occurring because of their excitement. Normally they played gin for two hours before lunch. On a good day they got about thirty hands completed. Today they played twice that number. For the most part they also knew what the next card was before they picked it, and they had some very strong feelings about what hand their opponents were playing, too. No one realized it, but they were reading each other's minds and thoughts. Much later they would understand why.

After lunch they met at Ben's. He had a corner apartment on the fifth floor and therefore a large balcony. Now the four men sat in chaise longue chairs and sipped iced coffee as they talked about their discovery and what it meant.

"I still feel super." Joe opened the conversation.

"Me, too," chimed in Bernie, "and I'll tell you a little secret. After lunch I took Rose to the bedroom . . . had a matinee. I haven't done that for . . . well, more than ten years, at least. And I could have stayed with her all afternoon."

The others laughed, but they understood what Bernie was talking about. The same feeling had crossed each of their minds. Bernie was just a man of action. They felt as though they had missed something and each made a mental note to give it a try.

"I think Joe was right this morning. We have found something that is extraordinary. This must be very new equipment, maybe even experimental stuff . . . but what it is . . . I don't know. Any ideas?" Ben asked.

Art spoke next. "I don't know what the stuff is, but I think we should keep it quiet for a little while. If everyone in this place began to feel like I do this afternoon, we would have a mob scene."

Joe Finley was quiet now. He stared out toward the pool and watched a man in his seventies struggle to swim a few laps. He recalled diving into the pool that morning and swimming underwater without taking a breath. It had felt natural. While he was underwater he had the feeling that he was a diver. He was no longer in a pool, but rather in the ocean. The water was warm and crystal clear. Below him he could see other divers, and below them objects that appeared to be long white tubes of some sort. Then the image had blurred and he had popped out of the water to greet his friends. Now as he watched the old man swim he decided to withhold his experience from his friends until he understood what it meant. Still, he spoke. "I think there is a proper sequence to the equipment," he said. "I don't know what that sequence is, but I believe we should experiment. Tomorrow, let's give it a real thorough going over and see if we can figure out the differences and find a sequence."

"How can we do that?" asked Art. "We don't know even what the damned stuff is!"

"Well," answered Joe, "I've been thinking about that. There are four of us, and as far as I can see there are six different pieces of equipment. The cabinets, the cots, the center table, and two devices near the screen wall, and maybe the wall itself. Notice how it changed color when Ben got onto the center table today? I think we should each start with a different piece of equipment and go through a particular sequence. Then let's wait a day and reverse the sequence. By that time we should have some idea of what each one does."

"Sounds good," said Ben. "Of course, another way to do it is to have one of us do a sequence and observe how he feels and what his reactions are. Then another can do it differently."

"That would take too long," said Joe impatiently. His voice was sharp and curt. The others looked at him questioningly. "Sorry, guys," he said. "Look, you know my problem. Well, lately I've been having some bad symptoms. I know you noticed and I thank you for keeping it to yourselves. I can't explain it, but somehow this room is a very special place. To me it's like . . . like being reborn in a way. I spent twenty minutes in that cabinet and a few minutes on the cot. Do you guys know I swam the pool underwater?"

"Sure," said Ben, "we saw you."

"No," said Joe, "you saw me at the end. I swam four laps underwater . . . without stopping for air."

"My God!" said Bernie. "Are you shitting us? Four laps underwater? How?"

"I don't know how," answered Joe. "That's just my point. It certainly has to do with the room, and I'm going to find out how it does and what that means. I tell you guys, and I wasn't going to say this, but somehow I believe that the answer to my troubles is in that room, and nothing is going to stop me from finding out."

"Amen," murmured Art Perlman.

"Amen," the group echoed.

• 19 •

Alma was surprised that Joe wanted to make such an early appointment with the doctor. Now, as they drove back to Antares, she contemplated the strange actions that her husband had exhibited in the past twenty-four hours. He was intent on getting back to the complex. He concentrated on driving. Conversation was nonexistent, so she had time to think.

He had returned from the gin game just after noon. He seemed preoccupied when she had asked him what he wanted for lunch. His request for a sizable meal stunned her. Then as she leaned to give him a peck on the cheek he embraced her with a strength she had not felt for years. They kissed and he had slid his hands around to her breasts, then bent down and kissed them through the soft cashmere of her sweater. This sensation alone had almost given her an orgasm. She had pulled away and made a joke about lunch. Actually, she was disoriented from the surge of passion that she had felt.

Joe wolfed down his lunch and was showering when she left for the mah-jongg game. She yelled, "See you later, honey," into the shower. A loud, "You betchum, Red Ryder," had boomed back at her.

Puzzled, she left Joe singing in the shower.

The mah-jongg game had been pleasant, but there, too, something was different. Alma finally realized toward the end of the game that the difference was Rose Lewis. Rose was a good player and kept things moving. Today Rose was in another world. She seemed preoccupied, almost in shock. Her excuse was that she felt as if she was coming down with something . . . perhaps the flu. The other women accepted the explanation. Alma didn't.

As the afternoon drew to a close, Rose seemed impatient. Alma, still confused by Joe's sudden surge of energy, felt the need to get home early. She suggested that they break early so that Rose could get into bed and try to fight off the flu.

Rose's reaction was violent, especially at the mention of bed. "Bed?" she had said. "I'm not going to bed. What would I do in bed?"

"Rest," said Bess Perlman. "Rest . . . take some aspirin and stop the fever. That's what you do in bed."

Rose stared at her for a moment, then smiled

and said, "Of course . . . you're right . . . I'll do exactly that."

Then the game broke up.

Alma returned to her apartment to find Joe sitting on their terrace sipping a gin-and-tonic. She had not seen him take a drink of hard liquor in months.

"Join me?" he had asked, and she had said okay. "One silver bullet coming up," he said as he got up and moved toward their portable bar. She noticed that he had a martini glass on ice and a small pitcher already mixed. He poured the drink and handed it to her.

"Joe, do you feel . . ?" But she didn't have time to complete the question.

"To us and to love and to this wonderful place," he toasted, interrupting her. "And mostly to the woman I love very very, *very* much."

They drank. She finished her drink in one gulp and he quickly filled her glass again. "You're going to get me drunk," she had protested.

"Not drunk, sweetheart, just a little warm." She blushed because she knew what was coming, remembering the noontime embrace. She had been right.

He took her around the waist and led her to the bedroom. The bedspread had been removed. The covers had been turned back. The curtains were drawn and the radio was tuned to an FM station playing classical music. He took her drink and placed it on the night table, then turned and kissed her softly. She was floating. She vaguely remembered her husband taking off her clothes and then his own clothes. They were sitting on the bed, lying on the bed. Then they were all over the bed and each other. It went on for three hours . . . loving . . . resting . . . touching . . . loving . . . resting. At one point he led her to the shower and they made love there, too. It was like a dream and she dared not interrupt it. Finally, he said, "Now, darling, this old retired actor would like something rare and juicy to eat. I'm starved."

As she prepared the steaks, he napped. Alma Finley, a woman who prided herself in having control over her life and her emotions, wept some very happy tears onto French-fried potatoes.

• 20 •

The car pulled into the complex and Joe drove directly to their parking spot. He was out of the car in a flash and headed toward the pool. "I don't want to be late for the game!" he yelled over his shoulder. "See you for lunch." Alma got out and watched him disappear around the building. *Lunch — who eats lunch?* she thought. Not when you're married to the last of the red-hot lovers!

Alma returned to the apartment. As she put the key in the lock, she heard the phone ringing. She rushed to answer and found a distraught Rose Lewis on the other end.

"Alma, I've been trying you all morning. I have to talk to someone. Do you have time . . . now?"

"We were at the doctor's early today," she answered.

"Can I come over?" asked Rose.

"Certainly. I'll put up some coffee."

146

The phone went dead. *Strange,* thought Alma. *Rose is always sensitive to Joe's illness. She usually asks what the doctor said, but not this time. It must be serious.* She went to the kitchen and put up a pot of coffee.

As Rose Lewis made a beeline toward the Finley apartment, Mary Green was waking up. She reached out her hand toward her husband but he was gone. She sat up and saw a note on his pillow:

You went back to sleep and you looked so peaceful I didn't want to wake you. I'm off to play gin. See you later. Kisses.

Mary fell back on her pillows and stretched. Her body felt a bit sore, but wonderful. Her back hurt slightly. She also felt the wetness of the sheet under her. *Ben Green,* she thought, *you are a dirty old man. But great . . . just great.* Twice last night and again this morning. They had always had a fairly good sex life, but this was different. He seemed stronger and younger. He was gentle and caring and patient. He was, she thought, like . . . like what? Like a lover? Yes. More. Like a stranger who knew her. She realized that she was the stranger to herself. She was happy and smiling like a schoolgirl as she fell back to sleep again.

147

Bess Perlman did not feel like a schoolgirl at all. She sat alone in the kitchen sipping her coffee. Art had left for the daily gin game after she had pleaded with him to leave her alone. "You are like an animal!" she had yelled. "Enough already."

Last night until two in the morning and then bright and early he wanted her again. "Arthur," she had begged, "please leave me alone . . . I can't now."

"I love you," he had answered.

"I love you, too, but it's been a long time and I'm just not prepared for this." She had begun to cry and he had stroked her head and held her close and apologized.

"I'm sorry, honey. I'm sorry. We'll talk about it later."

Talk about what? What had gotten into him? He had sounded so positive and strong. Was this going to be a new thing? Was she prepared to deal with it? Did she want it? Did she need it? There were too many questions bouncing around inside her head. She decided she needed to talk to someone. She reached for the phone, but there was no answer at Rose Lewis' apartment.

Rose related the story nonstop, almost without taking a breath. "This may seem personal and I'm sorry, but I respect you and your attitude on things . . . I mean, you and I are friends. Not old friends, but I feel good about you and I have to talk to someone. Yesterday. It began yesterday. At lunch. My Bernie came in for lunch and it was ready for him on the table. It was his favorite — chopped liver and potato salad. A new pickle. A Dr. Brown's Cel-Ray. He didn't even see it. He . . . he came at me . . . he grabbed me . . . not violent . . . but, like a young man grabs a girl. He didn't ask. Nothing. Just took me and carried me. I said *carried* me into the bedroom and put me on the bed. I'm sorry, Alma." She began to cry.

"It's okay," said Alma. She was stunned because in many ways Rose Lewis was talking about feelings that she had had regarding her own husband's actions, too.

Rose continued: "We have been married a long time. A good life, but my Bernie is a difficult man. Sex was sex. It was okay, but never a big deal. I come from an upbringing where it was never discussed. I was taught that a woman was there for a man. You know what I mean." Alma nodded.

"So suddenly, after a long time, I mean we are not spring chickens anymore, Bernie comes in and, out of the blue, sweeps me into the bedroom and undresses me and makes love to me in a way he never did in all the years we've been married. He was like a stranger. But kind."

She stopped again and sobbed. Alma moved her chair closer to Rose and put her arm around her. "I know what you are saying, Rose. Believe me, I know."

Rose looked up at her. "You do?"

Alma felt a tear in her eye, too. "Rose, dear, I really do!"

"I'm not finished," said Rose. "I called you because at the game yesterday I had a feeling that you somehow understood that I was uncomfortable. Somehow I felt that you knew."

"Yes," said Alma, "I knew something was wrong, and it wasn't the flu."

"When I went back to the apartment Bernie was there. He wanted to talk, but I cut him off. I told him I didn't want to talk about it. You have to know Bernie to see how funny that is, because that's his favorite line when he wants to end a discussion. Alma . . . I'm afraid. I'm afraid that after forty years of marriage I suddenly have a stranger living with me and I don't know what to do."

She looked down in her coffee and Alma squeezed her hand again and tried to think of something to say to her friend.

As their wives struggled and reflected on their newfound lovers, the four men had entered their private health club and now stood at the center table planning the morning's activities.

The wall screen was its familiar pale blue. The quiet hum filled the room. A fine mist rose from the cabinets. All of the overhead "lamps" were off.

"Let's have a look at those two things over near the wall," suggested Ben Green.

The men walked over to the first device. It was just three feet tall and cylindrical in shape with a diameter of about one foot. The color was silver, but dull, and there were no controls or cables. The device seemed solid. On the top were two round white dots.

The men circled it for a moment. Then Ben reached his hand toward the dots. As he made contact the thing hummed and glowed red. When he pulled his hand away it stopped.

"Nothing," said Ben.

"What the hell is it?" asked Art.

Ben was about to answer Art when Bernie Lewis let out a "Holy shit!"

The other three looked at him and then down to his bathing suit. Bernie was staring at his suit, too.

"What is it?" asked Joe Finley.

"My suit," said Bernie. "This morning I went in for a dip before we met. My suit was wet when we came here. Look now. The front of the suit is dry . . . bone dry, and the back is still wet. This thing must be some kind of dryer."

Ben touched his suit and agreed. "I think you're right. It makes sense, too. We use this before we leave to dry the sweat."

"Or before we start to dry our clothing?" suggested Joe.

In either case, they agreed they had found a dryer and it belonged at the beginning or end of the "health club" sequence.

The next device was farther down the blue wall toward the rear of the room. It was larger and, in fact, reached to the ceiling. It appeared to be a black cabinet, or storage locker of some kind. It was about six feet wide and they estimated at least fifteen feet tall. Its depth was only about two feet. They could not see a door or opening of any kind. The men began looking around the sides and base of the cabinet for a handle or control panel.

"Here it is," said Joe. His fingers were touching a slight bulge in the lower right panel. "Here goes nothing," he said and pressed the bulge.

Instantly, the front of the cabinet disappeared, as if by magic, and revealed row upon row of slim silver handles. Art did some quick mathematics and told the others that there were nine hundred forty one handles. Fifty were missing.

Ben grasped one of the handles closest to him and pulled. He could not move it. The others each tried various handles at random, but with no success. Then Joe Finley told them to back off. He studied the contents of the cabinet for a moment and reached for the handle next to the last missing one. Sure enough, it came sliding out. It was attached to a slim silver case.

They tried to open the case for fifteen minutes, but to no avail. Finally, Ben Green suggested that they replace it, since obviously it required a key or special device to get it open.

Joe was reluctant to give up. "It really bugs me," he said. "What could possibly be in here?"

"Lockers?" suggested Bernie Lewis.

They all laughed and Joe replaced the case in the same slot. He then bent down and pressed the bulge. Immediately, the front panel appeared and the case was sealed once again.

"I suggest we keep these two devices out of the cycle for now," said Ben. "Why don't we each start in a different place?" The others agreed and it was decided that Ben would take cabinet number one, Bernie would take cabinet number six, Art would lie on one of the small cots at the rear of the room, and Joe Finley would take the center table. They would stay for ten minutes and then discuss how they felt and what they felt.

The plan was good, they felt, but they weren't prepared for the changes that occurred when the blue wall turned red.

• 21 •

Arnie Fischer gave Judy a big hug at the door that lifted her right off the ground. Sandy called from the kitchen, "You two had better stop that messing around. He's a married man now!"

"Sorry, honey. Force of habit," answered Arnie. Judy laughed. "Want a drink?"

"Sure. Got any wine?"

"Coming up," said Arnie as he moved toward the small portable bar in the dining room.

Arnie and Sandy had been married for a few weeks, but they had lived together for three years, off and on. Arnie was an art director at a small advertising agency in Miami. He was a talented commercial artist, too, and made extra money doing illustrations. He was three years older than Jack, and had a very different personality. Arnie was solid and responsible. The few years' difference between the brothers had kept them separated until lately. Arnie had

155

missed Vietnam because of a college deferment and a subsequent career as a teacher. Jack had been drafted into the navy. He served on gunboats in the Mekong Delta and had been in the heart of the action. After his return to the States, Arnie had made an effort to know his younger brother and they had become very close. Their parents were dead and, apart from one aunt in Cleveland and two cousins in California, they had no family.

Physically, Arnie was shorter and lighter than Jack. He was a fitness nut, so he was in good shape. Jack, on the other hand, was a good six inches taller and thirty pounds heavier. Although Arnie was stronger, Jack could put a bear hug on him and immobilize his older brother. As youngsters Arnie and Jack always fought, and the three years' difference weighed in Arnie's favor until Jack was eighteen. Jack had received his draft notice and Arnie had pleaded with him to enroll in college for a deferment. Jack had refused and the discussion quickly turned into a pushing match that wound up as a knock-down, drag-out fight. Jack exploded on his brother and broke two of Arnie's ribs and put a hairline fracture in his jaw. Jack proved he was no longer "little brother."

"Ice?" asked Arnie.

"Fine," said Judy. Her thoughts were far away with Jack.

"You okay?" he asked, handing her the chablis.

"Sure, love. I just miss the bum."

Sandy came in from the kitchen and kissed Judy hello, then asked Arnie to fix her a glass of wine.

"Want a joint?" she asked Judy.

"Not now. I got ripped last night with Monica."

Arnie brought the drink to his wife and sat next to her on the fluffy sofa. Judy sat on the floor pillow opposite them.

"Tell me about this charter my brother, the captain, took on," Arnie said.

"He didn't tell me that much," answered Judy, "except that it was some kind of treasure hunt or something and they wanted him for three months. He'll be in on weekends."

"Where are they diving?" Sandy was interested. She was an amateur diver with a scuba license that cleared her for depths up to one hundred fifty feet.

"I don't know, but I think off the Bahamas. One of the Windward Islands. He was vague. I guess they don't want him to talk about it." Her voice was low. *Why am I so damned emotional?* she thought.

Sandy picked up on it immediately. "You want to call him on the radio phone?"

Judy looked at her watch. It was eight P.M. "Let's wait till after dinner." She perked up. "What's on the menu?"

"Stone crabs, mustard sauce, salad, and . . . Key lime pie," Sandy answered proudly.

"Wow! Aren't we the gourmet bride," joked Judy. "I'm starved and that sounds great!" They went out to the Florida room to eat.

The day had been a bit different for Jack and the band of Antareans. They had brought only three cocoons in from The Stones. These were slightly different from the rest in that they seemed larger and had a silver dome at the head and foot. Amos had telepathed that these were three of the group commanders. They were not commanders in the sense that All Light, No Light and the female, whose name was Beam, were commanders, but they did have special powers and training. Their cocoons were slightly different, too. Jack recalled the first day, when Amos had explained the structure of the little army. These commanders had ninety soldiers under them in groups of ten.

After docking and moving the cocoons to the orange room, Jack had gone to his room to shower and eat. He had just removed his deck shoes when he felt something was wrong. It was a small pain that went through him. Without knowing why, he went quickly out of the room through the orange door. *Something's wrong,* he thought.

Yes, answered Amos into his mind.

What? telepathed Jack. *Are the group commanders damaged, too?*

No, thought All Light. *We think perhaps someone was here today.*

Then Jack realized that the room was warm but they had not yet begun the processing. Everything looked normal. The wall was blue, the cabinets misting, the lamps off, but, yes, the room was normally cool before they began processing. Now it was warm. All their thoughts were attuned and Jack was with them. Amos broke the puzzlement by suggesting a possible overload in the electrics. Hal would check it out. While he went for the test equipment they began processing the three command cocoons.

It was no wonder the room was still warm. The four men had been in there for most of the day, and had, in fact, left only an hour before the Antareans returned. The day had started with a frightening experience followed by the most wonderful feelings that these men had ever had.

Ben Green noticed the color change first. "Hey, guys, look at the wall. It's going red!" he yelled from his cabinet. Art and Joe were under their respective lamps and didn't want to open their eyes.

Bernie looked up from cabinet six. "I'll be damned. Maybe the movie is starting," he said. Hadn't Ben told them it was a wall screen?

"I hope it's a porno," continued Bernie.

Then Art Perlman shouted from the rear of the room, "Hey! Who turned on the heat? It's getting hot as a son-of-a-bitch back here!"

"Oww!" yelled Joe Finley. He jumped off the center table. "I'm burning up!"

Ben called to Art to get up and open the cabinets. Art seemed in a daze and waved Ben off. Ben screamed at him, "Art, damn it! Joe's in trouble!"

Art sat up and his lamp went off. He was dazed for a moment, but then saw Joe on his knees near the center table and ran to him. Joe's skin was as red as a lobster under the fine white ash that covered him.

Ben yelled again, "Get us out of here!"

Art left Joe and opened Ben's and Bernie's cabinets. They slid out and gathered around Joe Finley, who was still on his knees, obviously in pain. The wall had begun to turn from red to blue.

"That damned wall must be some kind of sun lamp," said Joe, getting to his feet. "I feel like I've got one hell of a sunburn."

"Are you okay?" asked Bernie. They were all concerned.

"Funny," said Joe, "it was cool under the lamp. Then the wall got red and I felt heat like someone opened a furnace door. But, and this is going to sound weird, it was under my skin . . . the heat, that is. It was like I was burning from within."

Ben examined Joe's skin as he spoke. He did it gently first brushing away the fine ash. Once again the ash disappeared before it hit the floor. He poked Joe's forearm. "Does that hurt?"

"No."

"You don't seem to be burned, but your skin is definitely red." He squeezed the forearm and then released. It was white but then immediately turned red again. "Blood," said Ben, "your capillaries are full of blood."

"That's why he's red," added Bernie.

"Of course," said Art, grabbing Bernie's and Joe's arms. "It's like a super massage. It gets the blood flowing right up to the surface of the skin."

"Like a slap," added Joe. "I just wasn't ready for that thorough a massage." They all felt better.

"Let's take it easy with this stuff," suggested Ben. "Moderation is the name of the game."

For the rest of the morning they rotated with the equipment. One man stood by each time just in case something went wrong. They found that each had a different tolerance for the center table, and they could judge how long to stay on the table by the color of the wall. Art Perlman was able to stay the longest. They nicknamed him "Deep Red."

The foursome had passed on their gin game because they couldn't sit still. Ben suggested they go out to lunch, and he had called Alma and told her their plan. He also asked her to please call the other wives.

She was relieved because it gave her more time to talk with Rose. When she called Mary Green, Mary suggested that they all come over to her place for lunch. She said she was feeling energetic and would put out a light spread. Alma checked with Rose, who reluctantly said okay.

When Alma called Bess Perlman to invite her to lunch at Mary's, Bess was also reluctant. Then Alma told her that Rose was with her and that they were both going. Bess finally agreed, but still sounded strange.

The men took Bernie Lewis' big red Buick and drove over to Wolfie's on Collins Avenue.

They were starved. This time of day was always busy at Wolfie's. The boys got seated quickly because they were in the line for foursomes. Most of the other patrons were in twos. After they ordered, it was Art Perlman who opened the discussion. "How do you guys feel?" he asked.

Joe Finley answered first. "Like I'm twenty one. Did you see what I ordered for lunch?"

"Did you see what we all ordered for lunch?" quipped Ben.

"That equipment sure builds up an appetite," said Bernie.

Art and Joe said together, "It's more than an appetite!" They looked at each other and laughed.

"You a mind reader?" asked Art.

"Yes," answered Joe, "and so are you."

"So are we all," said Ben, "I knew you both were going to say that. I knew it before you spoke."

Bernie, who was looking around the restaurant, murmured, "Yeah, me, too." Then he turned back to the others. "Hey, guys, look at the people in here." They were already looking. "I feel funny," he continued. "I mean, they are our age, but they look . . . old."

"They are old," said Ben. "but I know what you mean. It's like we don't belong with them."

"Yeah," agreed Art.

"What?" asked Ben, looking at Joe.

"Nothing. I didn't say anything," Joe answered.

"I thought you said something about the ocean," continued Ben.

"No, but I was thinking about the ocean."

Then a strange and frightened look crossed Joe's face. "Let's stop the bullshit, guys," said Joe. "I'm going to say what's on all our minds. Something has happened to us. Something to do with that room, and that equipment. I'll bet we all made love to our wives last night and this morning. I'll bet we all feel like kids again. I'll bet we can read each other's minds. I'll bet we are all scared and confused."

No one answered, but each knew the other's thoughts.

Yes, they all thought.

"Right," said Joe aloud. "And I'll tell you something else. After we finish lunch, you guys are going to drive me to the hospital. I'm going to have my doctor do a blood test. I'll bet my leukemia is getting better."

"Wrong," said Bernie Lewis. "It's gone!"

• **22** •

Had the Antareans known about the unwanted members of their "health club," it would have made their life easier. Now they pondered the possibilities of why the room was warm. Hal, Harry, and Beam, the female commander, were busy running circuit checks on the equipment and power sources. They weren't having much luck. Everything seemed to be functioning properly.

Amos glanced at his watch and telepathed to the others that he was going to the condo office to meet with Mr. Shields. He had called the manager at home after they had discovered the warmth. He had asked Shields to meet him at the office on the pretext of a change in plans for construction that couldn't wait. Now he left the processing room and headed toward Building A. He could see the light on in the office, so he knew Shields was waiting there.

Since they had begun raising the cocoons,

there had been little contact with the manager. Amos had telephoned each morning to keep in touch. As he walked toward the office now, his thoughts went back to the time before the complex was Antarean.

They had brought the shuttle down at night and submerged near Key Biscayne. Amos, Hal, and Harry were on board. The commanders and the rest of the crew remained on the mother ship, parked on the far side of the moon. Aware of the technology that Earth beings possessed, they had jammed the radar during their approach and made the jamming appear to be an atmospheric disturbance. Their landing was undetected. The trio left their craft parked near a wreck and swam underwater to the beach. They emerged and shed their waterproofing. Underneath they wore casual clothes. Using the information gathered by several probes, monitoring of radio and television and life experiences of their agents who lived among Earth people, they had devised the plan to raise the cocoons with the least amount of disturbance to the natural order of Florida.

They knew that they had only two options. The first was to bring the mother ship in, submerge it, and remove all the cocoons at once. Then leave and process on board. With this approach, they would run the risk of exposing their presence on Earth. It would also mean processing continually, since the cocoons were perishable once they were removed from their large storage environment. If anything were wrong with the processing, or if the cocoons had been damaged in any way, they ran the risk of losing the entire army.

The second plan made more sense. They would find, or build, a facility near the storage area and process in a normal manner, under standard procedures.

When Antares Quad Three was a thriving community of space trade, the Florida peninsula was populated by primitive Indians. Now, sandbars and swamps had become a thriving resort community. However, the Antareans were a resourceful race and Amos enjoyed the challenge. Plan two was to be explored.

The three spacemen walked along the beach and onto the causeway that wound through Key Biscayne. Their appearance was that of vacationers out for an evening walk. The fact that several extremely wealthy people had residences near their location had escaped their intelligence. As they strolled toward the mainland a police cruiser pulled up behind them. The driver called out to them on the P.A. system to stop. Amos telepathed to the others to let him do the communicating. The two policemen stepped out of the car with their guns. "Will you gentlemen please identify yourselves?"

Amos spoke in a soft voice. "Good evening, Officer. My name is Bright, Amos Bright. We're taking a walk."

"You live in the Key?" asked the policeman.

"No, sir, we live in Miami." He thought for a moment and continued. "South Miami, that is. Is something wrong?"

"No!" He spoke to his partner. "They look okay, George."

Then back to Amos: "No, nothing wrong. We're just checking this section of the beach. You guys watch out for the cars if you're walking back on the causeway."

"We will. Thanks." Then he added, "It's good to know that you fellows are out watching things so well. Makes us feel secure. Good night."

They turned and walked away feeling pleased with their success with the first human contact.

Hal asked, "What are they guarding?"

Amos answered, "Wealthy people. In this country they get special protection."

Harry telepathed, *Why must they guard the wealthy?* Amos came back. *Because the wealthy demand it*, thought Amos to his companions.

The next few days were spent among Earth people. The three men split up and went in different directions. Amos went south toward Coral Gables, Hal went north toward Fort Lauderdale, and Harry went west toward the Everglades. They agreed to meet back at the shuttle in five days.

Hal and Harry arrived at the shuttle together. They took nourishment from their storage unit before discussing their findings. The north was heavily populated and all of the sections along the beach were used. They would have great difficulty bringing the cocoons into any facility. There was a possibility of some industrial property near the bay, but using it at night would draw attention. Harry found quite the opposite. There was a canal system that went west, but after a few miles of heavily populated areas he had run into a great swamp that stretched for miles. He had entered the swamp and explored it. Constructing a building would be impossible. They telepathed for Amos but received no answer. Now they rested and waited for their leader's return.

Amos Bright had found what he believed they needed. It was still under construction, but the location was correct. Two large buildings situated on a canal with direct access to the sea. The sign had stated that the Blamar Construction Company of Coral Gables was the builder. The owner was South Florida Land Development Corporation of Homestead. Amos entered the construction site and walked around for several hours. The layout was perfect. He slipped into the canal and swam underwater to the open sea. Upon his return the next morning he located the offices of the owners and telephoned for an appointment for the next day. When the secretary asked what the purpose of the appointment was, Amos had told her that he wished to discuss the purchase of the entire complex. She had told him it was not for sale. Amos thanked her and hung up. He then went to the offices and telepathed the secretary so that she wrote down the appointment for the next day. That part was easy, but in doing it Amos had violated his orders not to interfere in the lives of the inhabitants of the planet. He would have to get clearance from Antares to proceed with his plan.

Hal and Harry sensed Amos' approach and greeted him anxiously as he entered the shuttle. They were interested to hear how he had fared, but they also were excited about the near mishap they had experienced earlier. It seemed they had parked the shuttle near a favorite sport-fishing ground and all day there had been activity overhead. Three times their craft had been hooked by the trolling lines from the fishing craft. The last time, the line had been weighted, and very strong. It had hooked onto the antenna and nearly overturned the craft. Hal had applied power and they picked up the thoughts of the men above. The fishermen were sure they had hooked a very large fish because the shuttle had pulled back on their line. Harry had gone out of the ship and severed the line; however, the fishermen continued to troll over the same spot all morning. Finally, Harry had to go out and find a large fish, stun it, and attach it to the line. That seemed to have pleased the men above and they left after boating the fish. Amos listened with amusement but he felt badly for the fish. He sensed the underwater creatures were not unlike Antareans. They, too, lived an inner life, under the surface of the planet. Someday, when the Earth was ready, they would have to explain the importance of preserving life in the scheme of cosmic energy. He recalled how easy it was to find the planet because of the ambient life forces surrounding it. Planets that had high destruction, or death rates, always had these forces in abundance. It was the released energy of life departing from the host it had occupied. Here on this planet there was a great deal of unnatural death.

Amos contacted the mother ship that night and communicated with the commanders. He outlined his plan and requested they clear it with Antares' base. If approval was forthcoming, he would need a probe sent down with valuables to trade for the complex. The message was understood and he was told to wait for a response. The answer came an hour later. Permission was given for Amos to "sway" the humans to his bidding, but no physical force was to be involved. He was also authorized to use the valuables known as diamonds for the trade. The intelligence on Antares suggested that he sell the diamonds for the normal exchange medium, dollars. This could best be accomplished in a city called Amsterdam, in a country to the east known as Holland. Commander All Light would take a shuttle and sell diamonds. He would bring the money to Amos by morning because Holland was on a different time schedule from Miami and the commerce there began while it was still night in Florida.

All Light arrived after dawn with a single document that had a value of twenty million dollars. He suggested that Amos put that in a bank. It would take a few days for the actual dollars to come to the bank, but that was a reasonable delay. The intelligence also warned that large transactions such as his would draw attention of many government officials. He advised that they find a bank that would be able to withhold the transaction from public view in return for a share of the purchase price. Amos understood. He had been involved in many bizarre transactions all over the Universe. Since the basic drive on this planet was greed, it would not be a problem to cover the transaction for the period of time they required.

He chose a small bank in Coral Gables. When he entered the bank he scanned until he found the person in charge. The man was seated behind the last desk in an area with five other workers. The man's name was DePalmer. To ensure control, and because he had been cleared to manipulate the Earth people as required, Amos entered Mr. DePalmer's mind and prepared him for the transaction. It went smoothly. The secretary led Amos to Mr. DePalmer's desk. The man exchanged greetings and moved right to business. Amos told him that he wished to open an account in the sum of twenty million dollars. The man was pleased. Now that Amos was dressed in an expensive business suit, it all seemed natural. The account was opened and Mr. DePalmer told Amos he would process the Dutch draft immediately. If all went well Amos should have funds available within a week. The problem of keeping the transaction quiet was forced into Mr. DePalmer's mind.

"That might be difficult to do," he said.

"I'm sure there are ways," Amos answered.

"Well, yes, there are always ways, but they can get expensive," DePalmer replied.

"Cost is not an object," Amos stated. "I leave the details to you, and I trust you will use discretion."

"How much discretion?" the banker asked.

"Let's say two percent worth?" questioned Amos.

DePalmer brightened immediately. "Consider your business the most closely guarded secret in Florida, Mr. Bright." The banker had been pleased.

The rest was too simple, but it was a good lesson in why certain planets in the Universe were to be left alone. Without the ability to telepath, mind control, and therefore action control, was without challenge. Amos kept his appointment at South Florida Development and bought the complex, as it existed, for twelve million dollars cash. This gave the owners a profit of four million, and when Amos inferred that change of title could be "unofficial," the owners realized that their profit would not be taxed immediately, and possibly never.

The unnamed condo complex became Antares Condominiums. The construction company was not aware of the change of ownership. They were instructed to proceed on a suddenly accelerated schedule. Building A was nearly finished at the time that the Antareans bought it, and Building B was nearly done, too. Amos ordered that all efforts be put into Building A and that another construction unit would work on Building B. The contractor had complained and threatened a lawsuit. It took only half a million dollars to satisfy him. Fifteen days later the construction crews left Building A completed. Shuttles ran all that next night and the commanders, technicians, and equipment were brought into Building B.

By morning, what appeared to be a small construction crew was busy in Building B. Amos had Mr. DePalmer handle the sales office and staffing. He wanted to be sure that, at least on the surface, everything looked normal. He told the banker that for personal reasons he was not anxious to sell too many condominiums right away. DePalmer suggested a very high price and an inept staff. Amos was amused. They had both made the error of making Antares seem so unattractive that people were sure it was a great deal. However, the success of sales in Building A did not delay the Antareans.

It only meant that they would have to move the cocoons at night and with care. Overall, the plan worked well. As long as they kept Building B unfinished, they could proceed with their business. Their intelligence had been good, but had failed to understand the mentality of retired Americans and the boredom that drove them either to vegetate, or, in the case of Ben, Joe, Bernie, and Art, let their curiosity lead them to adventure.

Mr. Shields was behind his desk when Amos entered.

"Hi, Mr. Bright. Long time, no see," Shields said as he extended his hand.

Amos shook the little man's hand. "Nice to see you, Mr. Shields. I have a few things that can't wait. I'm sorry for getting you out at this late hour."

"Anytime, Mr. Bright. You're the boss."

"I'll come right to the point, Mr. Shields. My partners and I are pleased at the way you are running things. However, we did ask that moisture . . . uh . . . water . . . be kept out of the swimming area. I noticed that it was filled last week."

Shields had been prepared for this. "Yes, Mr. Bright. I did tell Mr. DePalmer about that. I guess he didn't speak to you. We had a problem

176

with one of our owners in the complex." Shields shuffled some papers on his desk and found what he was looking for. "A Mr. Green came in a few weeks ago and demanded that the pool be filled. I tried to stall him and avoid him, but he went to the authorities. I know that you and Mr. DePalmer and the others don't want any publicity, so I had to agree to fill it." He looked at Amos for approval.

"Yes," said Amos, "you did the correct thing."

Shields was pleased with himself. "Is that all?" he asked.

"No," said Amos. "Building B. I told you that I wanted it secured. We don't want any accidents over there since the construction has been delayed."

Shields was puzzled. "No one has been there, Mr. Bright. Wally and I keep a close watch on things. The old folks have been getting a little annoyed about the appearance of the place, and a few have inquired as to when the construction will be finished. You know those people don't walk too well, and they know it's dangerous near the construction site. I can't imagine any of them getting in there. Has there been trouble?" Shields was concerned.

Amos answered carefully. He didn't want Wally or Shields poking around, either. "No, not any trouble. We have some special equipment over there and we think someone may be tampering with it."

Shields thought a moment. "How about hiring a night watchman or a guard service? I can vouch for the daytime, but you know there could be someone sneaking in at night."

"I'll think about that, Mr. Shields. I'll let you know, but for now I would appreciate your keeping a close eye on things during the day, in case some of our Building A people are wandering in."

Shields answered, "Absolutely, Mr. Bright. Consider it done." He made a mental note to talk to Wally the next morning.

"Fine," said Amos. "Now I must go. Thank you again for coming in. I appreciate it, and I will show my appreciation in your next salary check."

Shields beamed and the two men left the office together. Amos watched him walk to his car and drive away, then turned toward the processing room.

A strong contact with a mind came from behind and above him. He reached a thought back in answer. Then it was gone. Amos couldn't find it. *Nourishment*, thought Amos, *I need nourishment*. He knew that there were no

Antareans above and behind him. All his mates were in the processing room. He didn't even hear Joe Finley trip against the chaise on his terrace as he ducked away from the railing.

• **23** •

That same afternoon, while the boys were at lunch, the ladies had their own revelations to discuss. Alma and Mary were thrilled by the sudden sexual interest of their husbands. Rose and Bess were yet to be convinced.

The menu was fruit and cottage cheese, cake and coffee. As they ate, they said little. Bess and Rose huddled together, staring down at their plates. Mary was bubbling over with small talk. She had doubts about telling how wonderful things had suddenly become in bed, and her own excitement and satisfaction kept her from noticing how depressed and upset Bess and Rose were.

Alma finally broke the ice. "Do you think that we might all talk about what we were discussing this morning, Rose?" she said, pointedly.

Rose looked up at Alma and then at the

others. Even Bess was curious. "I suppose so," she answered.

Alma addressed the group. "I'm going to ask a curious question and, although we have become friends, some of you may feel I'm getting too personal. So please let me know." She paused to gather her thoughts. Mary looked interested. Bess looked frightened. Alma continued: "You all know that my Joe is . . . well . . . a sick man. To put it frankly, he has had leukemia for almost ten years." They all nodded. Alma had never spoken about this before so she had their interest. "Lately he had been getting worse."

Mary reached over. "I'm sorry, Alma."

Alma smiled. "That's okay. Thanks. He's been tired and without appetite. This doctor thinks it's the beginning of the end. I knew this day would come, but it shook me . . . deeply." A tear came to her eye.

Rose Lewis looked at her with confusion. What was she bringing this up for? What did this have to do with their discussion this morning, and what did it have to do with Rose's problem?

Alma went on. "Today Rose called and came over. She had a problem, and frankly I would not have been in the mood to discuss it with her if something strange hadn't happened to me . . . to Joe and me." Suddenly they all became interested. "As I said, Joe has been tired lately and, among other things, our . . ." — she paused, then decided to jump in — ". . . our sex life hasn't been terribly active." She smiled. "Actually, it's been nil . . . zero . . ."

Suddenly Mary interrupted. "Until last night . . . no, yesterday afternoon?"

"How did you know?" Alma was puzzled.

"I know, honey . . . I know," she answered, "and I bet Bess can tell us the same about hers." They all looked at Bess Perlman.

She blurted out, "He's an animal! He nearly raped me yesterday and again this morning."

Rose gasped, "You, too?"

Alma answered, "All of us. Something has happened to our husbands."

"But what?" asked Bess. "What could affect them all the same way?"

As their wives pondered their predicament that afternoon, and as the Antareans were raising the three command cocoons, the four men had finished lunch, possessing exciting new knowledge. They hadn't even been shocked when Bernie Lewis told Joe Finley that his disease was gone. They somehow knew it. For the rest of the lunch the quartet communicated silently. At one point Ben Green tried calling the waitress with his mind. It worked. He had zeroed his eyes on to her as she walked toward the kitchen. She was about forty feet from them and moving in the opposite direction. "Watch this," he said aloud. The three other men turned their eyes toward the middle-aged woman. She stopped dead in her tracks, three feet from the kitchen door, turned, searched the dining room for a moment, and locked her eyes on their table, then made a beeline for them.

"Can I get you anything else?" she asked.

"Some coffee and the check," answered Ben, proud of his feat.

After the check came they divided it, paid, and left. Bernie turned the Buick up Collins Avenue toward Mount Sinai Hospital.

Dr. Feldman was waiting for them. Joe had called from the restaurant and told the doctor it was urgent that he see him. Because the doctor knew that Joe was coming to the end of his struggle, he was receptive to the visit. He wasn't prepared for the group meeting that occurred.

The four men entered the clinic and walked to the doctor's office. Dr. Morris Feldman was a tall, gray-haired specialist who had moved his practice to Miami in the late 1960s. He was the chief hematologist of the hospital. There was no doubt in his mind that Joe Finley's disease was progressing rapidly. He was sure it was a matter of months. The medication no longer could contain the rampant production of white cells. The last blood test had shown that clearly. Actually, the test prior to the last had shown it. Yesterday's test had been a freak and the doctor was sure that the lab had confused Finley's test with a perfectly healthy person's. The test had shown no sign of the disease, and Feldman knew that was impossible.

Now the foursome burst into his office. Joe quickly introduced his friends. The doctor was cordial.

"Doc," said Joe, "I know you're a very busy guy, and I appreciate your seeing me so quickly. Can you take some blood now and have a look?"

The doctor was taken aback. "Mr. Finley, we have procedures here. Why the rush for a test now?"

"Well," answered Joe, "it's really hard to say. I just think that this problem that I have . . . uh, *had* . . . is gone. I want to be sure."

The doctor was immediately convinced that somehow Finley had gotten wind of the erroneous report and it had given him false hope.

The doctor spoke. "Procedures, Mr. Finley. I'll be glad to do another test, but it will take some time for the results."

"How long?" asked Ben Green.

"Well, Mr. . . . uh?"

"Green," answered Ben.

"Well, Mr. Green, we should have your friend's results back tomorrow."

"No good," said Art Perlman.

The doctor was getting annoyed when Bernie Lewis broke into the conversation. "Dr. Feldman, you don't remember me. I'm Bernie Lewis. Used to live in Scarsdale. We played golf a few times. Maybe twenty years ago. I was a friend of Sid Blackman . . . God rest his soul."

Dr. Feldman studied Bernie's face and it came back to him. "Sure, you had a garment business . . . woolens. Sid invested some money with you. Sure, I remember. Sid was a good friend, one of the best surgeons I ever worked with."

"Well, doctor," Bernie continued, "Joe . . . the four of us . . . have become good friends here . . . in the autumn of our lives. We are close . . . you understand. We're concerned, and we know about Joe's problem. Understand that we are grown-ups and refuse to be treated like children. Being old doesn't mean stupid, and it certainly doesn't mean we can be ignored."

"I'm not ignoring you," answered the doctor.

"We know that," Bernie went on, "and we appreciate that, too. That's why we would like you to do a favor . . . just this once, and give Finley a blood test right now. You know what to look for. It won't take but a minute. Okay?"

The doctor knew he was beaten. "Okay," he agreed. "You guys wait here and I'll get a syringe." He went down to the emergency room while the boys made themselves comfortable. Thoughts flew back and forth among them without any verbal enhancement. The excitement made their hearts pound. Energy surged through each to the other.

Dr. Feldman spun on the stool. He looked at the four men gathered around him near the microscope.

Joe spoke up. "It's gone, isn't it?"

"Yes," answered a very puzzled doctor. "It's gone without a trace. But I don't know why."

The men hugged each other.

Joe was crying. "I knew it . . . I knew it." He stopped hugging, crossed himself, and prayed. "In the name of the Father, the son, and the Holy Spirit." He folded his hands. "Thank you, God!"

"Amen," said Bernie.

"Amen," they echoed.

Feldman shook his head as the men began to leave and muttered to himself, "Amen, all right. But why?" He yelled to them, "Joe, please stop by and see me in a few days?" Joe waved over his shoulder. Morris Feldman turned back to the microscope and peered through the lens at the very normal, healthy blood cells on the slide below. He leaned nearer and stared. These were not only normal cells, they were the healthiest cells he had ever seen. The platelets were perfectly formed. There were no damaged ones, no dead ones. The white count was normal, and the most astonishing fact was that the blood itself was clean as a whistle. There were no impurities, no bacteria, no indication of damaged cells . . . and above all no indication of leukemia whatsoever.

He knew he would not see Joe Finley in a few days. He suspected he would not see Joe Finley again. He was right.

• 24 •

The day had been exciting for the Greens, Perlmans, Lewises, and Finleys. The women had talked all afternoon about the new and strange energy their husbands possessed. The men had gone back to the health club and used the equipment until early evening. Thus, the room was warm when the returning Antareans had entered.

One other event had happened in Amos' absence. While the Antareans were checking the equipment for faults, Jack had suddenly felt the urge to go to the boat. Commander No Light picked up on his thoughts and communicated.

Jack didn't understand the feeling, so he spoke. "I feel as though I should be on the boat and I don't know why."

No Light telepathed back, *Yes, I feel it, too. A message is there. Someone is trying to reach you, but not on the boat. On the radio phone.*

Jack then heard the operator ringing his call letters. That was impossible, he thought. *The radio is shut down.*

You can hear it, anyway, thought All Light. *Go to the boat and turn it on. Beam will go with you.*

Sure enough, when Jack turned on the radio phone the operator was calling. He answered and then heard Judy on the other end. "Jack, is that you?"

"Yes, honey. How are you? Is everything okay?" He was concerned.

"Just fine. I miss you. Where are you?"

The commander shook her head at Jack and put her finger to her lips.

"I'm at sea, honey. We're working late, as a matter of fact. That's why it took me time to answer. I was out on deck . . . the charter people are doing some night diving."

The commander agreed with his strategy.

"Will you be in this weekend?"

He looked at the commander. She shook her head no. "I don't think so, honey. These folks are on to something. I can't talk about it."

"When will you be in?" she asked. There were tears in her voice. He looked at the commander again, but this time the thought was already in his head.

"Next weekend . . . for sure, honey."

"What about supplies?" she asked. "Do you have enough on board?"

You are a sneaky lady, thought Jack. The commander smiled.

"Yes, dear, plenty. Look, let me call you in a few days. I'll have a better idea of my schedule. Okay?"

Judy was put off, but could only agree. "Okay. Hold a minute. Your brother wants to say hello."

"My brother?" Jack was puzzled.

"Hi, little brother." Arnie came on the air.

"Hi, Arnie. Judy at your place?"

"Yeah. She came over for dinner. She's one hell of a girl. What she sees in you I don't know. You know, you could treat her better."

Jack was pissed off. "Arnie, not everyone lives like you. Some of us even like our freedom." Jack was immediately sorry for the dig and he hoped that Judy hadn't heard.

"Easy, little brother," answered Arnie. "She's worried about you, that's all. Where the hell are you?"

"I told her it was sort of a secret. It's a treasure-hunt thing."

"Okay . . . okay. Listen, if you're going to be out on the weekend, I could run out with my boss's boat. He offered it to me anytime I want."

"Not a good idea, Arnie. These folks are

pretty tight with the security. They think they're on to something big. It won't work."

Arnie gave in, but he was still curious. "Okay, Jack, have a safe trip. Let someone know how you are once in a while."

"Okay, Arnie. Love to Sandy. Put Judy back on."

Judy came on the radio again. "Hi, hon." She sounded better.

"Hi, babe. Listen, I've got to run. Thanks for calling. I'll try to call you over the weekend . . ." Silence. "Okay, honey?"

"Okay. But don't be surprised if I'm not in when you call." The receiver clicked off.

Sorry, thought the female commander. Jack was uneasy again.

They returned to the processing room. Amos entered shortly after. He let the others know that the manager was sure the security hadn't been breached. The others said they couldn't find anything wrong with the equipment, but they still had other power supplies to check. *Let's get the command cocoons processed,* communicated All Light.

Harry and Jack wheeled the first one in and set the first cabinet controls. They put the cocoon in and turned on the cabinet. Jack walked down to cabinet number six to prepare the controls. He reached for them and stopped.

Something was wrong. He had worked with them all last night and he knew how he had left them. Now the controls were set in a different mode. As the thought entered his mind, it also entered the minds of the others in the room. They all converged on the cabinet and stared at the panel. Hal telepathed that he had not touched the controls in his testing of the circuits. Neither had anyone else.

"Are you sure?" Amos asked aloud.

"Positive," answered Jack. "This isn't something that I would forget. Remember, I'm new at this so I am extra careful to do things the way Hal showed me. I know how I leave these controls each night. This one is not the way I left it."

Then we definitely have had visitors, thought Amos. But who? At this point the first cocoon was ready to be moved to cabinet six. They would have to wait until they completed their work to discuss who the intruders might be.

• 25 •

"Time and charges on that call, please, operator." Arnie waited.

"Four dollars and forty cents," she said.

"Four forty? That's not much for an overseas call to the Bahamas."

"That call was local, sir," replied the operator.

"Local? Just where was the boat?" asked Arnie Fischer.

"Coral Gables, sir," the operator replied.

"Are you sure?" asked Arnie.

"Yes, sir. It was received in the Coral Cables area."

"Thank you, operator." Arnie hung up.

Judy had been listening, "Coral Gables, huh?" She was furious. "Your brother is one hell of a liar!"

"Don't jump to conclusions, Judy," he answered. "Maybe he's in some kind of trouble. It isn't like Jack to lie, and he sounded strange to me."

"How strange?" Judy was getting concerned. She had been too upset with Jack to notice how he sounded.

"Well, he seemed distant. Like he was in a hurry to hang up."

Sandy chimed in. "You people are making a mountain out of a molehill. I think he's sworn to keep the location secret. He's just keeping a promise to the charter. We would expect the same if it were us."

Good old sensible Sandy, thought Arnie.

"Perhaps the operator made a mistake."

Judy was not sold on the idea. "I think he's in trouble. Call it intuition. I'm worried."

Arnie went to the phone. He dialed information and asked for the number of the charter boat *Razzmatazz*, docked in south Miami. The operator gave him a number and he wrote it down. He turned to the women. "It's too late now, but this is the number of Jack's buddy Phil Doyle. They fish together all the time. He'll know where Jack is. I'll call him tomorrow."

Judy was satisfied. "Call me when you know." She got up to leave. "Thanks for the dinner and for holding my hand."

Jack and Beam walked back toward Building B. They telepathed rapidly. Jack didn't think about his new skill anymore . . . he used it.

I am sorry your female is upset. She has an attachment to you.

I know. I feel very strongly about her, too, but your being here and my being with you must come first now.

We appreciate your cooperation Jack. It is quite helpful.

Things will work out. I hope we can find a way to solve the problem with the cocoons.

Yes, it will be a serious problem if we do not get the army to its new location in time.

Where is that?

It is a brilliant planet, and most unusual. The base is carbon but evolved to the crystalline form. We call it Parma Quad Two. It is fed by the star Sirius in the constellation you call Canis Major.

That's the star after which we name the Dog Days of August. It's a morning star in our summer sky . . . the Dog star.

Yes. Beam's thoughts went to the diminutive Parma Quad Two. She had been on the initial probe mission to the planet. At that time she was not yet a commander and served the same function as the copper men — scientific and technical service. However, because of her birth and training, she knew she was destined to be a commander. This mission was her first at that rank.

Parma Quad Two had been probed for ten time periods that totaled roughly two hundred Earth years. The Antareans knew that a life form existed on the planet. By their rules a life-form planet was studied for at least eight time periods before any contact or an actual landing was attempted.

The Parmans were basic crystal life forms. They were an old race and highly developed technologically. Their only nourishment requirements came from their star and they used only the ultraviolet spectrum of its light. They were completely peaceful, yet within their crystalline bodies they possessed an ability to unleash an extremely destructive force upon outsiders. But they never used their power in a negative manner.

The planet itself was brilliant. The surface was entirely glasslike in appearance. Actually, it was a silicone "skin" constructed by the Parmans. Its main function was to filter the starlight from the great star Sirius so that only the ultraviolet end of the spectrum passed through to the crystal beings below.

Picture a marble, smooth outside and honeycombed on the inside. That was Parma.

When Beam and her party had finally been allowed entrance to the planet, the Parmans greeted them warmly. They offered friendship and a sharing of their knowledge. One of the most exciting discoveries made by the Antareans was that because of the Parmans' extreme sensitivity to ultraviolet and their ability to extract it from universal starlight, they were, in effect, living guidance and propulsion systems. In other words, a Parman could be installed on an interstellar vehicle and it could guide the craft to any light source that contained ultraviolet light, no matter how weak or how far. Since the Parmans were able to extract ultraviolet from the source, they could then pull a spacecraft toward the source. As the distance between the Parman and the source lessened, the flow of ultraviolet increased and thus the effect increased as with a magnet. The discovery that Beam had made was that since the Parmans required no gases for life support, they could live in space freely.

Negotiations had proceeded and one time period ago the Parmans had agreed to let the Antareans build a craft out of Parmans. A living spaceship capable of zeroing in on any star . . . any planet . . . any galaxy, moving toward it rapidly in a geometric progression of acceleration. No fuel was required. No guidance system was required. The Parmans were the ultimate space vehicle.

Jack read all of Beam's thoughts as they

approached Building B. He was overwhelmed. Beam read him.

Jack, she telepathed, *our Universe holds wonders at every star. Yours is a strong race and one that will move among the stars as we now do. It will be time periods before that happens, but it will happen. The things you consider large here will become small. But that which is small, actually smallest — the atoms of your minds — will become large. Their energy is the energy of the Universe. It is the life spark. It is what makes us be.*

Jack understood and, for no reason he could comprehend, suddenly thought back to Vietnam and the war. He felt ashamed. Beam reached and touched his hand. It was a female touch, filled with caring. Jack thought a kiss to Beam, and she returned a formless thought to him that made his body warm and caused a tear in his eye.

They entered Building B and moved quickly to the processing room.

Joe Finley had been unable to sleep. He was supercharged for two reasons. The first was the long period of time the men had spent in the health club that afternoon. The second reason was that his leukemia was definitely gone. He was alive, more alive than he had ever been before. And he was not alone. Ben, Art, and Bernie was also more alive.

He did not tell Alma about his visit to Dr. Feldman. He wanted to in the worst way, but he had no reason for his sudden cure, and the men had decided to try to figure out what the health club was all about before revealing their discovery to their wives. He did, however, let Alma know that he was feeling much better and mentioned that he felt the disease had gone into a big remission.

They had had dinner and made love all evening, until Alma fell asleep. Joe could not sleep, and that was why he was on the terrace, sitting in the dark, contemplating the stars above when he noticed Mr. Shields arrive at the office. He did not know the stranger who entered the office shortly after Shields. When the two men emerged from the office later, Joe had backed away from the terrace railing and tripped over a chaise chair.

He had backed away because he felt he was being pulled toward the stranger with Shields, and he feared he would be pulled over the terrace. He also had the crazy idea that he could fly down to the stranger.

The noise awoke Alma and she noticed that Joe was not in bed. She could see him crouched on the terrace. That was the same position he had been in when they first met.

Alma McClain had been a beautiful woman. She had never married and was able to advance her career as a journalist to a position of editor for a major New York television station's news department. They had even offered her a crack at commentator, on camera every night, but she declined. She did do the editorial comment weekly and was a celebrity of sorts in chic New York circles.

She met Joe Finley at a party on Fire Island. She was scheduled to work the evening news that summer Friday, so she didn't arrive at the party until after midnight. By then things were in full swing. The first thing Alma did was make a beeline for the bathroom. Her bladder was ready to burst after the long boat ride from the mainland. It was there that she met Joe Finley. He was bent over, crouching on the floor, looking for a contact lens that his date had dropped. His date looked more like his daughter. She was a slim, pretty girl with long brown hair, and she wore a see-through blouse that revealed how young she really was. A thought about older men and young girls passed through Alma's mind and she immediately disliked Joe Finley. He had been extremely polite and explained the circumstances. It took a few more minutes until Joe found the lens and Alma could relieve herself. As Joe and Penny left the bathroom, Alma let them know of her discomfort by suggesting that they have their gatherings in a room other than the only bathroom in the damned house.

When she came out of the bathroom, Joe was standing there. Penny was nowhere in sight. He said three things. "My name is Joe Finley. You are a beautiful woman. You are a mean bitch, too." He then turned heel and left her startled.

In twenty minutes she approached him and apologized. She then found out that his "date" was just an attempt by their host, and it wasn't working.

After that night their relationship grew slowly. They didn't make love for six weeks, although they saw a great deal of each other. Alma began to doubt if they would ever be lovers. She liked Joe and felt she could love him deeply. But he seemed removed.

His new show opened off Broadway on a Wednesday night. The reviews came out that weekend and they were excellent. Alma had made sure that her friends in the press and television covered the show. She never told Joe that she had done that. The show was good and Joe was great.

After the Saturday night performance, Alma waited for Joe in a small restaurant in

Greenwich Village. He walked in at eleven p.m. He was glowing brighter than when he had read the reviews. He walked up to her, threw a ten-dollar bill on the table, took her hand, and led her out of the restaurant. He had a cab waiting outside and, without a word, he took her to his apartment. She had tried to find out where they were going and what he was doing, but he remained silent, holding up his hand and smiling.

They entered his apartment. Joe turned down the lights, opened a bottle of champagne, and poured two glasses. He then gave her a glass, clinked a silent toast, and drained it in one swallow. Then he took her hand and led her to the bedroom. "Alma, I love you . . . will you love me?"

She nodded and he took her in his arms. They made love for most of the night. He asked her to marry him. She agreed and they set a date.

Their life had been beautiful together until the illness changed things. Their love had never diminished and they both considered their marriage something to be cherished.

Now she watched as Joe slowly raised his body up to the railing of the terrace. She could see that he was holding on tightly. She thought that he was shaking and suddenly became frightened. Was he sick? Has he been stricken again by the disease? She got out of bed and rushed to the terrace.

"Son-of-a-bitch," he murmured over and over. "Son-of-a-bitch . . ."

She was quickly at his side and put her arms around him. "Are you okay, honey?"

He turned to her and saw the concern in her face. "Am I all right? You bet your sweet ass I'm all right."

Then she was crying and he held her as they sat on the terrace floor rocking back and forth. He realized that he must have given her an awful fright. Perhaps he should tell her. Joe Finley rolled that thought over in his mind as they went back into the bedroom.

• 26 •

Morning found Ben, Art, Bernie, and Joe at the pool. They just arrived without knowing exactly why. Each had felt a need to go to the pool. Each had not slept all that night. Two had left sleeping and happy wives behind. Bernie Lewis' Rose was reasonably happy, but confused. Another adjustment to make. Bess Perlman was nervous and refused to discuss her feelings with her husband. They had not made love that night.

The men approached the pool from different directions. Words were not uttered but they all met at their card table.

Ben spoke. "I called you all here. I used the new phone system that our health club seems to have given us."

The others understood.

"I know no one slept last night. And I know we are not in the least bit tired. Joe is cured, thank God."

Art Perlman spoke. "I'm growing hair." He bent over and pointed to a dark fuzz on his normally bald scalp.

Bernie Lewis sat down under the umbrella and put his left hand on the table. "See that, guys?" He pointed to a small scar on the side of his thumb. "I cut my hand this morning. Actually, I just picked up a glass of orange juice and it . . . well, I must have squeezed it too tight or something . . . because it broke in my hand and a large piece went into my thumb." The other three men leaned closer and stared at the scar. "It began to bleed and I thought that it was going to be the emergency room and stitches. I went to the bathroom to get bandages to try to stop the bleeding. By the time I got there it had stopped, so I ran some cold water over it to wash off the blood. When I finished the wound had healed."

"Healed?" asked an amazed Ben Green.

"Healed," answered Bernie Lewis, "healed and sealed as though it had been there for years."

Bernie didn't tell them what the sight of blood did to him. It was an old story and a deeply personal matter. One of those things that people bear silently all their lives. It had to do with the Al in Bernal Woolens.

Bernal Woolens was incorporated in 1948 in

the state of New York. Bernie Lewis, a tough kid from Chicago's South Side, had been through a war and survived. He returned from the war by troop ship and sailed into New York harbor in the winter of 1945. Two years of fighting and occupation in Germany left him drained and bitter. He was discharged at Camp Kilmer, New Jersey. The first thing he did was to petition the court to have his name changed from Lefkowitz to Lewis.

His mother had died shortly after hearing that her oldest son, Martin, was killed in Okinawa. His father had died when he and Martin were kids. There was nothing left for him in Chicago, so he decided to stay in New York.

When he met Rose Charnofsky she was young and beautiful. They married quickly. He worked in the garment center as a showroom salesman for a manufacturer of inexpensive dresses. Bernie was successful and became sales manager in a few years.

There was only one thing that Bernie Lewis never spoke about in those days. That was his experience of being part of the first unit to enter the Auschwitz concentration camp. He spoke Yiddish and was attached to a British unit. The sights that he saw and the deprivation that Jews had been put to so shocked and angered him that he could not speak to a German without the thought of killing coming to mind. He shook for a whole day after the liberation, then worked around the clock to try to help the poor souls who remained in the camp.

He told Rose about the experience only after he had another experience that replaced the concentration camp as the thing that he would never speak about. That was what happened to his partner, Al Berger.

Bernal Woolens was Bernie's and Al's dream. They met in the garment center and liked each other right away. They became good friends. Al ran the business, supervised the cutters, and kept things on schedule. Bernie did the buying and selling. It was a winning team.

The business grew through the prosperity of the fifties and into the sixties. Bernie and Rose had their son, Craig, in 1950. Life was beautiful: a good business, an honest partner, a beautiful wife, a son, and a new home in Hewlett, Long Island. Bernie was even thinking of buying a Cadillac.

But business was cyclical, and the garment business was especially prone to fads and fancies, as well as economic cycles. In late 1965, amid the Vietnam War escalation, Bernal Woolens had a setback. Synthetic fabrics were moving into the marketplace rapidly. Imports were growing. On top of all this, Al had talked Bernie into buying new equipment for the cutting room and three new trucks. The partners put their personal guarantees on the line.

Unlike Bernie Lewis, Al Berger was an introverted man. He had come to America as a boy in 1932. He struggled through the Depression. Deep inside him were the scars caused by his father's fears that the family would go hungry. When bill collectors came to the door, Al watched his father hide in the basement because he had no money. He watched Benjamin Berger, a proud man, turn into a vegetable. He swore that he would never live that way.

So when Bernal Woolens could not make its bank payments or its payroll, Al Berger, Mr. Inside, took the blame for their failure on his shoulders. He could see no way out of their financial predicaments. On a summer Monday morning he came to the office early. He neatly arranged his desk papers, then sat down and typed a letter to his partner. The quiet Polish immigrant, Albert Berger, born in Warsaw, then pried open the elevator door, carefully hid the tool he had used, and then jumped down the shaft, landing on top of the elevator fifteen floors below.

Bernie had to identify the body. It had ripped

through the top of the elevator car and a sharp edge had torn the body open. The elevator was filled with blood.

After reading the letter, Bernie realized that Al had killed himself to save the business because they had insurance on each other's life. He explained in the letter that he would make it look like an accident and even suggested that Bernie sue the building and buy the mill they always dreamed of owning.

Bernie destroyed the letter. He followed Al's instructions and bought the mill. It was in the quiet countryside of eastern Pennsylvania and was called Berger Mills. Al's wife and family always remained partners in the firm.

The night after the suicide Bernie went home and told Rose about Auschwitz. He cried and railed and beat his fists on the walls. Rose knew his tears were for Al Berger, but she remained silent. From that day on, when the subject of Al Berger came up, Bernie Lewis had only one answer: "I don't want to talk about it!" And he never did. It was only the sight of blood that brought Al Berger back and brought the secret to the front of his mind.

"Let's cut the bullshit." Art Perlman sat down and was serious. "This health club of ours isn't a health club at all. It's the goddamned Fountain of Youth and Mt. Sinai Hospital rolled into one."

Ben Green was half listening as he followed another train of thought. Then he blurted out, "I feel like I'm in a science fiction movie."

Joe Finley laughed. "We are, buddies . . . we are!"

They stared at him and asked him to explain.

"I'm an actor, so I know about movies. The things that have happened to us are impossible. But in the movies the impossible always happens. That place . . . that room in Building B is not . . . human."

"How do you know?" asked Ben.

"Facts. Here they are. My leukemia is gone. Art is growing hair. Ben swims a hundred laps in the pool. Bernie slashes himself and the cut heals in a minute. We are all trotting around like young studs and trying to fuck our wives' brains out. We can read each other's minds and thoughts. We can project our thoughts into other people's minds."

They all were enthralled as Joe Finley rattled off the accomplishments. "Now I'll tell you the weird stuff!"

"That's not weird enough for you?" asked Bernie.

"Listen," said Joe as he silenced Bernie. "You remember when I told you that I was under the water for four laps? Well, there is more to the story. I couldn't bring myself to tell you before. While I was underwater I had the feeling that I was in the ocean. I could see the bottom but I wasn't alone. There were others swimming below me. They were down deep, yet I could see them. They didn't have diving suits. They seemed to be pulling caskets or tubes out from under large slabs."

"Not caskets or tubes, Joe. They were bodies." Ben Green's interruption shocked Joe.

"Bodies? How do you know?"

"Because I saw the same damned thing two days ago when I went for a swim. I decided to try your underwater feat. It was lunchtime, and the pool was deserted. I stayed down for fifteen minutes. I saw the same thing. They were bringing up bodies. I thought I was hallucinating."

"Okay, that's number one. Now, last night I couldn't sleep," Joe continued, "so I was out on the terrace. It was late, after midnight. I saw a guy come out of B and meet our old friend Sheilds. They went into the office and had some kind of powwow. When they came out I suddenly felt . . . don't laugh . . . I felt like I could fly."

"Holy shit!" Bernie Lewis had his hand to his mouth.

"I had to drop to my knees and crawl back away from the railing because, I swear to Christ, I was about to take a header down to the parking lot."

Art Perlman spoke. "What do you think it is, Joe?"

"I think that place belongs to someone who doesn't live here."

"You don't mean here at the condo?"

"I mean here on this mother-loving planet!"

• **27** •

"Operator, I want to call a fishing boat named *Razzmatazz*. It's registered in the name of Mr. Phillip Doyle, Coral Gables."

Judy waited patiently as the ship-to-shore operator searched out the number.

"Please make note, that number is 22-4851-CG-11. I'll connect you. Just a moment."

The line crackled a bit and she heard Phil come on the phone.

"Doyle, the old man of the sea, here."

"Phil? This is Judy Simmons. Jack Fischer's . . . friend."

"Hi, Judy. How are you? Is something wrong?" There was sudden concern in his voice.

"No, dear, I'm just trying to raise Jack and I seem to be having trouble. Have you spoken to him?"

"Not for a week . . . no, two weeks. He told me he had some charter."

"Well, I thought I would try you, anyway. If

you see him at the dock, please remind him that he has a girl friend who is lonely."

"How about dinner with me? Jack hasn't been at the dock for a few weeks. As a matter of fact, Jimmy Patras told me he thought he saw Jack's boat over at the condo with the strange name . . . what the hell is it?"

"Where, Phil?"

"At the end of Red Lake Canal . . . Antares . . . it's called Antares."

"Why would he be there?"

"Oh, it's probably not him." There was a condescending tone to his voice. He was covering up for his buddy, in the male tradition.

"Thanks, Phil. How's the fishing?"

"Good in the Stream, but lousy over by The Stones."

"Nice to talk to you, Phil. Maybe we can have that dinner if the louse keeps me hanging on too long."

"Anytime, sweetheart. Anytime."

"Bye."

"Bye."

Judy slammed down the phone. Once again, she was furious. Minutes later she was heading toward the Antares condominium complex.

Wally Parker noticed the pretty young girl in the convertible as she parked in the visitors' lot. She wore tight jeans and her tank top was well filled. Probably a granddaughter of one of the old fogies, he thought, as Judy walked toward the pool.

Bernie Lewis looked up from his gin hand. The sight of Judy Simmons filled his eyes. He was immediately interested. He locked on her mind and guided her to their table.

"Can we help you, young lady?" he asked as Judy stopped next to him.

"Uh, yes, I think so." She was looking into the face of an old man, but the eyes were bright and burning right through her. What she felt was strange and extremely sexy. She giggled inside and thought to herself, *dirty old man.*

"Well, what will it be?" Art Perlman chimed in.

He, too, had that look. Judy was unnerved, then gathered her composure.

"I'm looking for the boat dock. A friend of mine is supposed to meet me here with his boat."

"Boat dock?" Bernie looked at Ben. "We have a boat dock?"

The construction at Building B blocked access to the canal and the residents had not been aware there was a completed boat dock. The plans showed the dock, but Tony Stranger had told them all that it would be the last facility built.

"Oh," said Art, "the boat dock. That's not finished yet."

"That's strange," said Judy, "because my friend told me he docked here regularly."

With that, Joe Finley stood and suggested that they all walk over and check it out. Bernie offered Judy his arm. Art took the other side. Ben and Joe brought up the rear.

"Stay out of trouble," yelled Paul Amato, the former stockbroker from Boston. "You guys are too old for that."

"Says you," answered Bernie. They headed for the rear of Building B.

After the discovery that the processing room had been visited, the Antareans decided to keep a small force back in the room to watch their equipment.

The rest went out early at dawn in the two boats.

Amos Bright, the two male commanders, and one copper man watched with interest as the four men and the very pretty girl climbed over the construction obstacles.

Where are they going? thought Amos.

To the dock, answered copper man.

But why? They were told it was not built. Also, the girl is not a tenant here.

Copper man concentrated. He reached for the hand of the two commanders. They formed a triangle and copper man's eyes glowed.

The triangle broke. He thought to the others. *She is Jack's friend. She is searching for the* Manta III. *Somehow she thinks it is here. The others are those who live here. They are taking her to the dock.*

How could she know Jack was here? thought Amos.

She does not reveal that, answered copper man. *Something else. The four men with her . . . they are very hard to read . . . two of them block as we do . . . the others remain clear, like a commander.*

Amos stared at the four men with special interest.

Rose Lewis watched the four men and the young girl disappear around the back of Building B. She was on her terrace serving coffee to Alma and Mary. The three were in their bathing suits catching the morning sun. They had decided to meet and continue their discussion about the changes in their husbands.

Bess Perlman would join them later. She had to visit her sister, who had suffered a stroke and was in a nursing home in north Miami.

As Rose turned to tell the others about what she had just witnessed, Bess Perlman turned her blue Olds on to the One hundred sixty-third Street causeway. She drove slowly and ignored the horns and shouts of other drivers. No one could accuse her of reckless driving. No one could accuse her of reckless anything.

Her life had been careful and quiet. Before Arthur Perlman there was the good life in Manhattan Beach in Brooklyn. Her father was a judge of the State Court of Appeals. He was an honorable man with political connections. He was also second generation and totally Americanized and assimilated. Her mother was a gentile and considerably younger than Judge Bernstein. Bess had her mother's looks and her father's intelligence. She was a beautiful girl. She met Arthur Perlman at a New Year's Eve Party at a friend's house. The Bernstein sisters, Bess and Betty, were the talk of Manhattan Beach and extremely popular girls.

After Art had revealed his business to her, Bess understood why her father had avoided them after their marriage. He had disliked Perlman from the beginning, but he never gave Bess an acceptable reason. Actually, his resistance to Art had driven the two closer. Judge Bernstein was civil to Art Perlman, but nothing more.

Then the business with the hearings and the Mafia hit the papers and Bess understood. The thing she never knew was that her father was deeply involved in Arthur's business and had been on the "Family" payroll for most of his career. Art never had told her, and he never would.

She was not thinking about her Brooklyn past today, however. Her concern was for her widowed sister, Betty, lying in a nursing-home bed, unable to speak or move. Bess visited her at least once a week, even though most of the time there was no communication. The state had moved Betty to the home because they had judged she would never respond to therapy. Prior to that she had been in a hospital.

The Perlmans had enough money to take care of Betty, and Art had suggested that they get a special nurse to live with Betty. Bess had refused. For some reason, when it came to her family, she didn't want to use Art's "dirty" money. It was personal and only between them. He never argued with her. Deep down he knew that she knew about things that could put several people in jail for a long time. He didn't ever want to aggravate her to the point where she might tell what she knew out of spite. So he kept quiet and she looked after her sister as best she could.

The home was a modest three-story building west of Biscayne Boulevard and north of One hundred sixty-third Street. She parked the Olds and walked up the stairs to the main entrance.

There were a few old people sitting on the porch. They were expressionless. One man, who looked to be well over eighty, kept dabbing his mouth with a wet handkerchief held in his right hand. His left hand rested immobile in his lap.

As she opened the door a tiny old woman using a walker stood in front of her. The woman motioned toward the door and Bess understood. She held the door as the woman tried to go outside.

Then a voice boomed out from behind the woman. "Mrs. Poland! Where do you think you are going? Stop right there." A heavy woman, fiftyish, who looked as if she had come directly from a Gestapo training school, put an arm on frail Mrs. Poland. Bess watched the old woman flinch in pain as she was grabbed. The matron pulled Mrs. Poland around and pointed toward a doorway. "You go in there. I'll talk to you later."

Mrs. Poland looked back at Bess for a moment. She had a tear in her eye, but she nodded a thank you at Bess.

Fear for her sister gripped Bess. She didn't realize the matron was talking to her.

"Can I help you?"

Bess looked away from the old lady directly into the eyes of the matron. "Help me? I don't think you could help anyone."

The woman ignored her sarcasm. "Are you here to visit someone?"

"Yes, my sister. Mrs. Betty Franklin."

"Oh, that one. She's on the third floor. Room 303. Take the elevator over there." The woman gestured, turned, and left.

As Bess moved toward the elevator and away from the door, the smell of the home reached her senses. It was the sweet smell of the old, mixed with disinfectant and rotten cooking. It made her even more afraid.

The door to room 303 was shut. Bess turned the knob and the door swung open. The room was dark. She reached for a light switch and found it didn't exist. Her eyes adjusted to the room. There was a faint light coming from a small window that had a drawn shade. Then she saw an overhead light with a string hanging down. She pulled the string and the light went on. *I don't know they made ten-watt bulbs*, she thought to herself, because the light made little difference in the illumination of the room. It was just as well.

Her sister, once the most beautiful girl in Brooklyn, was lying on a small bed that resembled a crib. The sides were up. She lay on her back. Her eyes were open. She stared at the ceiling.

Bess touched her hand and bent to kiss her on the forehead. There was a slight response and a sound. Not a moan, nor a cry. It was a whine, the whine of a hurt puppy. Bess leaned over the bed and cried. Tears rolled from both the sisters' eyes in that darkened tiny room, so far from Brooklyn, New York, and the wonderful days of youth.

The four men and Judy found the path leading to the dock. Copper man joined hands with the commanders again and read the minds of the quintet on the dock. He also listened to their words.

Ben Green trotted onto the dock and looked at the two slips. "I'll be darned, young lady. You were right."

Joe knelt to examine the bumpers along the dockside. "This place is being used, all right. These bumpers are worn."

Art Perlman checked the other side. "These, too," he shouted.

"Two boats?" Ben muttered to himself, then noticed the tractor and flatbed parked behind some bushes near the path. He walked over to examine it. The others read his thoughts and turned to look.

Copper man gasped audibly. "They telepath," he blurted out.

Yes, thought Amos and the commanders simultaneously. *They telepath. But they are dwellers, and we know dwellers cannot do this!*

Commander of All Light broke into the minds of the others. *Clear*, he ordered. *Quickly*. But it was not quick enough.

Ben and Bernie caught Amos' thoughts at the same time. They looked at each other after stopping dead in their tracks.

"You get that?" asked Ben.

"You bet," Bernie answered verbally. "It's like being tuned into a radio station. Who was it?"

Judy didn't notice the strange behavior of the four men. She was sure that Jack had been here and that he would return. She made up her mind to check back that night, but now she was wasting her time. *Manta III* was out somewhere on the ocean.

The men walked back to the car with Judy. She asked them to keep an eye out for the *Manta III* and told them she would be back later that afternoon. Just in case, she left her phone number with them.

Above the parking lot, three very angry wives watched their husbands get the phone number of a pretty young girl. No one had to guess what they were writing.

"The last of the red-hot lovers," quipped Rose Lewis.

"All of them," said Mary.

Alma watched. Joe didn't really seem interested in the girl. He was looking left and right as though he was searching for the source of a sound. Ben joined him. Art opened the car door for the girl. Bernie helped her in, but abandoned her quickly.

Then the four men made a beeline toward Building B.

"Not lovers," said Alma. "Something is going on."

The doorbell rang, interrupting her train of thought. When she opened the door a very distraught Bess Perlman was standing there. Her eyes were red and she seemed to have aged ten years.

• 28 •

The calm water broke as Hal and copper man popped to the surface. They swam rapidly to the *Manta III*. On board, Jack was already preparing to weigh anchor. Harry had ordered him suddenly after receiving a telepath from Beam on the *Terra Time*.

The message was sharp and clear: return to base immediately.

Terra Time was already under way off to the port side.

"What's wrong?" called Jack.

"We must go back to the dock immediately. The commanders have called. They do not say why."

Copper man and Harry slid on deck. Jack revved the engines and turned toward the coast in the wake of the *Terra Time*.

Back at Building B Hal spoke to Amos. "Why did you call them?"

Amos looked at him sternly. He thought to

225

himself: *they are like us, yet they are not Anta-reans. I do not know their kind. They have powers. Perhaps they are Ferons, but we know of no Feron expeditions in this quadrant. They come quickly; therefore, they understand.* He gestured for all to move back to the corner of the processing room.

A moment later the four old men popped the lock on the processing-room door and entered their "health club."

"Bess. Come in, dear," Alma took her arm. Bess leaned against her heavily and sighed. The two other women came to her.

"What happened, Bess?" Rose was sitting next to Bess, holding her around the shoulders. Bess sobbed.

"We should all die quickly in our sleep." Bess spoke to no one in particular. Her voice was soft and weak. "I went to see my sister today at the new home. The new home is a nightmare. She's in a room like a closet. She's alone. No one there . . . just lying in the dark . . . she can't speak . . . she can't ask . . . she's alone . . . alone . . . oh, God . . . she's alone." Bess cried and the others let her cry. She would feel better after she had shed her tears.

Thoughts flew around the room like

bees outside a hive.

Where are they?
Who are you?
You command nothing!
I see them in the corner.
How many?
Four.
Four.
They are human.
Of course I'm human.
What are you doing here?
We ask the same.

Oddly enough, it was Ben Green who over-came the confusion. He reached deep inside his mind and blocked the chatter. Then he shouted, "Shut up!" aloud.

There was silence. Amos moved out from the corner of the room into the blue light emanating from the wall screen. He spoke aloud to Ben Green. "May we speak?"

"Of course."

"You've been in this room before, haven't you?"

"Yes, many times. Is it your room?"

"Yes."

"What is it?"

"That I cannot say yet. Will you talk with me first?"

"Watch it, Ben," Bernie cut in. "These

guys don't live here."

The commanders moved into the light. Copper man stayed back.

"Holy shit!" remarked Art Perlman. "Look at those two!"

Ben looked over at the commanders. Then the four men felt them, but only briefly. Again thought flew, but this time only among the four men.

Watch it.

Ow!

Block them, guys.

Suddenly Bernie Lewis grabbed his right arm. *Hey, that hurts!*

The commanders were directing energy at the four men. What happened next was not expected.

Joe Finley started it. He turned to the commanders and thought a punch at them. All Light hit the floor. No Light doubled up in pain. Ben had thought a punch in the stomach at the Shiny Black at the same time that Joe had mentally hit Shiny White. Amos spoke again as he stared in disbelief at the hurt commanders. Copper man was frantically sending a message to Beam for them to hurry back.

"May we talk, please?" asked Amos.

"I thought that's what we were going to do." Ben answered.

"Tell your buddies that that shit won't work with us, and if they try it again we'll really kick some ass."

"I am sorry. It won't happen again."

The commanders got up slowly.

"May I have a moment to see to my friends?" asked Amos.

"Go ahead, and tell the other guy back there to step out here where we can see him."

Copper man moved into the light.

"Good God!" said Bernie, rubbing his arm. "Look at that one. He looks like a piece of plumbing."

A few moments later Amos guided the commanders onto one of the cots. The copper man helped. The lamps above the cots came on and the commanders rested. Their faces glowed as the beams hit them.

"Are they okay?" asked Ben.

"Yes," answered Amos, "but I am not sure why they were hurt."

"We did it," said Joe.

"I know, but their power is strong. Now it is weak. I don't think you did that . . . make them weak. Let us talk."

Amos moved toward the large center table. The four men met him there.

"Let us speak with our tongues. In verbal language. If we use thoughts then I fear we may

229

hurt the commanders more. It will be less confusing."

Ben agreed. "Who are you?" he asked.

Amos considered his answer carefully. His thoughts were totally Antarean now and deep inside. No one could read them. *What shall I tell these humans? They have used the equipment and gained powers that they do not understand. Yet they can use them. The other thing is worse. We are weakened. Have they done this? Or is it an outside force? If I tell them who we are, how will they react? What will they do? Do they know how strong they are? Do they know how weak we are? I wish Jack would get here. They would believe him . . . he is one of them. He is the only one they will believe.*

• 29 •

"The man is telling the truth. I swear it." Jack had just finished what was, for him, a long speech. Ben Green, Art Perlman, and Bernie Lewis stood at the center table staring at Jack Fischer. They believed him.

Joe Finley had moved over to the cots where the commanders were resting. His thoughts went to a copper man and Hal. *Will they be okay?*

Your concern is welcome. Yes, they will be. These were the thoughts he received.

Ben Green spoke first. "It's fantastic. What can I say? What does one say to people from another planet? Welcome?"

"Thank you," said Amos. "That is a good start."

"What are you going to do about your army?" asked Bernie.

"That is a problem we must solve, but right now . . ." — Amos hesitated — ". . . now we have a greater problem."

Shocked, Jack Fischer asked, "What now?"

"Something has weakened us. We are losing abilities. Normally the commanders would have been able to protect themselves, but they were not able. I don't know why."

As they talked, Beam moved around the group at the center table. One of her functions was that of medical officer. As the men and the Antareans talked, she scanned them. She discovered two interesting facts. One was that Amos, Harry, Hal, the copper men, and the commanders were experiencing a molecular breakdown of the protective shield that they wore. It was a super-thin spacesuit of sorts whose main function was to keep their bodies within a specified temperature and atmosphere. That explained the weakened state of the space party.

The second fact was just as interesting. As she scanned the bodies of the aging Earth men, she realized that, by some freak accident of nature, the processing equipment meant for the cocoons was transforming them into perfect space soldiers. These thoughts she kept blocked, and then she stored them in her mind.

Beam moved around to the commanders on the cot. She transferred her knowledge to them at close range, much like one might speak to a baby. Her thoughts were soft and whispered.

Commander of All Light stood and moved to the center table.

Amos moved aside.

"I am All Light, commander of our expedition. I am sorry that we tried to attack you before. Your response was deserved. It will not happen again."

The four men nodded.

"We were here a very long time ago. That was when we left our cocoons buried. Florida was a primitive place. Now it has changed. Our intelligence is good, but it seems we have overlooked some rather important facts."

Amos could not read All Light. All of the Antareans gathered around the table. Everyone listened as the commander continued.

"Jack has seen our faces. Later we will show you. The human covering we wear is so that we may work among you. I am sure you understand. You will not find us ugly. We are humanoid, too."

Commander of No Light picked up the discussion from Shiny White. "The covering we have serves another purpose. It has, underneath it, a thick skinlike substance that allows us to keep our bodies at the correct temperature and pressure. It is an environment like Antares, our home planet. Beam is our medical officer. She is a commander, too. She has discovered our problem."

Beam now stepped forward and continued. Bernie Lewis wondered what a female Antarean really looked like. If she was anything like the attractive blond woman facing them now, he thought, he might like to take a trip to Antares. His thought was not missed by anyone in the room.

Beam smiled at him and spoke. "The protective skin is one molecule thick. That is very thin, but normally it is enough. It was enough when we were here before. Something has changed in the atmosphere. Your air has become caustic. It is breaking down the protection. The molecules are being changed by outside chemicals. I have sampled the air now. It is filled with these chemicals."

"We not only kill ourselves with bad air . . . we also screw it up for visitors from outer space." No one laughed at Bernie's joke. "I mean, I'm sorry." He shrugged.

Beam continued. "It has taken three of your Earth weeks for our protection to deteriorate. We can visit our mother ship and obtain new skins, but they will last only for the same period. Then we will have no protection."

"Is there some way we can help?" asked Ben.

Amos answered. "You do not have a technology capable of making these skins. We do not have the material on board that can accomplish the task on time."

"What temperature and pressure do you require?" asked Bernie.

"We need one hundred forty of your Fahrenheit degrees and five hundred of your pounds per square inch."

Jack Fischer now understood why the room had been so unbearable for him when the cocoons were opened. Although each soldier had a protective skin, it had to be activated when the last layer of the cocoon was peeled away. For that moment the room pressure and temperature were brought to Antarean conditions. Thus, the red wall and the feeling of being hit with a shock wave.

He spoke. "But, Commander, when we release the soldiers you simulate those conditions in this room." Then he realized that he might be telling the Earth men something that the Antareans didn't want them to know. He didn't continue, but the four men understood what he was trying to say.

Beam spoke again. "There is another matter we must discuss." She looked toward Amos and whispered thoughts about the conditions of the humans who had used the equipment. The four men strained, but could not read her.

Amos spoke. "I want to tell you what Beam has discovered. Before I do, we will need to agree on a method of private conference. I am sure that you dwellers realize that we wish to remain undetected by the rest of your race. It would be disastrous to our mission and to the delicate balances that exist in your world if our presence were discovered."

Joe Finley was way ahead of him. "Mr. Bright, I think that we need to talk among ourselves as much as you do. The solution could also show good faith. I know that if I don't want to listen in on your thoughts, I can block them. Each time I try to do it, it gets easier. I am sure you can do the same."

"Yes," said Amos.

"Well, then let's agree not to eavesdrop on each other."

Amos smiled. He liked this man. "Agreed." Then he continued. "You four men have used our equipment. We know that this has affected you in earthly ways, shall we say? Mr. Finley has been cured of a disease. All of you are extremely healthy and energetic. Our readings show that other changes have occurred in your bodies and minds that are of great interest to us."

"What changes?" asked Art.

"You have become, or are becoming, capable

of . . ." – he paused because he was about to break one of the cardinal rules of contact with other planets – ". . . capable of accepting the programming originally scheduled for our cocoons."

A hot flash surged through Ben Green's body. Immediately the four men grasped the enormity of the information Amos Bright had presented.

"What exactly does that mean?" asked Ben.

Deep inside, Amos decided to tell them everything. He had broken the rule. There was no turning back. Only the copper men resisted. Harry and Hal were neutral.

"Our Galaxy . . . our Universe . . . is a vast place. In time, your race will learn to travel through space . . . they will learn to survive other environments, they will learn to be with other races. In time. Much of what is required for space travel and for communication with other beings depends on the full development of the human mind. Your race is barely one-tenth of the way to that goal. But that is not true of the four of you."

Amos was telling them facts they had only begun to suspect. The four listened intently

"You have become superhuman. You are superior to your fellow dwellers, and you will always be that way. We cannot reverse the process that changes your bodies and minds."

"My God!" gasped Jack Fischer. His expression was one of fear and exhilaration.

"God of us all!" answered Amos Bright.

• 30 •

Judy left her exercise class at five P.M. and drove to Arnie's and Sandy's apartment. She had called Arnie twice at his office earlier to tell him that she had found out where Jack was. But she could not tell them over the phone. She would tell them in person. As she drove she couldn't get the four old men out of her mind. There had been something weird about them, and although they were obviously well over sixty, she had found them exciting and sensual. The thing she didn't know was that they found her exciting, too, and the feelings that she had were due to their newfound ability to telepath thoughts and physical emotions.

The four wives had spent the afternoon talking, once again. Their first goal was to calm Bess Perlman and promise to help her get her sister out of the home. It became a pact among them and this brought them closer to each other. They spent the rest of the afternoon trying to understand what was happening to their husbands.

The four men spent their afternoon on the *Manta III*. It had been decided that the Antareans would remain at the complex to discuss their problems while the Earth men used Jack's boat to have their meeting. By separating it would make the blocking of thoughts a little easier. It was also imperative that the Antareans feed and try to regain some of their strength. They could set the processing room to the proper atmosphere and pressure. That would help, but they all knew it was only a temporary measure.

With the excitement of the day, Amos Bright had forgotten his conversation with Mr. Shields the night before. But Shields had not forgotten. Most of all, he remembered Mr. Bright's telling him that his appreciation would be shown in his paycheck.

Shields had called Wally Parker at home early the next morning and told him to be in by eight A.M. They had met in the office and Wally had spent the day sneaking around following the four men while they were on the condo property.

Wally had been aware of the fact that his employer, Amos Bright, used Building B from time to time, and that he had several friends who used it, too. His instructions were definite. He was never to go into the building. Therefore, when he saw the four men leave the young girl in the parking lot and go into Building B, he had stayed outside, pretending to inspect the shrubs that had not yet been planted along the walk leading to the main door of the building. He had watched the two boats arrive and tie up in a hurry. His curiosity was peaked as the crew from both boats ran to the back door of Building B and disappeared inside.

The four old men and the captain had boarded the *Manta III* in silence. Wally watched the sleek cruiser back out, turn, and proceed slowly up the canal. Then he watched Building B for a sign of the others. After twenty minutes he walked back to the office to report to Mr. Shields on the strange happenings at the unfinished Antares building.

Dr. Morris Feldman sat in his office waiting for Dr. Fred Breedlove. He had called his colleague and asked him to come to the hospital at five-thirty. The Finley case was on his mind all day. He couldn't shake it. How had this miraculous recovery occurred? But it was more than a recovery. He looked at the microscope slide again. Joe Finley's blood was perfect. No disease, not a hint of foreign bodies. Perfectly formed platelets. He was sure there was something else, but he couldn't get a handle on it. So Fred Breedlove would have a look, too, because Fred was the top . . . *numero uno* . . . when it came to lab work in hematology. Fred would find the answer.

Marie Amato finally said what was on the others' minds. She sat by the pool with Andrea Hankinson. Their husbands came out of the pool and toweled themselves. Paul Amato had yelled a remark at the four men as they took the pretty young girl behind Building B. Now the group had returned and the girl was leaving. Marie looked up and saw Alma and the other wives watching from the terrace. Then the men had moved quickly to Building B again. She also noticed that the handyman seemed to be following them.

"Those old men are getting stranger every day!" Marie said.

"I'm glad you said it," remarked Andrea. "I think they have flipped."

Paul Amato smiled and chided his wife. "Can't you let a couple of old guys have a fling? They aren't hurting anyone."

Marie attacked immediately. "Not hurting anyone? Did you see their wives watching them?"

"No . . . poor old guys . . . haven't got the sense to play off the grounds."

"You're impossible . . . such a chauvinist . . . think of those women. It must be humiliating for them."

Frank Hankinson didn't comment. He knew Ben Green, and Ben was not the kind of man who would flaunt an affair in his wife's face. He also knew that the other three men were solid citizens and very intelligent. No, something else was happening, and Frank's background, as a reporter before becoming a partner in the St. Louis radio station, pushed him to decide to do a little investigating of his own. When he saw Wally make a beeline for the office, Frank excused himself from the group and followed Wally into Shields' office.

• 31 •

Bernie, Art, and Joe sat quietly as the *Manta III* passed the sea wall and turned north toward Miami Beach. Ben Green finished his phone conversation with Mary on the ship-to-shore. "It's a business deal, honey, nothing more. All we want to do is check out the boat. We were going to surprise all of you, so don't say anything to the other wives if you can help it. Just tell them we are going to be late for dinner. Tell them it's business. Bye, love."

He switched off before she could answer back. He felt guilty knowing Mary would tell the others the whole story, but that was part of the plan. At least they wouldn't worry when the men were missing. Ben didn't know that the women had seen them talking to the young girl in the parking lot that afternoon. Now Mary was convinced that the men were going to meet the girl and her friends to practice their new-found sexual prowess.

244

Ben moved over and stood next to Jack Fischer. He had taken a liking to the lean young charter captain. "You must have had quite an interesting time these past few weeks."

Jack, glad to be among his own kind for a change, chuckled. "Interesting isn't the word, Mr. Green. It's been downright weird, but, to tell you the truth, I have never been so excited in my life. These people are good and they sure know a lot about things we can't even imagine. It's screwing up my private life a bit, but I really feel honored to be part of all this."

Ben understood and agreed. Now they were part of it, too. But how much a part? That had to be decided this night. He turned back to his buddies. It was time to begin.

Ben spoke first. "I would like to preface our discussion with my personal feelings about who we are, and where we are . . . and why. If you don't mind, I've been thinking about this little speech since Mr. Bright told us what we have become and what we will remain.

"I know we are friends and have become very close in the past few weeks. I consider you guys my best friends — after my wife, that is. I want to tell you about my feelings . . . they are mine, and I don't profess to speak for you. Just bear with me . . . please."

"Go ahead," said Joe. Bernie and Art nodded.

"I never thought of myself as an old man — never, that is, until we moved down here and were cut off from business, from the hustle of the big city, from the day-to-day action that we call work. Then I began to feel old, and more, I began to feel useless. Tired. Bored. The space-man called us superhuman. Ten times more ability than the rest of humanity. Well, let me tell you that I always felt that way . . . maybe not ten times better, but I certainly knew, and know, I am a capable man. But for some reason, that, today particularly, seems really ridiculous, we live in a society that tells us that old is useless . . . old is being finished . . . old is being unable to make a contribution . . . old is ugly. And we believe it!"

The other three men listened and felt Ben's anger as their own.

"I don't know what I really feel now, except I am more alive than I have been in years. It's not only the physical awakening. We know the room did that. No, it's a mental awakening, and that is part of me that was always there. I don't ever want to lose it again. I guess what I'm trying to say is that we have been touched by something special . . . perhaps by God. I feel singled out . . . unique . . . and I don't want to blow it."

Art, staring out the porthole at the setting

sun, spoke. "What don't you want to blow, Ben?"

"The greatest, most important event to take place on this earth since the birth of Christ."

Bernie Lewis stood and walked to the stern. He was deep in thought. Joe Finley got up and walked out to the ladder that led to the flying bridge. He began to climb slowly. He, too, wanted to be alone for a moment. Ben's words had shaken him.

A quiet settled over the boat. The hum of the diesels and the slapping of the bow onto the calm Florida water mixed with the evening cries of gulls and pelicans to create a background for thought.

Twenty minutes later Jack heard their minds come alive and call to each other. They gathered in the cabin.

Art Perlman spoke first. "Jack, we know you have some ability to read our thoughts. But you are nowhere as advanced as we are, because we have used the Antarean equipment. We would like to be able to speak freely here and know that you will respect our desire that what is said tonight be kept confidential."

"Okay. But they can read my mind, so they may pick up some things involuntarily."

"We'll take that risk. You know things about them that we need to know, too."

Jack began to feel as though his brain was community property held by the Antareans and these four old men. But he also felt like a middleman . . . an intermediary, and that felt good.

"The way I see it," said Bernie, "we are in a negotiation . . . a business negotiation."

"Like a contract?" asked Art.

"Yes," Bernie replied.

Ben stood. "Before we get to the terms, can we agree to go all the way with these people?"

Joe Finley held up his hand as though he were in a classroom trying to get the teacher's attention.

"What, Joe?" asked Ben.

"When you say all the way, what exactly do you mean?"

"I mean that Mr. Bright exposed two problems to us and, I believe, inferred the solution to both rested on our cooperating with them."

"I have no problem helping them operate the room and conserve their strength. We can certainly do that," said Art.

"You miss the point, Artie," Bernie interrupted. "The man, Bright, and the shiny white commander – All Light – told us something else."

"Right," agreed Ben. "They don't think they can get the army up and running. *Spoiled* is what they said."

"Water damage," Jack chimed in.

"Right, water damage. So in addition to helping them, I think they were saying that we . . . the four of us . . . and people like us . . . would . . . or could . . . become their army." Ben sat down.

Jack put the controls on auto pilot and sat with the four men. "Holy shit! You mean they want to take you guys into space?"

"You got it now, Jack."

"I wonder where," Joe remarked. "I wonder what kind of place. And what would we do there?"

Art Perlman was up and pacing. "To tell you the truth, physically I feel like I could fight a whole army myself, but . . . mentally . . . well, I'm too old to be a soldier."

"Wait a minute, gentlemen." Jack got their attention. "Last night I was alone with the female commander, the one they call Beam — the one who examined you guys while we were talking earlier? Anyway, she told me a little about the planet where the army was to go. It was called Parma Quad Two. It's near the Dog star — the one we call Sirius. But it wasn't for war. It was like an army of education . . . something like that. The inhabitants of the planet are quite advanced technologically and have agreed to let the Antareans onto their world."

Ben interrupted Jack. "You say for education, not war?"

"Right. These beings on the planet are crystals . . . like rocks, but they are alive and they feed on ultraviolet light. The Antareans want to use them as spaceships. It's a little beyond me, but what I'm trying to say is that I don't think this army is for war as we know it, anyway."

"That's good to know," Ben thanked Jack.

"This planet is near Sirius, you say?" Art was on his feet.

"That's not like going to Detroit."

"Not even Beverly Hills," said Joe.

"Not even Disneyworld. We are talking about light-years . . . about millions and billions of miles." Art was serious.

Ben leaned back against the bulkhead. "We are talking about forever."

• **32** •

The room was glowing bright red. The atmosphere was thick. The entire Antarean expedition crew lay on the cots with the lamps turned on full. They communicated silently with one another, each projecting thought without interruption; each absorbing the previous thoughts into one pattern; each building on the pattern until it became one thought for all.

Shall we block out their thoughts?

We promised.

We should.

Agreed and done.

They are good men.

I like them.

Strange that their race rejects them because they have age.

It is common in primitive societies.

Not always. The Sengs in Galaxy Outer Seven revere their old ones and ask them to rule.

True, but the Sengs are descended from the First and are closest to Touching.

True.

These are not Sengs. They are dwellers who are called human. I will trust them.

And I.

Will it be right to take them to Parma Quad Two?

That is the mission.

Then you are sure the cocoons are useless?

I am certain.

We must replace them for another time.

If the dwellers — humans — agree, can we program them in time?

I believe we can.

We have only four of them. We need nine hundred forty-one!

Where will we get them?

The four will find them.

They must be old like our four. Of that I am sure.

Explain.

It will not work on the young tissue like Jack. I am not certain exactly why. It is a chemical reaction.

So they will be old humans?

There are many in this area.

They gather here before they die.

We will need to make commanders of some of them.

Yes.

Shall it be these four?

They will tell us.

Remember, this is an army of nines and threes. We will need more than four commanders.

True.

Amos will speak with them. Beam will assist.

Agreed. Agreed by all.

Now we must feed and prepare for new skins.

The Antareans rested as the overhead cones fed them and prepared their outer skins for the trip back to the mother ship. As they rested an entire row of Antarean soldiers died. Their glowing eyes dimmed slowly and finally went dark.

• 33 •

The ladies met at Alma Finley's car. They decided to have dinner out as long as their husbands were going to be home late. Mary had suggested that they treat themselves to the fancy French Restaurant that had recently opened in Coconut Grove. Mary Green told the other women that Ben had called and that the men were going to be late. She had not told them about the "business" deal, because she didn't believe it, and she knew the others wouldn't, either. However, she felt that perhaps after a drink or two she would work up the courage to tell them exactly what Ben had said. Buying a charter boat, indeed!

Bess was still quiet as they drove north to the Grove. The women had been helpful. She felt some hope in that she and her sister were not alone. She even considered asking Art for a loan to pay for private nursing care. All she knew was that Betty had to be out of that horrible place, and soon.

Judy Simmons was not quiet. She was angry and let Sandy and Arnie know it in no uncertain terms. "Your brother is a lying fink. He's been in Coral Gables all of the time."

"Are you sure, honey?"

"Don't 'honey' me, Arnie Fischer. I am as sure as I can be."

Sandy tried to calm her down, but Judy wouldn't have it. "I didn't see the *Manta*, but he was there, all right. Some men told me that two boats were there. I also spoke to Phil Doyle on the *Razzmatazz*. He tried to cover up, but he let it slip that Jack was seen over at that place, too."

Arnie tried to reason. "Look, Judy, maybe he's really tied up with these people and they want him to keep things secret. He did say that it was some kind of treasure thing. Maybe he's only doing his job."

"He knows he doesn't have to lie to me. He knows I'd keep my mouth shut. It's not the goddamned CIA, you know!"

"Maybe it is."

That stopped her for a moment. Then she looked them both in the eye and, in a slow and deliberate manner, said, "Maybe it is the goddamned CIA. If it is, then I want to know, because if he is working for them, then I don't want to know him . . . ever again!"

They took Arnie's car and drove toward the Antares complex.

Frank Hankinson had been trying to call Ben Green since seven P.M. It had been that late by the time he went home. It had been a strange afternoon. Perhaps Ben could answer his questions. Wally and Shields certainly didn't know the whole story.

He had followed Wally into the office at five-thirty. The secretary was gone and Wally was in the inner office with Shields. Frank had decided to wait and listen.

"Mr. Shields, the boss is playing you for a sucker."

"What are you talking about?"

"Well, I followed those old fogies like you told me. They left this morning and came back about one. They went into Building B."

"I knew it . . . I knew it. Mr. Bright was right."

"Mr. Bright knew they were in there!"

"What? Bright knew?"

"That's right. They went in for a few hours and then came out. Then they met some young chick by the pool and took her down to the dock."

"The dock? No one is supposed to go to the dock!"

"Yeah, well, they did. Before they went down I saw Bright and a few of his strange buddies watching from a window. They didn't stop them . . . and since you told me just to watch, I didn't stop them, either."

"What happened?"

"It was strange. They checked it out. Then they all jumped up . . . not the girl, but the old men. They looked up at Building B and hustled the girl away . . . like someone yelled at them to get off the dock. But no one yelled. Anyway, they took the girl back to her car and came back to Building B."

"Did you follow them in?"

"No, sir. You told me to stay out of there. I hung around for about an hour. Then I saw the two boats come in and all of those weird people make a beeline for Building B."

"Maybe they caught the old farts. You don't think they would hurt them, do you?"

"No. No way. About an hour later Mr. Bright comes out the back door with the four old guys and the captain of the charter boat. He walks them down to the dock and they take off. Then Bright goes back to the building. I hung around for a while and then came right here."

"Did Bright seem to be friendly with them?"

"Like buddies, especially the big guy who reamed us about the pool."

"Green."

"Yeah. Oh, also, you know who was with them? The guy from the D.A.'s office."

"You mean the old lawyer who pushed us to fill the pool?"

"You got it. He's one of them?"

"Son-of-a-bitch! What the fuck is going on here?"

"Beats me, boss."

Wally sat staring at Shields. Outside, Frank Hankinson understood the silence and realized that he didn't want to speak to these man at this time. He slowly opened the office door and left. Instead of going home, he walked around Building B and made his way to the dock area. It was on the *Terra Time* that he met his first Antarean.

As Hankinson approached the dock, copper man number one turned off the cone above him.

"Someone approaches *Terra Time*."

"See who it is."

He left the processing room and went out the back door toward the dock. Frank had already boarded the *Terra Time* and was in the lower cabin when copper man one came aboard. Suddenly he was frozen in his tracks. He was awake and aware, but couldn't move. Then he felt himself turned around and stood facing the strange-looking man.

"Who are you, and why are you on my boat?"

Frank felt his vocal cords release and he could talk. "Hank . . . Hankinson . . . Frank Hankinson is my name. I live here."

"Why are you on my boat?"

"No harm meant. I was just looking . . . around . . . for my friend."

"Who is that?"

"Ben Green. Do you know him?"

"He is not here. He went out on our other boat."

"Oh . . . do you live here . . . if you don't mind my asking? I don't think I've seen you around."

"No. I work here. On construction."

"Oh . . . well, I hope you guys finish soon." Frank felt the unexplained grip on him loosen. But he was not completely free to move. The stranger, who remained in shadow, backed away and swiftly moved up the ladder to the deck above.

Frank then shook and was free. He moved toward the ladder but his steps were heavy, as though his feet were filled with lead. When he finally came on deck the man was gone.

He stood for a moment and then distinctly

heard a voice say, "Please leave my boat!"

It frightened him because the voice was inside his head, yet as clear as if someone was shouting at him. He jumped off the boat and headed for home. It was then that he realized it was almost dark and what seemed like a few passing minutes on the boat must have been at least an hour. He knew he had to talk to Ben Green as soon as possible. He was sure that Ben was in trouble.

• 34 •

The *Manta III*'s running lights played on the calm water of the canal as the cruiser slowly made its way toward the Antares dock. Ben opened his mind and reached out for the Antareans. Commander No Light answered.

We are decided.

And so are we.

Are you rested?

Enough to meet.

Where shall we gather?

Ask Jack to take you to his room. We will find you there.

Good.

All the Antareans, as well as Art, Joe, and Bernie, heard the message. Jack got most of it.

Ben had put things in perspective. In a word, they were talking about forever. How do you leave your home, your life, your planet, forever? It had been only a few years since the people of Earth were able to view their planet from space.

It was just becoming familiar. Now these four elderly men were talking seriously about leaving Earth and never seeing it again.

It is, however, human nature to rise to an occasion when either opportunity or circumstances dictates action. None of the men could deny the excitement and wonder they felt. They were mature and were able to weigh their emotions against the facts that faced them. But it was still a fantastic thought: to travel through space to a distant star and live with a totally alien life form.

Once they began to discuss it, they could not control their minds. The excitement was too much. Their deepest thoughts were laid bare for the others to see, yet, in an almost magical way, it was just that phenomenon that allowed them to reach the final conclusion. Bernie's mind opened first. He could not help himself. Visions of Auschwitz and the horrors of that experience burst upon the minds of the others. They turned to him in disbelief, and then immediately understood. Joe Finley cried. Art Perlman put his arm around his friend. Ben gritted his teeth in anger. Then they saw the bloodstained elevator car and the torn body of Al Berger. They gathered Bernie Lewis' pain inside themselves and forever after that his burden would be lighter.

Joe Finley had few secrets. He had looked death in the face and had seen it removed from his body. For him there was little doubt about what he owed to the Antareans. But there was more than just a debt. He was filled with the idea that they would be explorers – the first humans to venture to other planets . . . to meet other beings. To learn. He told the others that as far as he was concerned, he had died on planet Earth from leukemia. His future lay in the stars.

Ben opened still another train of thought to the group. His excitement came from the challenge. He was a bitter man and although the others had suspected his anger at a society that forces its aged to retire, they let him vent his feelings. He was born again in a way that was different from Joe's. He was in the midst of a discussion . . . a business discussion. He was needed. The Antareans were depending on them for help. And, most exciting, they would return for a meeting and negotiation of terms of their future. He felt that to deny this opportunity would be to admit that age made one useless, and he was far from useless.

The last to open was Art Perlman. He knew that he must, and that it must be the truth, but he was not sure how the others would react to his past life and deeds. He didn't really care one way or the other about the Antareans and their problem. He didn't care about traveling in space, or about being useful to others or himself. He was a selfish man. That was what he told his friends. They had turned to him in silence. Ben asked him to explain. It came out slowly, in dribs and drabs, in disconnected thoughts and deeds, as the whole ugly story of his life trickled into their minds as the blood from the hundreds of contract victims had trickled onto the streets of America for decades. He told them of his part in this and they were shocked. The mild, quiet accountant was a mobster.

It was Art Perlman's revelation that had taken the most time to discuss. At one point Art and Bernie nearly came to blows. Bernie asked Art about his involvement in the garment business. He asked whether Art might have been involved in a manipulation that caused Bernal Woolens' financial trouble. Art denied any knowledge of those activities. Bernie read Art's mind through to the thought that Art's friends did, in fact, control a larger part of that industry, especially the trucking and union organization.

Ben became the mediator and calmed them both. Joe Finley suggested that the burden of Art's life was really his own business. If Art was satisfied with his position today, then so be it. If Art didn't want to help the Antareans, that was his business. Certainly it was too much to ask anyone to leave the Earth against his will.

It was also interesting that Art Perlman found the answer that satisfied himself.

"Joe," he said, "you are right. You can't ask me to leave the Earth against my will." Then he let the thought continue. "It's really the same as when I was active in the business . . . I couldn't leave against their will. Once I was in, I was stuck for life. You may not believe it, but for many years I did want to get out . . . to leave it all . . . but you never can, you know. In my case I know too much. To this day I am sure they watch me. They come from time to time . . . a note . . . a call . . . a visit. It never ends."

"It can now," said Ben.

Perlman stared at the big adman. It was a cold stare, penetrating, but he could not crack through Ben Green. They were both, in their own ways, extremely tough men.

"Yes, it can," said Art.

They were agreed. Bernie Lewis made it official by placing his hand on top of Art's and then moving both hands toward Joe. Joe and Ben got the idea.

Four old men. They stood on the deck in a circle, hands joined in the center and silently swore an alliance . . . forever. Then they began to discuss their wives and families.

• 35 •

"That's the girl," said Wally. "The one who the old men took to the dock." He was pointing toward Judy as she led Arnie and Sandy Fischer from the parking lot toward the dock. Shields and Wally cut across the rubble-strewn, would-be lawn of Building B to cut them off.

"Can we help you folks?" asked Shields. He stood on the path blocking their way.

"I don't think so," answered Judy. "We are meeting a friend on the dock. He parks his boat here."

"No one parks his boat here, miss. The dock isn't opened."

Arnie stepped forward in front of the two women. "Who are you?"

"I'm the manager of this place and, to put it directly, you people are trespassing."

Arnie sensed hostility in the manager's voice, so he tried to be diplomatic. "Look, friend, this young lady was here before. Her boyfriend is a charter-boat captain, and apparently he is running a charter for some people who live here. She is supposed to meet him this evening."

"Well, mister," Shields answered, "I don't know where your young lady got her information, but our dock isn't finished and there are no boats down there."

"Do you mind if we have a look?"

"Yes, I mind. Like I said, you're trespassing. Wally, please show these people to their car."

Wally stepped forward and gestured to Arnie that it was time to leave.

"Can't we discuss this?" asked Arnie.

Wally spoke. "There is nothing to discuss. Why don't you have the young lady call her boyfriend on the radio? I'm sure she is mistaken about our dock. Let's go."

As they drove out of the Antares complex, Judy, who had been silent up to now, spoke. "Arnie, can you get your boss' boat tonight?"

"Not tonight, but you can bet I'll have it tomorrow after work!"

They drove for a few more minutes before Sandy spoke. "Let's be careful. I don't want to get Jack in trouble, and to tell you the truth, that place gives me the creeps."

Wally watched the car clear the gate and walked back to meet Shields. "They're gone. Funny, she didn't argue with you. She was on the dock today, you know."

"Yeah, well, she didn't see any boats down there, so she's not sure. What she didn't know was that there is no way I could call the police. The boss would have a fit."

As they spoke a slightly dazed Frank Hankinson came up the path from the dock toward them. They stepped back along the shrubs, but he was distracted and never noticed them.

"That guy looks like he saw a ghost," commented Wally.

Shields watched Frank for a moment. "Maybe he did." Then he turned toward the dock and listened. The faint hum of diesel engines grew louder. The *Manta III* was docking.

Mary ordered a second round of martinis with her escargots. The ladies were quiet and Bess' depression hung like a cloud over the table. *Now is the time*, thought Mary. "Ben told me that the boys are thinking of buying a fishing boat," she said quietly.

"What?" Rose Lewis asked.

"A fishing boat. That's where they are tonight. Out on a fishing boat . . . to try it out."

Alma was smiling. "Joe would get seasick in a bathtub. What would they want with a fishing boat?"

"To have parties on," answered Mary. "We saw

them with that girl in the parking lot today."

"What girl?" asked Bess. She was suddenly interested.

"Oh," said Alma, "it was before you came back from seeing your sister today. The boys were talking to a young girl in the parking lot. We saw them from my balcony."

"Talking, my ass!" said Mary. "They walked behind Building B with her and they took her phone number before she left."

"My Arthur did that?"

"Your Arthur was the one who wrote down the number."

"So the sex maniacs have decided to go outside for their action." Bess was furious.

"Let's not jump to conclusions," suggested Mary.

The martinis arrived, and the ladies paused, for a moment, to drink.

"It may be innocent. Perhaps the girl has something to do with buying the boat." Alma was proud of her logic, but as she looked around the table she saw that her story had convinced no one.

"Maybe . . . I didn't think of that," said Mary. "I suppose it's possible. All I can say is that Ben has some explaining to do. I don't like surprises!" Mary had softened a bit.

"I'll second that," said Rose.

The rest agreed, and dinner was spent discussing how to help Bess get her sister to another nursing home.

Jack docked the *Manta III* smoothly. Ben tied the boat to the dock and the five men headed toward the back door of Building B. Wally and Shields crouched behind the shrubs and watched. Ben sent the messenger to the others. *That creep Shields and his henchman are hiding in the bushes. What should we do?*

I'm going to stop and tie my shoelace. You think ahead to Bright and tell him they are out here . . . but not for long. As Joe Finley telepathed to Amos Bright, Ben Green knelt on the path and faked tying his shoelace. When the others had entered the building, he turned toward the bushes and sent a mental jolt into Wally's stomach. The handyman fell over in pain. Shields was stunned as he watched Wally roll over in pain. Then Ben sent him a kick in the ass and he jumped up yelling. They both turned and ran toward the parking lot, got in their car, and took off without looking back once.

Ben Green chuckled to himself and headed toward Jack's room.

• 36 •

It was the beginning of a night they would remember always. Amos, All Light, No Light, and Beam were in the room when Art, Bernie, Joe and Jack arrived. Copper man two stood outside the door. Ben followed a moment later.

They greeted each other out loud and kept their thoughts blocked inside. Joe felt something and spoke.

"Some of your soldiers have died . . . is that true?"

"Nine more, a short while ago," answered All Light. "We have said the words for them."

"Serve the Master as you did your own." Joe spoke first.

"You have taken your reward," Art continued.

"Guide us if you can as you move among the stars," Bernie added.

"We love you." Ben finished the words.

"Thank you," answered all the Antareans.

Ben sat on Jack's bed and spoke to Amos

directly. "We have come to some decisions, but no conclusions. For one, we need more information. Two, we have to speak to our wives. They are a part of this, too."

"Understood. How shall we proceed?"

"Let's talk about this army business first. Just what kind of army is it?"

Amos and the commanders explained about the Antarean base on Earth and how and why they came to evacuate Earth, leaving the army buried in their cocoons. The damage to the cocoons was not foreseen. This army was one of many left throughout several galaxies. It was one of the reasons why the Antareans have survived so long and why they were universal travelers. This particular army was designed and trained for diplomatic service. That was why they were on Earth to begin with.

The Antarean base here was a diplomatic center as well as a trading center for their Galaxy. The role of the army was that of service, translation, education, and supplying comfort to the huge variety of visitors who came to the base. They were not a fighting army. Their purpose was not war.

Ben waited for Amos to finish his description of the army. Then he said, "We know that your equipment can do things to our bodies so that we are able to travel in space, but from what you describe, this army has very special skills and knowledge that we don't possess. How do we learn?"

"It will require programming and training. We have the methods to accomplish that task, and Beam has assured us that your race is capable of assimilating the knowledge."

Joe asked, "How many soldiers do you need?"

"Nine hundred forty-one," answered No Light.

"Who will command?" asked Bernie.

"We will have to make nine commanders," answered All Light.

"How will you do that?" Art was interested.

Beam could see what his personal intentions were. "It will require special training and some . . . well . . . changes have to be made in part of your nervous system . . . that is the nervous systems of the ones chosen for command."

"Surgery?" asked Art.

"Only for some special implants and one small device that activates a portion of your brain," she answered.

"Brain surgery?" Bernie was concerned.

"In what you call the medulla . . . the center . . . it must be enlarged and attached directly to certain nerves. But it is quite safe."

"Safe? Screwing around with the brain is never safe!" Ben was adamant.

"But," Amos said, "you men have been screwing around, as you put it, with your brains for the past week. This procedure is as safe as what you have been doing accidentally to yourselves."

Mary Green heard the phone ringing as she opened the door to the apartment. "Hello?"

"Hi, Mary . . . it's Frank Hankinson. Is Ben there?"

"No, Frank. He's out with the boys for a while. Can I help?"

"No, dear . . . just ask him to phone me when he comes in . . . okay?"

"Sure, but he may be late."

"Tell him no matter when he comes in . . . I'll be up and waiting. It's important."

"Is everything all right, Frank?"

"Yes . . . no problem. It's business. I have some information for him."

"Okay . . . bye. Oh . . . Frank. Is this about the boat?"

Frank was stunned. How did she know what happened to him on the boat? "The boat?" he asked. "What boat?"

"Oh, nothing . . . I thought it was something else . . . I'll have him call you. Bye, again."

"Bye."

Mary felt better. She was sure that Frank was involved in buying the boat. It was true, and he almost let the cat out of the bag. So it was supposed to be a surprise of some sort. She called the other wives and told them. They all felt better.

The discussion continued for over an hour in Jack's room. Ben was in his glory. It was an actual negotiation, but this wasn't pitching a new advertising account . . . it was their life and future that was being discussed. They were coming to final terms, all of which would depend on their wives, not to mention the fact that if a deal was struck, they would have to find nine hundred thirty-three more people willing to leave the Earth.

It was Ben who gave the summary of the discussion. "So this is where we are. We will most certainly help you with the immediate problem of your protective skins. We will work with you to get the remaining cocoons reprocessed and put back under the water. We will certainly keep all of this secret and help in any other way we can. As far as becoming your army, if it were up to the four of us you would have no problem. But this is about the most far-out thing that has ever happened on this Earth, so I am sure you will understand our need to proceed with some caution . . . for ourselves and for your sake, too. Step one will be our wives. I think that our plan for tonight is good . . . perhaps a bit unfair to the ladies, but certainly dramatic. If they are convinced, then we should be able to raise the rest of the army rather quickly. If not, then the Parmans will have to be disappointed. Let's think positively. Any questions?"

Bernie, Joe and Art had none. Neither did the Antareans.

"Then we will see you in an hour in the, uh . . . health club."

The four men headed home, and the Antarean party went to the processing room to prepare for visitors. As he walked down the hallway, Amos took a moment to discuss how they would handle Shields and Wally Parker tomorrow. It was clear that Beam couldn't wait to play her role in the plan.

• 37 •

The four couples met at the pool. It was after nine. The area was deserted. Each man had returned home to an argument. Each had played innocent. They did not argue, but rather took a verbal beating from their wives. The only one who ran into unexpected problems was Art Perlman. Bess broke down and told him about Betty. He immediately offered to pay for private nursing, which surprised Bess. This time she didn't refuse, but didn't accept, either. At least she knew that if the women couldn't solve the problem, then Art's money could. It relieved her.

Ben Green called Frank Hankinson as soon as Mary told him about the urgency of Frank's call. He told Frank it was too late to meet him that night, but that they could meet by the pool at nine the next morning. Frank kept asking if everything was okay, and Ben assured the snowbird that things were fine. After the phone conversation he telepathed the strange call to his three friends.

Now, sitting at their husbands' card table, the four women felt certain that the men were about to announce their purchase of the silly fishing boat. They could not have been further from the truth.

Joe Finley stood. "Tonight is going to be a very special night, and we ask that you lovely ladies allow us to present, to tell you . . . to show you . . . what we have discovered. If you possibly can, please hold your questions." He raised his hand dramatically and, with a flourish, continued. "First, I would like you all to reach over and touch Art's bald head."

Each woman slid her hand across his scalp.

Bess spoke. "You got a transplant?"

"It feels fuzzy . . . like a baby . . ." The ladies smiled.

"Next, Mr. Green will perform his famous aqua-show."

With a flourish, Ben stood and took off his pants and shirt, revealing a bathing suit underneath. In one swift movement he ran to the head of the pool. Joe gestured the women to poolside. Ben dove into the water and swam four laps underwater in just thirty seconds. He leaped out at the spot where he began. Bernie threw him a towel. Joe asked the ladies to sit down again. Mary shouted to Ben to see if he was okay. He wasn't even out of breath.

"How did you do that?" asked Mary.

Joe interrupted her. "No questions, yet, please. Now, for our third trick, oh, event . . . Mr. Bernard Lewis will take center stage."

Bernie stood and took a sharp penknife from his pocket. He placed his hand on the table and slit his palm in one quick motion.

Rose screamed.

Alma jumped up. "This isn't funny. Are you crazy? Have you all gone mad?"

Calmly, Joe Finley answered, "Ladies, we asked that you hold your questions. Please watch Mr. Lewis . . . this is his favorite trick."

The women looked back at the table and watched Bernie wipe away the blood. There was no cut. It had healed.

"They went to a magic store tonight," said a relieved Rose Lewis. "Just little boys with some new tricks trying to give us heart failure so they will be free to play with the young cuties."

Joe sat them down again. He put his arm around Alma. "I have no tricks to show you myself." He was the talented actor again and had the audience in his grasp immediately. He flashed a thought to the others: *Am I overdoing this?*

Do what you feel, they flashed back.

"I have no tricks, because as you know . . . I am not a well man." Alma was shocked. The other women were embarrassed. He held Alma tighter, as if to say, "Bear with me."

"But I do have of trick of sorts. A few days ago, Art was bald, Ben got headaches underwater, and Bernie had cut his hand like he did, we would all be in the emergency room getting ready to be donors. Except they wouldn't take my blood because it was full of white cells . . . leukemia."

"Oh, Joe," said Alma, but he silenced her.

"I said a few days ago that would have happened. My trick is to tell you all that it is gone. My disease is completely and irrevocably gone . . . vanished . . . *fini* . . . *kaput*. I am well again."

Alma threw her arms around him and hugged him. The others, including the men, wiped tears from their eyes.

Finally, Mary spoke up. "But how . . . why . . . what is going on here?"

"That is what we've been trying to discover for the past few days," answered Ben. "Now, without answering any questions, we would like to show you something."

He stood, and so did the other men. Each took their wives by the hand and the group moved toward Building B.

"Are we going to the dock?" asked Mary.

"No, not the dock," answered Ben so that all of them heard him. "We are going to the damnedest health club you ever saw."

"Yeah," said Joe, "with some pretty far-out attendants, too!"

• 38 •

Arnie and Sandy Fischer sat at their kitchen table sipping coffee, trying to speculate on what Jack's mysterious behavior was about. Sandy was sure there was a logical explanation. Arnie, knowing his brother, wasn't convinced.

Judy smoked a joint and called Monica. She spent over an hour complaining to her friend about Jack. Monica listened and tried to soothe Judy's anger.

Mr. Shields and Wally Parker sat at the bar of a small local chop house and waited for Tony Stranger, the worst salesman in Miami, to join them. They ordered their third drink but still hadn't decided how to deal with the weird events at the Antares condominiums. They were hoping that Tony, a devious man in his own right, might have some ideas.

Frank Hankinson was more confused than ever. He watched the four couples at the pool from his balcony. He watched them touch Art's head and move to the pool while Ben Green swam. The screams filtered up faintly as Bernie cut his hand. Then there was some hugging and kissing and the four couples walked toward Building B. He felt left out of what appeared to be a private party.

"It's cold in here," commented Bess Perlman as they walked down the hall toward the health club. No one answered her.

The door to the health club was slightly ajar. As the group reached the door, Ben halted them for a moment. "What we are about to show you is, to say the least, different. We would like you all to keep an open mind, and trust us. That's important because we are going to ask you to . . . well . . . sort of do things. I promise you nothing will hurt, and the results will be terrific."

The women looked at each other in confusion.

"Lead on," said Alma.

The wall was blue. The center table was bathed in soft green light. On the left, all of the cabinets were misting and opened, as though they were waiting for customers. In the rear of the room four of the cots were turned on, and they were bathed in green light, too.

"What?" said a startled Mary Green. "Did you say something, Ben?"

"No," he answered. "It was Mr. Bright."

"Who?"

"Amos?" called Ben. "Are you there?"

Amos stepped into the light of the center table. He was wearing a pale, one-piece jump-suit. Even the men were startled by his appearance. They were used to seeing him in ordinary Earth clothing. His head was in shadow.

"Yes, Ben, I'm here. Before we go any further, we thought that it would be better to do this introduction properly. We have removed our camouflage so that you will all see us as we really are."

"Do you think they are ready for that?" asked Art.

"We think it is the best way."

"Who is that?" asked Bess.

"Okay, ladies." Joe Finley took over. "This is the bottom line ... believe it or not. We found this room by accident two weeks ago. We thought it was a health club, so we began to use the equipment. Well, it isn't a health club, and the equipment you see in the room is not ... well ... not really .."

Bernie interrupted. "Not of this Earth. It belongs to that gentleman and his friends."

As Bernie spoke the others joined Amos at the center table. All their faces were in shadow, too.

"Who are they?" Rose was getting nervous.

"They are visitors," answered Ben, but he felt uneasy. He wasn't sure that revealing their actual faces to the women at this time was such a good idea.

Amos read him and telepathed a calming word to him. *The sooner they see us, the faster they will become used to us. It is better this way.*

"Look, girls." Joe was back in control. "These people are from another world."

"What . . . ?" "Oh, my God . . . !" "You guys are crazy!" "This game is getting nuts!" The women were all talking at once.

"Hold it," Joe continued. "I'll say it again. These people are from another world . . . again, so it sinks in. These people are from space . . . they are from outer space . . . they are from far away . . . another planet . . . UFOs . . . all that stuff . . . is true."

At this point the group at the center table moved into the light. Bess screamed; Alma grabbed Joe's arm; Mary stared and began to shake . . . Ben held her; Rose Lewis moved away from the rest, and with a courage that none of them knew she possessed, she approached the group of Antareans. It was a magical moment. She reached the near side of the table and looked at each of the Artareans individually. When her glance came to Beam, she stopped. "Are you a woman?"

"Yes."

"You are beautiful."

"Thank you."

She was. The men had not seen them all together like this, and had never seen Beam as she really was. There was a difference. No doubt that she was female.

The shape of her eyes was different from the others. They wrapped around her head and tapered to a fine point past where the temple would be. At that point there was a faint red spot. It began there and ran down her neck, circling back and joining at her throat. Alma thought of a ruby-throated hummingbird. Joe read her thought and agreed silently to himself.

Bess reached out her hand to Beam. Beam reached for Bess with her hand. It was attached to an arm that was longer in proportion to a human arm. The hand had four fingers, three of equal length and a longer thumb. When her hand reached Bess', the three longer fingers separated and became six and enveloped Bess' hand.

"Oh!" Bess exclaimed, feeling the warmth and friendship that Beam passed to her. "How pleasant!"

After that display the others needed no more convincing. Beam didn't come from a magic store. Not with a hand like that.

The other Earth people moved to the center table and exchanged greetings. Ben handled the introductions. All Light and No Light, commanders of the highest grade, were actually shy with the women. Amos explained they were showing respect. Historically, the females of the species encountered were treated in this manner because they were responsible for the young and the continuation of the race.

Alma marveled at the physical makeup of the commanders. They were smaller than the others. Their heads were larger and appeared to have appendages growing out from the sides and rear of their skulls. The two side bumps were red in color and glowing. The bump in the rear was white and kept expanding and contracting, as though it were breathing. Their arms were long and tapered, with hands similar to Beam's. Their legs were short and stumpy, and their feet were flat and spread on the floor for support. They appeared fragile and weblike.

Hal and Harry had shed their blond, beach-boy covering. They, too, were Antareans, but had no bumps on their skulls. Their eyes wrapped around their heads and glowed like the others. They were a bit taller than the commanders, but much shorter than they had appeared when disguised as humans. The copper men were still metallic. Now, however, their heads were Antarean.

Amos, whose eyes were larger than the rest, had a long bump extending from between his eyes over the top of his skull and down his back. Otherwise, he, too, was an Antarean.

Their skin appeared cream-colored and translucent. They had no mouth, no ears, and no nose.

Amos spoke. "The copper men, as you call them, are soldiers in the sense that you use the word. They are specially suited for combat and thus have the metal skin. We ask that you do not touch our skin, only our hands, if we extend them."

Then he addressed Ben. "Shall we show the ladies our equipment?"

"Fine. Let's start with my wife." He motioned Mary to follow him, and thought to Hal and Harry for their help. "Honey, how is your back today?"

"Stiff, as always. Why?" Mary asked.

As the others gathered at the first cabinet, Ben helped Mary into it while he explained that she should relax. Harry set the dials and they enclosed Mary in the cabinet. It turned on and the mist began to rise.

"Hmm . . . that feels good." Mary was smiling.

While she relaxed and enjoyed the sensation, Bernie Lewis took Rose's hand and guided her to the second cabinet. Amos opened it. "Rose, when was the last time you could bend and touch your toes?"

"Longer than I care to remember."

"Okay, try this cabinet. I guarantee you will be as supple as Nadia Comaneci in a few minutes."

"But will I be as young?"

Amos thought a smile to the human men. Alma Finley reacted to the thought, though she didn't know where it came from.

Joe and Beam were guiding Alma to the third cabinet when Joe had a thought. "Alma is physically quite healthy, so I propose we show her a different piece of equipment."

Beam picked up on his idea. "Good. Put her on the second cot. I will adjust the lamp." They took Alma to the cot and as she lay down, Beam reached to the lamp above and set a dial. The lamp turned on and its laser beam descended down to Alma and spread over her body in a weblike pattern that duplicated her nervous system.

"Relax, honey," said Joe.

"It tingles," she said, "but it's wonderful."

Bess stood apart from the rest. She somehow knew that a miracle was taking place and was surprised at how easily she accepted the strange happenings.

Art came to her side. "I know what you are thinking."

"How can you know that?"

"Because I can read your thought. This stuff isn't just for the body. It affects the mental powers, too."

"Can it cure Betty?"

"I believe it can, but don't get your hopes up too high. We have more to discuss after you all see what this place can do."

Amos Bright listened to the conversation between the Perlmans. He came over to them. "Let me be with Mrs. Perlman alone for a moment, Arthur. I think I can answer her questions."

Art moved away.

"Place your hand on my forehead, Mrs. Perlman."

Bess put her right hand on the bump between Bright's eyes. She felt her hand adhere to his skin. His eyes glowed for a moment and her body shook, then relaxed. "Oh, God," she said softly, "how beautiful!"

Then his eyes glowed again, brighter this time, and Bess saw her sister sitting up in bed in the dingy room. Betty was smiling. She felt Amos Bright's skin release her hand.

"Can you do that?" she asked.

"What you saw we did together. Now your sister rests comfortably. She is not cured, but she feels us. I have given her rest. You have given your thought of love. She knows we will help her."

"Thank you."

Mary and Rose were moved to the second set of cabinets to complete their physical treatments. Alma was up and around and having the time of her life reading everyone's thoughts. Joe kept sending her thoughts of love and she began to get embarrassed because she knew that everyone could feel her loving responses to him. They were like children with a new toy.

Suddenly Alma felt a jolt to her body. Then sadness. She was confused. Panicked.

"A leader is gone in the second group," said Amos.

"They will go quickly. We must replace them in the cocoons soon," replied Beam.

"Who died?" asked Alma. "I feel someone has died. It's so sad."

Joe came to her. "One of their army . . . up on the roof."

Then he thought to the commanders. *I think we should do what we have to as quickly as possible. The ladies will believe.*

All Light directed Harry and Hal to remove

the two women from the cabinets. Mary's back-ache was gone and she knew it immediately.

Then they watched Rose Lewis get out of the cabinet and proceed to stretch her arms in the air. Then she bent and touched her palms to the floor.

"Wow, do I feel good! Like I'm fifteen again."

They all gathered at the center table.

Amos spoke. "I know that the women now believe who we are. Allow me to tell them why we are here and what has happened. Then we can discuss the future." He told the story to the four wives.

It was dawn when they all came to an agreement. The hardest part was to figure out how they would tell their children that they were leaving Earth.

Amos had assured them they could return for a visit sometime.

Bess agreed only on the condition that Betty could join them, and that she would not be a commander. However, she was sure that Betty would want to command.

The only person in the room who was disappointed was Jack Fischer. Beam had explained that because of his age, he could not go with them. The equipment and processing would work only in human bodies that had reached a certain stage in the aging process. The muscles, tissues, and bones of the older Earth people had begun degenerating. It was only at a stage of fairly advanced aging that rejuvenation and change would be effective.

When Amos felt Jack's disappointment, he moved over to the charter captain, who had been so helpful to the Antareans, and whispered a promise to him. "When we return you will be old enough. If you keep our secret and help us to the end, we will take you with us next time."

The promise of eternity, with only a small price to pay for it, cheered Jack immensely.

• 39 •

No one was tired as the four couples sat in the Greens' apartment and discussed their commitment to the Antareans. How radically their lives had changed, and how calmly they accepted their decision. That was the marvel they couldn't get over.

"We are really going into space!" Rose Lewis kept repeating her feelings. "I remember watching Neil Armstrong on the Moon. It all looked so forbidding and cold and barren."

Her husband looked at her as though she were a stranger. He couldn't remember when she had seemed so alive and excited. The others let her go on. She was expressing all of their thoughts.

Alma helped Mary with the coffee and Danish. It was nearly eight o'clock in the morning. Mary called over to Ben. "Remember, you have to meet Frank Hankinson in an hour."

"Right. I think we should start recruiting

as soon as we can."

"How do we decide on whom to approach?" questioned Joe.

Bess took over. "We have certain criteria that will narrow the list, and remember nine hundred forty-one people is a lot of people."

"Exactly," chimed in Alma. "I figured that if we got everyone in Building A, assuming they are all old enough, we would have only about one hundred thirty. So we have a lot of lists to make up and only a short time to accomplish it."

The ladies were in their element and quickly gaining control of the logistics.

"It's like a big wedding reception," Rose said. "I think each of us should make a list of all the people who we think would be old enough, and whom we think would like to go. Assuming we all have about the same number of friends and family and people like that, I guess that would give us about a hundred or more."

Arthur did some fast calculating. "So that leaves about seven hundred more people to find. I think we are going to have a problem."

Rose and Bess spoke at once. "I can think of . . ." They laughed.

"Go ahead, Bess," Rose deferred.

"Well, I was only thinking of the home where

my sister is. If there was some way to get those people out of there . . ."

"We could buy it," said Art.

"And how do you explain the disappearance of all those people?" asked Ben.

"We don't," answered Art. "We won't be around to be asked."

The others laughed.

"I had a little different idea," said Rose. "A few months ago I went to see my Aunt Ruth down on Collins Avenue. There must have been hundreds of old people down there, living a meager existence. Maybe there is a way to organize them. Aunt Ruth certainly knows a lot of them and they look up to her."

Ben was serious. "I know we all have good ideas. We also have to remember that if the word gets out and the authorities get wind of what has happened here, there won't be any space trip for anyone. So let's be real careful of how, and who, we approach. Okay?"

They all agreed.

They spent the next hour eating breakfast. Each of the women took a piece of paper and began making their lists. The men added a name now and then. Within the hour, much to their surprise, the four couples had over two hundred candidates. They also knew that it was going to be extremely difficult to find the remaining number of people to complete the army.

"We are assured that they can be trusted, these dwellers, and that they will serve well on Parma Quad Two. It is our belief that others of their age will adapt. It will be of no help to communicate to Antares or to the Parmans for permission. We must be on our way before the message will reach our councils. Send a probe with my message and a history of what has transpired here. Once we are on our way, we can confirm the probe and pass on the details."

No Light knew that his superiors would be understanding when they knew all the facts, but messages that spoke of interference with life forms, and radical changes in plans, were best presented in person. He paused in his communication to consider the coincidence of the damaged cocoons and the ability of the aging dwellers to adapt. He had traveled in space for a very long time. Coincidence and purpose had often been partners in his experience. These events served to strengthen his conviction that there was a universal plan, guided by a force that they believed in, but did not understand.

Above him, on the roof, the second row of soldiers died, their eyes flickering, then glowing bright, then dimming slowly until life passed from them, and their eyes turned dark and lifeless. He reported the event to the mother ship and uttered the prayer for the departed.

Now they would have to move quickly to replace the remaining soldiers in cocoons and back under the sea. He slid from the table and faced his sleeping companions, then raised his hand and turned off the lamps above the cots.

The Antareans awoke and set about their work.

Tony Stranger sat in his car in the parking lot of the bank and waited for it to open. He mulled over the story he would present to Mr. DePalmer. Shields and Parker had been vague about what was going on at the complex, but through their drunken muttering, Tony was convinced that something had scared them. It wasn't his business, or so he told them, but he knew that he would make some good money when they opened Building B. So he was interested. He also saw the possibility of getting rid of Shields and managing the complex himself. So he had gone along with the two men and told them he would find out what he could from Mr. DePalmer because DePalmer had hired him. What he didn't tell Shields and Parker was that he would keep the information to himself if it proved to be useful. He had a feeling that this was going to be his lucky day. Then he flushed with excitement as Mr. De-Palmer's car pulled into the lot and he saw the banker enter the front door of the bank.

Judy awoke to the ringing telephone. It was Arnie reminding her that he would have the keys to his boss' boat by the afternoon. Sandy and he would pick her up at four P.M. She agreed and hung up, then went back to sleep. The events of the previous day and too much grass had knocked her out. She knew she would need her strength later.

Frank Hankinson sat at the pool and watched the four men walk toward him. He wondered why Ben had brought the others. "Hi, guys," he greeted them. "Good morning."

Ben was smiling and reaching out his hand, and Frank extended his thinking that to shake hands was a rather formal thing to do. The men read his feelings and communicated to each other to put him at ease.

Frank began his story after they were seated in a circle on the lounge chairs. "Look, guys," he began, "it may be none of my business, but there have been some weird things happening around here . . . weird to me, that is, probably because I'm an old reporter, so I have a nosy nose."

The others listened calmly.

"When you guys took that chick down to the dock yesterday, I was sitting here . . . so I was kind of interested . . . and I kept an eye on you."

Joe Finley tried to keep it light. "Dirty old men, huh?"

"No, Joe, I mean I know you guys and, like I say, it's none of my business . . . except the caretaker . . . Parker . . . he was following you, real sneaky like."

Art thought to Bernie: *How did we miss that?*

"Anyway, he was really sneaking after you, so I kept watch. After you came back with the girl and then went back to Building B, I really got interested. I stayed at the pool all day. Parker watched for a while, then went to the office, so I followed him. He met Shields there."

Ben asked, "Did they speak about us?"

"Yes, and, boy, were they pissed . . . but they were also confused. They kept talking about some guy named Bright and how he was your buddy, Ben. They also talked about a man from the D.A.'s office being with you."

Joe laughed. "The infamous Mr. Bonser!"

"Yes, that's what Parker said . . . Bonser from the D.A., but I didn't understand."

Joe explained that it was a long story, but not

a problem. He thought that would satisfy Frank. He was wrong.

"Well, I'm glad that's okay. I thought you guys had some problem with the D.A. or something."

Ben reassured him that it was part of the swimming pool scheme and not a problem with the police.

"Good. That's not all. After I left the office . . ."

Art interrupted. "Did they see you?"

"No . . . anyway, I went down to the dock."

Bernie jumped in this time. "Dock? You know about the dock?"

"No . . . yes . . . well, I didn't but they were talking about it, so I thought I would have a look. They were pissed because no one is supposed to go down there. Then when Parker told Shields you guys were buddies with this Bright fellow, the man was really confused. So I sneaked away and went to have a look at the dock."

The four men just sat and let him continue.

"There was a boat down there. A real nice cruiser . . . *Terra Time* . . . and I went aboard to have a look." He paused to gather his thoughts because he wasn't sure how to explain what had happened to him.

Ben read his thought. He was about to recruit

his first soldier. The others agreed.

"Frank, how long do we know each other?"

"A few months, I guess. Why?"

Frank wanted to get on with his story, unaware that the other men already knew it. "Don't you guys want to hear what I have to say?"

Ben was patient, but firm. "Yes, we do, but to tell you the truth, we already know."

"The guy told you?"

"No, you told us."

"What . . . when?"

"Just now."

"Are you nuts?"

"No, Frank, but we want to tell you whom you met and what you saw and why. It's difficult, and it's the first time we have had to do this, so bear with us. I promise you the most fascinating day of your life."

"Are you guys okay? I mean . . ." He was upset.

"We are more okay than we have ever been in our lives, Frank. Please listen and try to believe us. First, let me ask you how old you are."

"Fifty-six."

"How is your health?"

Frank looked at the four men facing him and smiled a very nervous smile.

"Relax, Frank. How's your health?"

"Okay, I guess . . . a little arthritis . . . an ulcer . . . wear and tear . . . you know."

"Good."

"If you guys think that's good, you are nuts. I have a lot of aches and pains . . . nothing good about that."

"I know. How about your business?"

"What about it?"

"Well, do you like it? How long before you retire?"

"Sure I like it. I've been in the radio business all my life, just about. I built that station up from nothing to the fifth biggest in St. Louis."

"Do you think you'll keep working at it, or will you retire?"

"Sure, I'll retire. To tell you guys the truth, it's not as much fun as it was in the old days. Then I was a reporter and D.J. and engineer all in one. It was exciting. Now, well, now it sort of runs itself. I don't get the chance to get my hands dirty anymore. Maybe that's the way it should be . . ." His voice trailed off. It was a sore point with him. He had had a hard time adjusting to growing old, and had really not yet accepted the fact that he was no longer young and energetic. What bothered him the most was the arrogance of the young people. They were always telling him that he wasn't "with it" and didn't understand the young people and today's marketing techniques. "This is a country that worships the young . . . you have to cater to them . . ." Deep inside he always said "bullshit" to himself, but they really got their way and ran the business. All he did was own it.

The others read his thoughts and knew they had their first recruit.

Ben repeated Frank's thought out loud to him.

Frank was struck dumb. "How the hell did you do that?"

"Do you really want to know?" asked Ben.

"Yeah, I really want to know, and quick, before I lose my mind."

Ben laughed. "You won't lose your mind. I promise. Not only that, but I am about to give you the biggest news story you ever had."

"And eternity to boot!" said Joe Finley as he reached over and squeezed Frank's arm.

Ten minutes later Ben and Frank headed toward Building B while the others returned to Ben's apartment.

Shields had a hangover. He sat with Wally in his office and sipped his black coffee. The secretary banged away on the typewriter in the outer office. He motioned for Parker to close the door because the typing was jangling his nerves.

"You think Tony will get some answers for us, Mr. Shields?"

"I think Stranger is an asshole. But he knows that banker DePalmer, and DePalmer is Bright's buddy. Anyway, I'll give him till noon."

"And if nothing comes up?"

"If he has nothing for us, then I'm going to take matters into my own hands and find out what the hell is going on here. I am the manager . . . I have a right to know."

"Okay, you're the boss."

"Yeah, boss. Meanwhile, you keep snooping around and try to keep an eye on those old farts. Check back with me later."

Wally left the office in time to see Ben and Frank walk toward Building B. He had a funny feeling in the pit of his stomach. It was a fear of Ben Green. He made believe he didn't see them and walked in the opposite direction toward Building A. His office was in there and he would lay low for a while, maybe even catch a nap.

Mr. DePalmer excused himself and left Tony Stranger sitting at his desk. He went to the head teller's desk, out of sight of Stranger, and telephoned Amos Bright.

"Mr. Bright, this is John DePalmer at the bank. . . . Fine. How are you? Good. The reason I called is that Mr. Stranger, the sales-man I hired for you, is here at my office. He seems to have some information regarding the other building. He says that you are beginning to occupy the building and he wants to know why he wasn't hired for the sales office."

"I appreciate your call, Mr. DePalmer, but Mr. Stranger is wrong about Building B. We are far from completing it."

"That's what I told him, but he says he knows that it is practically occupied."

"How does he know that?"

"He won't say, Mr. Bright. I know you like to keep things quiet over there, and I have tried to fulfill your every request."

"Yes, Mr. DePalmer, I'm very pleased with the way you have handled things."

"So I thought you would want to . . . uh . . . deal with Mr. Stranger, rather than have him nosing around and bothering people over there."

"You are absolutely right. Have him come by this afternoon to see me. And thank you again, John."

"Yes, sir, Mr. Bright. Good-bye."

Tony Stranger wasn't surprised that Mr. Bright wanted to see him. He was quite pleased and felt sure that he would be making big commissions shortly. Now all he had to do was make up a story to tell Shields and Parker. He wanted some time to think it through so that he could move right' into the manager's job after Building B was sold out.

He drove a few blocks from the bank and pulled over to a pay phone. He called Shields.

"Ralph? Tony. How's your head this morning?"

"Larger and pounding. What did you find out?"

"Well, my friend at the bank tried to put me off, but I just pressed him. He told me they were ahead of schedule on the construction and didn't want to open the building for sales before the season began. It seems some of the people in Building A have lined up their friends for apartments in the new building, so they are pressing Mr. Bright for a date. He's being nice to them and humoring them along. Understand?"

"Yeah, I understand, but he could have told me when I saw him the other night. I hope he doesn't blame me for those old bastards' poking around."

Tony thought to himself: *Thank you, Ralph Shields . . . you just gave me the ammunition I need to get you fired . . .*

"No, Ralph, I'm sure he doesn't blame

you . . . or Wally. I'll keep in touch. Let me know if anything happens."

"Yeah. Thanks for the call . . . I'll see you."

Shields hung up, leaned back in his leather armchair, and closed his eyes. He needed a short nap.

As Wally Parker and Ralph Shields napped, the world — their world — was changing radically around them. They would never know what hit them.

• 40 •

Phil Doyle held the *Razzmatazz* against the current in the channel. He had no charter today and was going to bring the boat over to the yard in Miami to replace the propeller shaft on number two. He had entered the main channel and was running toward the sea when he caught sight of the *Manta III* coming out of the Antares canal ahead of him. He cut the engines and turned toward shore so that Jack Fischer would not see him. Now, when he was sure the *Manta III* was well down the channel, he started up again and eased out to follow his friend's boat. The new shaft would have to wait.

It had been a long night for the Antareans. A probe craft had arrived with material for the cocoons. They worked all night and well into the morning repacking nine soldiers and a leader. *Terra Time* and *Manta III* now carried the precious cargo of ten cocoons back out to

310

The Stones. There was a sadness on both boats.

Jack had tried to cheer the Antareans as he read their thoughts. "You guys haven't failed. You couldn't help what happened to the cocoons. And you're going to get a great army here. Humans can do the job . . . you'll see."

All Light answered. "Thank you, Jack. It is not that we are unsure of the humans. It is that we are returning our own to another long rest. We would like them to be among us."

"Well, next time you come back you'll have the right equipment to dry them properly. At least you didn't lose too many."

"To lose one is tragic."

"Yeah . . . I know and I'm sorry." He kept his mind on running the boat. Strange how their loss upset him, too. He liked these people, but until now he really didn't think of them as people. They were outsiders, from another world. Now he knew they felt sadness and loss just like humans.

As the *Manta III* cleared the breakwater and turned south toward The Stones, Hal, looking like a beachboy again, climbed the ladder to the flying bridge. "We have someone following us, Jack."

Jack turned and looked behind toward the breakwater. The *Razzmatazz* was behind him. "Phil Doyle, my fishing buddy. He's probably

311

got a charter. You think he's following?"

"Yes, we do."

"Let me give him a call on the radio." Jack turned the bridge over to Hal and slipped down the ladder to the radio in the cabin. He keyed the mike. "This is KAAL-9911 to *Razzmatazz.*"

"Hi, Jack. Phil here."

"You following me out today?"

"I thought I'd have a run near The Stones. Is that where you are heading?"

"Yeah. But the fishing is lousy over there."

"Judy called me the other night. She was looking for you."

"Yeah, I know. We spoke after that."

"Well, I hope I didn't cause any trouble. She's a nice lady."

"No . . . it's okay."

"Are you okay, Jack? I mean, is everything all right?"

"Sure."

There was an uncomfortable pause. Jack keyed back on. "Look, Phil, I haven't been ignoring your calls. It's just that this charter is sort of special. They don't want a crowd around. Understand?"

"I got it, buddy. I just wanted to be sure you were okay."

"I appreciate it."

"Roger. Okay, I'll take your word for it about The Stones. I'll take these folks over to the Stream. See you later."

"Roger . . . good fishing."

"Over and out."

Jack climbed up to the flying bridge and took the wheel from Hal.

"You sure no one else is on that boat?"

"There is only one human aboard. Why?"

"Nothing . . . he made like he had a party on board, that's all."

"Do you think he suspects something?"

"He was worried that I was in trouble of some kind. I think I convinced him otherwise. Maybe he was embarrassed that he was following me, so he made like he had a charter."

"Do you believe him?"

"Yes."

"Fine. Then we will not worry about it." Hal left the bridge as Jack turned the bow toward the morning sun, headed southeast for forty minutes, and then steered toward The Stones.

Ten cocoons were going back to sleep for a while.

Frank took it quite well. He trusted Ben all the way through the long explanation of the processing room and was prepared properly for Amos Bright to remove his face. Now the

Antarean and the two humans sat in the half-finished Building B office. There were five deck chairs from the *Terra Time* placed in there.

"Gathering nine hundred some-odd people is no small task, Ben. Have you formulated a plan?" Frank was concerned.

"Nothing firm. We are open to ideas."

"Well, we are certainly in the land of the old, so we know the bodies are here. The problem is that as people begin to disappear you are going to have the police poking around."

Ben was pleased to hear the "we" coming from Frank.

Amos spoke. "Your nation is large. Couldn't we get a few dwellers from each city?"

"That would take too long, Amos," Ben answered. "We have to be out of here, according to your schedule, in no more than five weeks. It's a logistical problem."

"And," said Frank, "we don't want to kidnap people. Somehow we have to expose the proposition to each one, or at least a couple at a time, so we don't blow the lid off this thing. One negative person and we have a problem on our hands."

"There has to be a simple way to do this," said Ben.

Frank thought for a moment. "Let me try

something. The Amatos from Boston are good friends. Let me try a little question-and-answer session with them and see if I can develop the conversation to the point where they admit that this situation would interest them. I'll keep it on a fantasy level. Then I'll hit them with the fact that I'm talking about reality. I make my wife part of it, too, so she will be just as surprised. If I can get them to bitch about the life they have now, perhaps they will be more open to the proposition."

"I think you're on the right track, Frank, but remember, we can't afford a failure or the cat is out of the bag."

Amos listened silently to the two men, realizing that raising the army was going to be more difficult than he had imagined. This was precisely why the rules about interfering with alien societies were so important. The Antareans had thrust a problem upon the humans that they were not prepared to deal with immediately. He knew that by mind suggestion alone they would raise the army, but it was a moral issue. The men had used the term "kidnapping." He read their thought as the stealing of a being against their will. They had great respect for the individual on this planet. But he knew that the society at large had little respect for individuals. Look how they shunned their old, their

315

poor, and injured ones that they called unfortunate. In addition, there were the other nations and the primitive jealousies among nations. He would have to let the men work it out themselves as best they could for now. However, the failure to raise the army must remain a possibility. In that case they would return to Antares humiliated. And who knew how the Parmans would react? Would they believe Antarean promises in the future? Would they once again close the Quadrant to outsiders?

• **41** •

Tony Stranger parked in the far corner of the lot. He didn't want Wally or Shields spotting his car. He then cut through the brush and construction at the side of Building B to the outside door that led to the office. It was locked. The windows were dirty so he could not see if anyone was in the office. Mr. DePalmer had told him to meet Amos Bright here at three o'clock. It was three on the nose.

Beam felt Tony approaching. She decided to make him wait a moment while she read his thoughts. Now, as he cast a shadow through the dirty glass, she read his anxiety. Then she probed deeper and found his greed. *So,* she thought, *he is out to get Mr. Shields and Mr. Parker in trouble. Well, Mr. Stranger, we have different plans for you . . .*

Tony was surprised to see the beautiful woman open the door and greet him.

"Mr. Stranger? I'm Laurie, Mr. Bright's

317

secretary. He will be a few minutes late. Please come in."

Tony was taken by her beauty. She was tall and slim with powder-blue eyes. Her body was full and round. The top three buttons of her silk blouse were open and revealing. Blondes in Florida were a dime a dozen, but blondes like Laurie were rare anywhere. He came on immediately. "That's fine. I have time."

"Come in, please."

He entered the office. Beam, now known as "Laurie," set the room in his mind. In reality it was still an unfinished office with five deck chairs scattered about and a small bridge table against one wall, but Tony saw it as a plush office with a large and inviting couch. He even heard soft music and sensed the faint smell of very expensive perfume in the air.

"You been with this outfit long?" Tony asked.

"I work for Mr. Bright in his other ventures. I'm just filling in over here for a few weeks."

"Terrific!"

"You used to work for Mr. Bright, too?" she asked innocently.

"I sold the entire Building A for him."

"Oh, yes, he was really pleased about that, I remember. You must be a terrific salesman."

Tony beamed with pride. "I do my job," he

remarked. "I do lots of things well." He stared at her.

I'll play him a little more, thought Beam, enjoying the game. It was rare that they were allowed to manipulate others this way. She knew it was innocent and harmless, but still it was fun.

Tony began to make his move. "You people really fixed his place up nice." He moved toward the imaginary couch. Beam projected pure sex to him. He felt a rush pulse through his body. Now Beam was ready.

Later, when Tony discovered semen all over his underwear, he was confused. He knew he had made love to Laurie, better than he had ever made love before. The fact that Mr. Bright had come into the office and caught them in the act seemed a colossal screw-up, and in fact it was. But Tony felt he could approach the man in a few days after he cooled down. God, she was beautiful. It was worth it.

Beam and Amos had a good laugh as the salesman had stumbled around the bare room attempting to put on his pants, which, in fact, were already on. He had never taken them off. Beam had projected the entire affair into his mind. As he tried to dress, imagining himself naked, Tony had pleaded with Amos that it was

319

just one of those things. Animal and magnetic attraction . . . Laurie had just left the room, which Tony thought was strange, considering he was bare-ass naked, so she wasn't there to support his story.

"I don't know how it happened, sir," he pleaded. "She was just here and I was here and then suddenly it was happening."

"I don't care to hear about it, Mr. Stranger." Amos played his part well. He was cool and aloof. He kept the images of the office in Tony's mind.

"What about our meeting?" Tony was a bit panicked.

"Meeting! Mr. Stranger, in view of your attitude regarding my office . . . my employees . . . I don't think we have anything to discuss." His word was final.

"Okay, I understand you are upset. I'll call in a few days. I'm really sorry. Please believe that." He moved toward the door.

"Yes . . . yes, Mr. Stranger, you do that if you wish. Now, good-bye."

The work out at The Stones went slowly. It was one thing to open the seals and bring out the cocoons, but a much more difficult task to replace them, particularly because they had been removing the last few squads vertically to assess the water damage to the cocoons at the bottom of the vaults. Now they had to replace the bottom cocoons first, which meant they had to remove some of the top layers, set them aside on the ocean floor, replacing the resealed cocoons, and then set the top layers back in place. It would take them most of the day and early evening to put the ten sleeping soldiers back in place.

Phil Doyle had felt the uneasiness in Jack's voice. He had turned the *Razzmatazz* north toward the boatyard in Miami with all intentions of getting the shaft replaced. It was a mild autumn day. If Jack Fischer wanted to keep things to himself, then that was his business . . . but if he was in trouble . . . well, Phil would have to think about that. It would have passed if the radio hadn't suddenly crackled with the familiar voice of Jack Mazuski, chopper pilot, freelance fish finder and all-around lunatic. "How about you worm drowners this morning?"

Phil keyed the mike. "Good morning, Maz. *Razzmatazz* here. I'm heading up to the yard to get a new shaft. Where are you?"

"Over at the pad. I thought I might have a peek around to see if the sailfish are moving in yet . . ."

"When are you going up?" Phil asked.

"After lunch, probably. Will you be out there?"

"No. Things are still slow for me. Want some company?" An idea had suddenly popped into Phil's head.

"Sure, Doyle. Grab some Jack Daniels and we'll go for a ride."

"Okay. I'll drop the boat off and cab it down to the pad. See you about one." Today obviously was not the day to get that new shaft.

"You got it, baby. Don't forget the booze. I'll bring the cups. Over and out."

"Roger. Out."

Phil knew that after a few swallows of Jack Daniels, Maz would fly his chopper to Europe if he asked. So going over to The Stones would be no problem. Perhaps he could get a better idea of what Jack Fischer was up to. In any case, Jack wouldn't know it was Phil spying on him. He opened the throttle as much as he dared and moved north to the boatyard.

Judy awoke to the ringing phone again. This time it was after one. She had slept all morning. The voice at the other end was unmistakably her agent, Carole Kress. The affected drawl and lisp of the aging agent and den mother always sickened Judy a bit.

"Good Morning," Judy said sleepily.

"Morning, dawling? It's the middle of a glawious day."

"It is? What's up, Carole?" Judy was not in the mood for her sweet talk.

"Cwanky, awn't we? I just cawlled to tell you that you have . . . that is, that I got you . . . an awdition faw the Flawida Powwa and Light Commerciawls . . . that's all."

"Oh . . hey, that's great." Judy was honestly excited. The local power company always did a pool of several TV commercials each year. It meant several thousand dollars to whomever got the job.

"Gweat, you say? I think it swoperior."

"Do you think I have a chance?"

"Absawlutely. They woved your pictawes."

"Great. Where and when?"

"Well, sweethewart, the only time they can see you is tonight. At the agency at six. Can you be thewre?"

"Yes . . . oh . . . a problem."

"What cwould pwossibly be a pwoblem?"

"I have an appointment late this afternoon."

"Well, bweak it, honey, bweak it. This only comes along once a decade faw you."

"How long do you think I'll be?"

"I hawve no idea . . . as lawng as they want. They have to make a chawice by Monday."

It was Friday. The trip on Arnie's boss' boat would have to wait a day. This was more important. "I'll be there . . . with bells on. Tell me about the part."

"Spowkespwosen . . . faw *all* the commerciawls."

"Holy shit! That's the big tamale . . . a gold mine!"

"Now you gwot it, howney . . . go to it."

"Okay, Carole . . . and thanks. Let me know when you hear."

"I'm on the case, dawling. Be your nawtraul self and you hawve it made. Ta . . ."

"Bye. Talk to you later."

Carole was gone. Long ago Carole had read that agents in Hollywood always got off the phone abruptly when they had no more to say. She had practiced the ploy until it became instinctive. She had no idea how much that pissed off the advertising people, but, oddly enough, as a ploy it still worked. They treated her with respect that few agents in Miami received.

Joe, Art, and Bernie had returned to the Finley apartment. Their wives, plus Mary Green, had gathered there after a quick shower and change. Each woman had a list neatly printed. The names totaled over three hundred people. Bess had estimated that there were at least fifty men and women at the home where Betty lived. Rose Lewis had called her Aunt Ruth and casually, in the context of their conversation, had asked how many people she really knew on Collins Avenue. Aunt Ruth had guessed over a hundred. Most of them were living on the edge of poverty.

Art calculated again. With the people in the building, plus the lists, plus the nursing home, plus Aunt Ruth's friends, it gave them a total of nearly eight hundred. Now they were cooking.

"We can certainly count on everyone in this building to know at least one other couple," suggested Joe.

"Right," said Bernie, "and that makes one complete space army."

"More like a geriatric brigade," said Alma Finley.

Joe laughed. "Geriatric Brigade . . . I like that . . ."

They all had a good chuckle. Then, with their newfound energy, they spent the rest of the morning and early afternoon discussing how to contact the people on their lists. It was decided that someone from each family would have to make a trip back home to speak to some of the people in person.

Bernie was on the phone making plane reservations when Ben Green and a rejuvenated,

mind-reading Frank Hankinson rang the doorbell of the Finleys' apartment. He didn't have
to. Joe had sensed their approach and opened
the door as the bell rang.

"What the . . ." said Frank.

"Hi, guys. You have to get used to being a
superman, Frank."

"I guess so. You startled me."

"Sorry. Come on in. How did it go, Ben?"

"Fine, as you can see . . . Frank has joined us."

They entered the apartment. Ben waved a
hello to Bernie, then walked into the kitchen,
where the ladies were gathered. "Welcome
Frank to the army."

"We have a new name for our gang." said
Alma. "Your wife conceived the title. We are
now known as the Geriatric Brigade."

Ben roared with laughter.

Frank said, "Perfect . . . I love it."

When they had settled down, Art gave Ben and
Frank the count and their projection for completing the Antarean requirements for personnel.
Ben and Frank agreed with the assessment, but
they were skeptical about getting the total cooperation of all the people in the Building A. Frank
explained his plan with the Amatos. Meanwhile,
the women would pack and head for their respective hometowns that night.

• 42 •

The wheels were set in motion for recruiting the army as Saturday morning dawned. Bess, Mary, and Alma were already in New York City. Andrea Hankinson was on the morning Eastern Flight to Atlanta, where she would change for a Delta flight to St. Louis. Marie Amato would catch the noon plane to Boston.

Frank had not expected to convince his wife and the Amatos so easily. He had set up the meeting as a normal Friday night card game. They had wanted to play cards and began to get annoyed at Frank's wanting to talk so much. But it was the card game that convinced them. Initially, they thought he was crazy and drunk. They were playing bridge. He simply read their cards out loud to them. At first they were sure he had stacked the deck, so they shuffled and dealt again. But he did it again. "Isn't that a bitch?" he asked them.

"How the hell do you do that?" asked Paul Amato. The Boston stockbroker was impressed.

"I can read your minds."

"Bullshit!" said Paul.

"You want to try it again?" questioned Frank.

"No, I believe you can do it . . . but *how* you do it is the question."

The women were silent. Andrea was embarrassed because she thought Frank was showing off. She liked the Amatos and she was afraid they would get angry with Frank.

"You really embarrassed about this, Andy?" asked Frank. She was shocked. "I'm a mind-reader, too," he boasted, enjoying his power for the first time.

"Okay, smartass," said Paul, "I'm thinking of a number." "It's 2,347.66" said Frank.

"My God!" Paul Amato was shocked.

"What's going on here?" Andrea Hankinson was disturbed.

Frank didn't hesitate. He went right into the story, asking them not to interrupt until he was finished.

An hour later, after he had finished, Andrea and the Amatos agreed to join the Geriatric Brigade. Now the six couples gathered in the meeting room for the Friday night function with one thought in mind. They would spread out among the other people from Building A and begin to size up the chances of activating more recruits.

Ralph Shields was in jail. Wally Parker was in the hospital. It had been hysterically funny, but Beam felt guilty. True, it had to be done, and she never did anything halfway, but somehow she would have to make it up to the two men before she left.

Beam had gone to Wally's office in the basement, where she knew he was sleeping off the night before. She had knocked to awaken him. From that point on she had mentally seduced him under the guise of Laurie, Mr. Bright's assistant. Once again, physically nothing happened, but Wally was sure he had gone to heaven as the beautiful young girl appeared like magic and made love to him.

At the same time, Amos Bright stormed into Shields' office and, in an uncharacteristic manner, reamed the manager for allowing his employees to turn a respectable residence into a brothel. Shields begged ignorance. "I don't know what you are talking about, Mr. Bright."

"I'm talking about that damned Wally Parker and my assistant shacking up in the service office below here — that's what I'm talking about!"

"Wally? Shacking up? With who?"

"My assistant, Mr. Shields. A sweet young girl. He must have given her drugs."

"Drugs? Wally Parker?" The little manager was not only confused, but was sure Amos Bright had gone out of his mind. Wally drank a little, and went out with a woman now and then, but never drugs, and certainly never young girls. He had never seen Wally with a woman under forty.

"Please, Mr. Bright. Let me check it out."

"You'd better do something, Mr. Shields. I'll see you later." Amos stormed out of the office, chuckling to himself. He felt a bit weak and knew he had better get back to the processing room for an hour under the lasers. Beam would take care of the rest.

Shields knocked hard on Wally's door.

"Wally, open up!" He could hear Wally moaning in ecstasy and the sound of a female laughing.

"Not now, boss. Not now."

"You open this goddamned door, or I'll break it down!"

"Bug off, Ralph. I'm busy!"

Shields reached into his pocket for the master key. Wally had double-locked the door from the inside. Beam heard the key in the door and moved to open the inside lock. Shields burst into the room and Beam gave him the image of Wally naked with a sixteen-year-old girl. "Oh, Christ, Parker! You're out of your mind!"

All Wally could see was an angry Shields staring at his lovely, newly arrived date.

All Shields could see was Wally raping an innocent young girl.

Beam then had Wally pronounce a loud and abusive "Fuck you, Shields!" to his boss, and the rest was history.

The police arrived within five minutes, brought by a call from Amos Bright, before the Antarean lay down to rest and feed.

The police found a crazed Ralph Shields sitting on top of an unconscious Wally Parker, punching away at the caretaker's face, which by now was a swollen, bloody mess. Shields was incoherent as the two Dade County officers lifted him off the larger man and cuffed him. One of the cops then called for an ambulance and a backup unit. Within fifteen minutes the Antares complex was quiet again, minus two of its employees.

Beam found her way back to the processing room and lay on the cot next to Amos. She, too, needed rest and food. They had ten more cocoons to process that night. After that the humans would begin their own unique processing and the Antareans would have to prepare the way. There would be little rest for any of them for a while.

Madman Mazuski lifted the aging Sikorsky EA-155 slowly off the pad and swung to the southeast, up, up over south Miami, over the inland waterway, up, up over south Miami Beach, up, up and out over the blue-green water of the Atlantic.

Phil Doyle poured their third Jack Daniels into the paper cups that Maz had supplied. The Madman belted his drink down in one smooth gulp. "Fill 'er up one more time, old *Razzmatazz*, old buddy . . ."

"Just remember you're the pilot . . . okay?"

"I'd better remember, or we both go into the shithouse." He laughed, making Phil even more uncomfortable. "Have another drink, Doyle. You're uptight today."

"Yeah, well . . . just keep your eye on the road."

"No sweat."

Jack Mazuski had served with the 101st in Vietnam. In those days he had flown a Medivac chopper and then had been transferred to a carrier for search-and-rescue operations. The reason this rare occurrence had come to pass was that he had seen a downed F-105 from the carrier *Hornet,* in the river. The Viet Cong were firing at the trapped pilot as he scrambled out of his fighter where it sat, ditched in the shallow riverbed. Mazuski had swooped down over the V.C. throwing hand grenades out of his small chopper. Then he turned up over the river and brought the chopper down on the river on the far side of the fighter plane, allowing the pilot to jump aboard after he had set the destruct device on the plane. It was a crazy and heroic action. Maz then took the pilot with him to pick up the wounded soldier, which had been his original mission. Against regulations, he brought both his passengers out to the carrier. He was ordered to do so by the pilot, who turned out to be a wing commander and a full colonel. Maz got a Distinguished Flying Cross, two Clusters, a recommendation for a presidential citation, and mention for a Congressional Medal of Honor. In addition, the colonel had Maz transferred to the carrier for the remainder of his tour. There Maz worked to train search-and-rescue pilots and flew several missions himself. But he never took chances after saving the colonel. No one expected him to. Not even the colonel.

Now the chopper chugged its way out over

the Gulf Stream. The greenish-blue water turned blue and they knew they had reached their destination.

After an hour in the air they had spotted six sailfish and a marlin. They had directed five boats that were out on the Stream to the fishes' locations.

"Well, not much action, but those boats will cover the gas today, anyway." Max was drunk, but steady.

"Want to take a little detour for me?" asked Phil.

"What you got in mind . . . Bimini?"

"No such luck. I want to have a look over at The Stones."

"Why?"

"Well," said Phil, lying, "the fishing has been lousy over there for a few weeks. I think it may be a big shark or a whole school of them. Something is screwing up the fishing, and I'm curious."

"Jaws, huh?"

Phil played it cool with the volatile pilot.

"Okay . . . let's head over and have a peek. But that will cost you another bourbon."

Phil gladly poured.

The work aboard *Manta III* and *Terra Time* continued to be slow and tedious. Six of the ten cocoons were in place. Two were in the works below, and two remained on deck. Both were on the *Manta III* as the helicopter's rotor noise caused Jack and Hal to look up toward the north. Hal saw it first. "There's a helicopter coming this way."

"Coast Guard?" wondered Jack.

Hal gave his attention to the sound. He then telepathed to Harry, the other blond "beach-boy" on *Terra Time*, asking him to zero in on the chopper and triangulate thoughts. Jack picked up their thoughts, but it became too painful for him to listen in on their intense thought waves. The sound, translated into his brain, was a high-pitched whine. He tuned them off and watched. Hal broke it off as the chopper came into view.

Looking up, Jack spoke. "It's the Madman."

"You know the pilot?"

"Yes, he spots fish for us from time to time. He's harmless."

"He is not alone. Your friend from the boat this morning, Mr. Doyle, is with him."

"Phil? Damn him!"

Hal knew he could not interrupt the commanders below. He sensed danger. Then he realized there were still two cocoons on deck. Turning quickly from the aircraft, he jumped onto the deck and yelled

335

to Jack, "Help me with these, quickly!"

Jack was startled by Hal's sudden move, but he caught on fast. "Over they go?"

"Yes, but quickly, before they come too close."

It was too late. In the chopper, the Madman recognized the *Manta III* immediately. Then the rest. "Hey," said Mazuski, "that's your friend Fischer. I don't know the other boat."

"Right," said Phil. "I wonder if he's catching fish."

"Don't look like he's fishing to me."

"Let's have a closer look."

The pilot responded and swung the whirlybird in closer. They came in above the *Manta III* from the west, out of the sun. It was an old combat pilot trick. "They won't see us right away." The Madman slurred his words.

Phil leaned over and peered out of the bubble. "What the hell is that?" He was watching Hal and Jack dump a cocoon over the side.

Mazuski hovered the copter and turned so that he could look down onto the deck of the *Manta III*. As he did this, Hal and Jack lifted the second cocoon and carried it to the bow of the boat. "Looks like some kind of buoy."

"No, more like a big white torpedo."

The Madman dipped the chopper so that both men could look out of the front of the bubble. Two of the copper men popped to the surface, grabbed a cocoon, and disappeared below the water in a matter of seconds.

It was at this point that Harry, the Antarean on the deck of the *Terra Time*, reached out with his mental powers and froze the minds of the two men in the helicopter. The Sikorsky began to spin out of control.

"No!" Jack shouted aloud. "Don't hurt them!"

Hal mentally took over the controls of the copter while Harry kept Jack Mazuski and Phil Doyle frozen in time.

"Let them go," said Jack. "Please . . . they are my friends."

"They saw the cocoons," Hal answered. "They will tell others."

"Listen," Jack pleaded, "they don't know what they saw. I'll talk to them tonight. I'll straighten it out . . . somehow, but don't hurt them!" He was emphatic.

Thoughts passed rapidly between the two Antareans. Then the shiny head of All Light broke the surface of the water below the hovering aircraft. Hal telepathed to the commander. A tense moment passed. Finally, the commander ordered the Antareans to release the intruders and their helicopter.

Above, Madman Mazuski jolted awake. "What happened, Doyle?"

"I don't know, but let's get the hell out of here!"

"That's a roger . . . we're on our way." The chopper took off at full throttle to the east.

· 43 ·

Arnie was disappointed when Judy called to say that they would have to put off their spy mission until the following morning. Sandy was ambivalent. She still felt that Jack was simply doing his job and protecting his clients. Arnie felt differently. He called his pretty wife and told her he had to work late. Then he was going to go over to the yacht club and get the keys to his boss' boat. In fact, he already had the keys. If Judy and Sandy wanted to wait until tomorrow, that was their business. He was going to have a look tonight.

They had arrived at the decision to send the women back to their home cities easily. It was the women who kept the social and family contacts. There were only a few business associates whom the men had who might be potential soldiers. That could be handled on the phone, or with an invitation to visit in Florida.

After the wives, with the exception of Rose Lewis, whose mission would take her to lower Collins Avenue and the ghetto of the old, had been delivered to the airport, the men gathered at the Green apartment. Rose took the red Buick. She would spend the day with Aunt Ruth.

Now the men sat and assessed their inquiries from the Friday night social. About half of the occupants of the condo had been there. Of the thirty couples, eleven were definitely out. They were in their fifties, active in business and part-time residents of the Antares complex. They were too young, anyway, and naturally kept apart from the other, more permanent residents. That left about fifteen couples, not counting the six couples that made up their own group.

Each of the men had chosen two or three of the couples as targets and had spent time talking about the life in Florida, their feelings about being retired, their families, and how they looked at the future. They were laying the groundwork for the more complicated conversations that would come later.

The probe had brought the spacesuit skins for the Earthbound Antareans. They would last a month or so depending on how long they were exposed to the caustic atmosphere of polluted south Florida.

Amos and Beam were rested and refreshed as they met Ben Green. The new suits were working and the atmosphere in the processing room had been brought up to a point that humans could tolerate, and the Antareans, too. The large wall glowed pink, the pressure was about three Earth atmospheres, and the temperature a warm one hundred five degrees Fahrenheit.

"We will probably be bringing some volunteers in today."

"We will be ready," answered a pleased Amos Bright.

"How many do you anticipate?" asked Beam.

"Hard to say, but figure on twenty or thirty."

"We will need your help with the equipment." Beam was concerned.

"Joe and I will help. Bernie and Frank will be available late this afternoon, and Art will be back tonight."

"Good," answered Amos. "We finished the last of the cocoons. They are being placed today. Then we will all be in position to begin full-time processing."

Beam interrupted. "The others have not yet put on the new skins. They are working slowly and will not be back until late tonight."

Ben was concerned. "There isn't any danger, is there?"

"No," she answered. "Only that they will be very tired when they return. They will need the cots for a while, and we will have to bring the room to Antarean atmosphere while they change skins." She thought for a moment and a message passed between her and Amos that Ben could not read. It was transmitted in a different language.

"What was that?" he asked.

"The language of the Parmans," answered Amos. "Soon you will know it."

The men had taken names and apartment numbers from the people at the social by telling them that they were forming an exciting senior citizens corporation that would start a business in which all the residents could work and contribute their talents. It was exciting to the older people. Retirement, in most cases, was a forced thing, or a result of illness. Some of the people had spent their lives at jobs they hated, scrimping and saving for the glorious days of retirement. The big payoff they called it. Now they found it was boring and isolated. A bitter dream come true. The new business was going to be done with federal funding based on a new law attached to the Social Security bill pending in Congress. The plan was in the early stages of development awaiting the passage of the bill. Once the funds were available, the men had lied, they wanted to be ready to apply immediately. So the planning had to take place now. Arrangements had been made for each of the men to call on their chosen neighbors that Saturday morning. They met at Ben's apartment, went over the strategy, then dispersed to their appointments.

Ben Green delayed his meetings for a half hour in order to meet with Amos and Beam.

A probe ship had come down early Saturday morning. Joe Finley had seen it as he left to drive some of the ladies to the airport. The small probe, glowing slightly blue as it descended directly onto the roof of Building B, was barely noticeable. Joe saw it and pointed it out to the women because he felt its arrival. His senses, now more tuned to the Antarean world, than the human world, were able to pick up the guidance sent out to the probe by Amos and Beam. In fact, Joe pitched in and helped a bit. It amused Amos to feel Finley's powers join their own. It also felt good to know there was help for them on this planet.

"I wanted to ask you about that. We have sort of decided on who will be our commanders. When do we begin changing to be commanders?"

Beam took over once again. "That will be done last. I will have a schedule programmed by tonight so that we can process the humans as you bring them. They must understand that once this begins they cannot roam about outside anymore. Since they will come in mostly as couples of male and female, I will program that one of them can be out of this building for a short period of time for one day. This time can be used to finalize their business transactions and gather any possessions they may wish to transport."

Amos interrupted. "Nothing bulky, but we thought they might wish to bring some mementoes of the Earth ... perhaps pictures or books."

This is really happening, thought Ben. *We are actually going to leave the Earth.* It was staggering. Beam came into his thoughts. She reassured him, stroked him; comfort flowed to him.

Amos spoke. "It is not difficult for us to tell you that this is a proper thing for you to do. We do understand your concern and, yes, fear of the unknown. I told you that we could help you better understand when the time came. Perhaps for you, Ben Green, the time has come to see more of what we know and feel more of what we are."

They led Ben to the center table and lifted him onto it. Above the cone glowed and for the first time a beam of soft yellow light extended from the core of the cone and enveloped Ben. This was not the hot ash-producing light that the center table had previously emitted onto the men.

"We have begun to change the programs to what is actually required for your processing," said Beam. "Relax and allow your mind to be free."

Ben closed his eyes and relaxed. He felt warm. He felt as though he were filling up with a glowing substance, like a balloon, his body filling with warmth, or so he felt. Opening his eyes, he expected to see himself bloated, but he had not changed shape.

Amos' thoughts reached him. *You are growing inside. Your nerves are being tuned. Your mind is expanding. You are sensing parts of your body and mind that you have never felt before. We believe that this internal growth reaches to the part of you that you call the soul.*

Ben relaxed again, comforted by Amos' thoughts. His mind filled again . . . it rambled at first . . . bits and pieces of insight . . . feelings . . . sensations of anger and love . . . frailty and strength . . . random explosions that coursed through his mind and body

. . . touching emotions . . . then slowly, or so it seemed, they gathered in one place, deep inside. He felt as though his body were a shell, an outer covering for a delicate, living, existing, important being that was himself. The thing was without gender or form. Its power was enormous. Its love almost brought him to tears . . . what he felt . . . so very big and consuming . . . far-reaching . . . clear!

He knew. *It is not important what that primitive part of me thinks or fears for itself. We have, inside of us, human and Antarean alike, a life force larger than our existence. We are a part of each other, of the Universe. If it is a plan, then we are part of the plan. If it is existence alone, it does not matter, for we are part of the existence, too. We must always reach and grow. It is a thing we can do together. Now, filled with knowledge of myself, I can be a part of all the others who will join. I can meld with them and we are together a part of one another. We are great together. We are wonderful. To leave the Earth is not to leave the Universe, for we are irrevocably a part of the total wonderful occurrence. We are life. We carry the seeds of tomorrow onward to the stars. We are life. We are together, all life, together we are God.*

"Thank you." Ben rose from the table. His eyes glowed; so did Beam's and Amos' under their skin suits. The light was the same color and intensity.

Ben was aware of other things. His thoughts were too full and new to be expressed. Oh, the futility of humanity's effort to express the knowledge he now possessed. But he was compassionate, because he knew, as he had never known, that the struggle to express would eventually bring the race to understanding. Ben knew it would be a slow process, spread over millennia. Yet, as slow as it might be, inexorably, he knew humanity would someday, on its own, unaided by outside influence, find the meaning to existence that, thanks to the Antareans, he now possessed. This knowledge was beautiful. "We will all feel this way . . . know these things?"

"Yes," answered Amos Bright. "Those who make the journey will have to be this way; otherwise, they would not be able to comprehend the Parmans, or, for that matter, the Antarean race, either."

"That's wonderful," said Ben. He reached his hands to Beam and Amos and they permitted him to touch them. It felt natural and human to Ben.

As he left the room Amos called to him. "There are some things that have happened that you should know."

Ben turned to listen. Beam had moved to the

cabinets to make programming adjustments.

"Three events. The first is that our Mr. Shields and Mr. Parker will be away from the grounds for some time . . . at least until after we depart."

"You fired them?"

"No, let's just say they have taken some much deserved time off. The second event is that the boats were followed today by some of Jack Fischer's friends. They came in a helicopter looking for Jack. He has spoken to them and assures us that their curiosity has been satisfied. However, it may be necessary for you to pay them a visit if they become curious again."

"Whatever you say, Commander."

"Good. The final matter is a bit more distressing. When the boats returned here last night, they were followed by another boat. The person on board was not known to us. Hal and Harry wanted to capture it, but the commanders needed to be brought here quickly. They have been using too much energy and were in need of rest and food. Their skins are almost destroyed. So we had to let the boat escape. The man aboard could not have seen anything extraordinary. I am not concerned. The boat is called *Banshee*. It is owned by one Mr. Robert Miner of Coral Gables. Perhaps tomorrow you can call on Mr. Miner and find out why he was following our boats?"

"Okay, Amos. Mr. Robert Miner will get a visit the first chance we have."

"Good. Then we will see you later."

Ben turned and left the room as Amos and Beam prepared to meet the first recruits of their new army.

Arnie honked the horn again. Sandy told him to be patient. "Judy will be down in a minute. She said she had a long session at the agency last night. She's excited about the job. It pays a lot of money."

Arnie, still mulling over the strange sights he had seen the night before, didn't pay attention. "For someone who wanted to find out about her boyfriend, she sure is taking her time."

"What's eating you, honey?" Sandy was concerned. "Everything okay at the office?"

"Fine, fine," answered Arnie. "It's just that Judy got me so worked up about Jack that I'm curious . . . and worried."

"Well, I still think it's all silly. I'm sure Jack will have a perfectly reasonable explanation."

"I hope so." Arnie clammed up and began figuring how long it would take them to get to the marina, get the *Banshee* under way and around to the Antares complex. He estimated an hour and a half. That would make it after one P.M. He blew the horn again, as Judy appeared at her front door. She waved, checked her mailbox, and hurried to the car.

Ben Green noticed Shields as he walked back to Building A. He wondered about the manager because Amos had told him that the man would not be around. *Now here he was.*

Amos didn't know about bail. He assumed the police would detain Shields indefinitely, or, at the very least, for several days, because he had struck another being. Ben walked out of his way and confronted the little man. "Good morning, Mr. Shields. How are you?"

"Good morning, Mr. Green. I'm fine." Shields was apprehensive about Ben Green after spying on him the other evening. "Have you seen Mr. Bright around?"

"Mr. Bright?"

Ben picked up his thoughts. "Oh, Amos, sure. We just had some coffee together. Nice guy. We were old friends back in New York."

"Funny, he never mentioned that to me, Mr. Green — especially when I told him about that pool business."

"Pool business? What pool business?"

"Surely you remember when you wanted me to get the pool filled. It's only been a month or so."

"Oh, *that* pool business. Well, there are a lot of Greens in the world. We met a few weeks ago by accident. Sort of a reunion. Small world, isn't it?"

"Yeah, small world." Shields wasn't buying it.

Ben decided to hold him for a moment and contact Amos. "How's the construction coming in Building B, Mr. Shields?"

"You should know. You're in there often enough."

Ben was trapped. *Okay, Mr. Shields,* he thought, *time to get you off the premises permanently.* Ben quickly relayed his plan to Amos, and they agreed upon it. Then he made Shields swing at him and knock him down. Shields didn't know why he had done it, but here he was again, in a fight, and this time with an old man. Ben kept the blows as soft as possible. Amos had the Dade County sheriff on the phone quickly and they dispatched a car. Ben refused medical attention, but he assured the police he would press charges. There would be no bail for Shields now. It was medical observation time, and that was good for at least a week. As the police took him away, Shields was almost incoherent, yelling about a man from the D.A.'s office, a swimming pool, and a conspiracy. *Explain that one to the doctors,* thought Ben Green as he lay under the cot

351

lamp for a minute to heal the bruises from his fight. Then he went back to Building A. It was conference time with the neighbors.

By the time Arnie docked the *Banshee* at the Antares complex dock, twenty people had begun processing in the large room above them. The dock was crowded with the *Manta III* and *Terra Time*, so Arnie nosed the *Banshee* in as close as he dared and threw an anchor fore and aft to steady the cruiser. He then helped the two women onto the dock.

Upstairs the activity in the busy processing room was interrupted for a moment. "Visitors," said Hal, who had been designated as a guard. "The young lady who was here looking for Jack and two others. One male and one female."

All Light questioned Jack. "Why are they here?"

"Looking for me, I guess. I'll go down and talk to them."

"We will monitor through you," commented All Light.

"Here he comes," announced Judy as she watched her boyfriend make his way down the path to the dock.

"He looks okay," said Sandy.

Jack stepped onto the dock and waved a big hello. He approached Judy to give her a big hug.

"Not so fast, Mr. Slippery. You have some explaining to do."

Jack backed off and turned to greet his brother and sister-in-law.

Sandy reached and gave Jack a kiss on the cheek. Arnie shook hands, but he remained silent. "We were worried about you, little brother."

"Worried about what?"

Arnie decided to be straightforward. "No deceptions, okay? We know that when you called us you were not where you said you were. Phil Doyle called and told me you were avoiding him and the rest of the charter boats . . . so we are worried."

"I appreciate your concern, but I don't think you people are listening to me. I told you that I had a special charter." Jack looked around, adding a conspiratorial atmosphere to the conversation. "These people are on to something big. They are spooky about outsiders. I gave them my word that there would be no leaks through me. I have to tell you . . . this is embarrassing. I could lose my charter."

Jack felt All Light send him a message. *Good going, Jack.*

Sandy turned to the others, "See? I told you it was that way."

Arnie wasn't buying it.

353

"What can be so secret that you have to lie to your girl friend and your family?" Judy was still pressing.

"Treasure, baby . . . treasure," Jack whispered.

"Treasure with shiny eyes and copper skin?"

"What?"

Judy and Sandy looked at Arnie.

"That's what I said — shiny eyes and copper skin. How about it, Jack?"

"What are you talking about, Arnie?"

Jack tried to buy time to think. How did he know? What did he see? The questions raced through Jack's mind up into All Light. All Light telepathed back: *I will send help*. Hal and Harry were already out the door of the processing room making tracks to their quarters to put on their beachboy coverings.

Arnie let his knowledge sink in. "I'm talking about the people, or whatever they were, on your boat last night. I followed you into the canal. I saw them."

"You were here last night?" Sandy asked the question.

"You bet I was here. I took the boat from my boss, but when Judy had to go for the interview I decided to have a look over here last night, anyway. The captain here had some very interesting passengers on his little yacht. It looked like a Halloween party. Who were they, Jack?"

"I don't know what you think you saw, Arnie. The divers have some new type of diving suits. That's all, and that's all I can say."

An awkward moment of silence passed on the dock. Judy noticed two young blond men coming down the path. "We've got company."

"Oh, damn," said Jack. "Thanks a lot, *family*. Now I'm in for it!"

Hal and Harry joined the group. "Anything wrong, Mr. Fischer?"

"No. These people are friends. This is my brother and sister-in-law, and this is my girl friend."

"You know the conditions of the charter, Mr. Fischer." Hal was acting annoyed. "I think this is a clear violation of our agreement."

"Yes, I'm really sorry about this. It won't happen again."

As Hal spoke, Harry read the minds of the three humans on the dock. The two women were convinced. He felt reluctance on the part of Jack's brother. He also knew that this was the same man who had spied on them last night in the canal. These thoughts were beamed back to the commanders. They were to detain the group.

At that time, Ben Green and Joe Finley were

sitting in Robert Miner's Florida room.

"It's not a serious problem, Mr. Miner. We just like to know who is on our property, and why. I'm sure you understand." Ben Green tried to be friendly, but firm.

"We've promised our clients complete privacy," Joe added.

"I'm sorry, gentlemen, but I don't know what you're talking about."

"We are talking about last night, Mr. Miner." Ben sharpened his tone. "Last night, your boat, the *Banshee*, followed some of our clients to our private dock on Red Lake Canal."

"Is there a law against that?" Robert Miner was a tough man. He had built his advertising agency from scratch to one of the biggest in Miami. At this point in his life, he felt he didn't have to answer to anyone, and if Arnie was in some kind of trouble, then he would protect him.

Joe and Ben read the man. Now they knew who had been in the canal, and that they were talking to the wrong man. "No, Mr. Miner, there is no law against that . . . per se. We have some rather special guests at the facility and they value their privacy. No harm done. No harm intended."

Miner was surprised at the fast backoff these two old men were making. It aroused his curiosity. "Who are these special guests?"

"That must remain a secret."

Joe Finley was standing, preparing to leave. "Thank you for your time."

"No problem. Glad to help, gentlemen . . . anytime." Driving back to the complex, Ben and Joe knew they had acted too hastily. That was not the last they would hear from Mr. Robert Miner.

The Madman listened as the phone rang at Phil Doyle's home. "Phil . . . ? Hi . . . Mazuski here."

"Hi-ya, Madman. Sober up yet?"

"I haven't touched a drop since yesterday afternoon. I've been trying to figure out what happened. Still drawing blanks."

"Me, too. It's all a blank . . . I mean, what happened when we saw the *Manta Three.*"

"I'm worried about Jack. He knew it was me up there. He sure looked like he was trying to hide something."

"Want to have another look?"

"What do you mean?"

"I know where he docks that boat of his. Let's go over and have a little talk with him."

"Okay, but I can't do it today. I have a party to take up to Lauderdale. How about tomorrow morning?"

"Okay. I'll meet you over at the pad. Hey, Mazuski?"

"Yeah?"

"You have a walkie-talkie we can hook up in my car?"

"Sure. I got you. A land-and-air attack. Good idea."

"Right. See you tomorrow around ten."

"Roger. Bye."

"Bye.

Ben and Joe received the message from Beam as they parked in the Antares lot. *Go to Jack's room to help with captives.*

"Your own brother, Jack — I'm your brother, man. Can't you convince your friends I'm telling the truth?"

"I'm sorry, Arnie, but I can't. Like I told you, these people mean business. They are afraid that you will spill the beans about their discovery."

"What discovery? I don't know anything about a damned discovery."

"I'm sorry, Arnie, but you brought this upon yourself." "So what happens now?" Judy sat on the bed. Sandy sat next to her.

"I don't know, honey. They're talking it over now."

"Don't 'honey' me, Jack Fischer. I've had it

358

with you." Judy was fed up.

"I'm sorry you feel that way. I only asked you to trust me."

"With lies?"

"With whatever. That's what trust is."

"Bullshit!" Judy yelled.

Sandy felt this was not the place or time. "I think we'd better figure out how to get out of here and save the lovers' quarrels for another time."

Ben and Joe entered the room. Judy recognized them right away. "Hi. Are you men part of this?" Judy was on her feet, approaching them.

"Hi, Miss Simmons. Hi, Jack."

Jack introduced Arnie and Sandy to the men.

Arnie spoke up first. "Mr. Green, you seem to have some authority here. Why are we being held?"

"I'm sorry for the inconvenience. We have some business here that must remain confidential. My partners and I feel you may have compromised our security by coming here."

Judy stepped back from the two elderly men. "I was right . . . damn it, I was right! Treasure, my ass! This is the CIA."

"CIA?" Jack was smiling. "What about the CIA?"

"He gave it away. I heard him . . . 'compromise and security.' That's the way they talk."

"Who talks, Miss Simmons?" asked Joe Finley.

"The goddamned CIA talks, Mr. Finley!" She was a child of the sixties and a member of the SDS at Columbia. They had been infiltrated by FBI and CIA agents, and the whole thing had blown up. Members were exposed and asked to resign from the college. It had been kept out of the papers, but Judy harbored an intense resentment toward government agencies.

"You are mistaken, Miss Simmons."

Arnie spoke up. "I don't think she is, Mr. Finley. This detainment smacks of CIA tactics."

Ben and Joe excused themselves. This was out of hand. They had to talk it over with the Antareans. As they left they locked the door from the outside. Jack went with them.

"Jail . . . goddamned jail," said Arnie.

Sandy began to feel frightened.

Amos, All Light, Beam, Jack, Ben, and Joe met in the hallway outside the processing room. The hum of activity from the room filled the hallway.

"It is a problem. What do you suggest?" Beam addressed Ben.

"I think we can't hold them too long. The question is: What can we tell them that they will believe?" Ben was concerned.

"How about the truth?" suggested Jack.

"I don't think so," said Joe. "Too many people are nosing around as it is, and when others begin disappearing around here it's going to get tougher and tougher. I think we have to hold them."

"We can't hold them for three or four weeks." Jack was disturbed. "Judy has a bunch of TV commercials to do . . . Arnie has a job . . . they have his boss' boat. Don't forget that. If that boat isn't back by Sunday night, we are going to have the Coast Guard on the case, too."

"Good point," said Ben.

"Perhaps we can try images . . . like we did with Shields and Parker and Mr. Stranger?" suggested Beam.

"Go on," said Amos.

"Well, we told them it is a treasure discovery. Why not show them some treasure? That will be proof and they will have to believe us. Tell them Jack gets a large share. That will keep them quiet."

"I like that," said Ben.

"Agreed," said All Light. "Beam will prepare a room to show them."

"Fine," said Beam. "Let's use the storage area in the basement. Bring them down in ten minutes." She began to move away, then stopped and spoke to Ben Green. "What kind of treasure should it be?"

"Gold," he answered. "Old gold coins and some gold bars."

Beam moved away to the stairwell leading to the basement.

Tony Stranger was not surprised to get a call from Shields. He was, however, surprised that it came from the psychiatric clinic at the county hospital. Shields explained his problem. It had a familiar ring to it, especially the part about Wally Parker and the girl.

"I'm going to be here for at least a week, Tony. Wally is in the hospital here, too. He doesn't know I'm here. I don't know what happened. It's all too confusing."

Tony knew Shields as a volatile man, but not a violent man. He decided not to tell Shields about his adventure with Mr. Bright's secretary. "Look, pal," he told Shields, "you hang in there. I'm going to have a look around that place. I get the feeling that our Mr. Bright is something more than he appears to be. It's bugging me."

He hung up, then called the hospital. "I'd like to inquire about Mr. Wally Parker. I believe he was admitted two days ago."

"Just a moment, please." The operator put him on hold.

A few seconds later a female voice came on the phone. "Fifth floor, Miss Burns speaking."

"Hello. I'd like to check on the status of a patient . . . a Mr. Wally Parker."

"Yes, sir. Are you family?"

"Yes, his brother."

"Yes, Mr. Parker. Your brother can't speak on the phone. He can have visitors tomorrow. His condition is satisfactory and he's resting, but under sedation. We had to wire his jaw. It was broken."

Tony was surprised. "Thank you. Please tell him I called . . . tell him Tony called. I'll be up tomorrow to see him. Good-bye."

"My God! Will you look at that!" Arnie Fischer stared at the pile of gold bars and chests of coins that Beam projected in the small storage room.

"Can I touch them!" asked Judy.

"We'd rather you didn't," answered Beam. "The authorities might be interested in finger-prints if they ever got wind of this."

Arnie was impressed. "Sure, I understand. Hey, I'm really sorry about being such a pain in the ass. I don't blame you for being so careful," Arnie said.

Beam, who stood off to the corner of the room, read the thoughts of the humans. They were all convinced. She felt satisfied.

Ben spoke. "Now, folks, let's take a walk back to the dock and talk about this a bit more. We agreed to show you this room in order to convince you. Now I would like to hear you convince me that what you saw will remain a secret. If you can't, then Jack will be out of a job and a most generous share of the profits."

They left the room and went out the back door toward the dock, convinced that silence was the order of the day. Ben and Joe felt satisfied as they watched the *Banshee* turn and head slowly up Red Lake Canal.

Jack felt Ben's thoughts. "I'll visit with them tomorrow night."

"Good idea," said Joe. "I think the little viewing of the treasure room will hold them for a while."

"All right," said Ben. "Now let's get to work. We have an army to prepare!"

Far to the south, in an area of the Atlantic known as the breeding ground of tropical storms, the *Tyros* satellite observed a depression growing. Within eighteen hours the weather service attached to the National Oceanic and Atmospheric Administration would name it Ellen. It would become the fifth hurricane of the season, and it would leave its mark on south Florida before dissipating out over a nation that would be missing nine hundred forty-one of its elder citizens.

• **44** •

Robert Jastrow, a NASA scientist, once wrote that scientists actually have the ability to match the human brain in memory capacity. But the memory bank would be so large it would take up most of the Empire State Building. It would consume electricity at the rate of one billion watts – half the output of the Grand Coulee Dam. It would cost about ten billion dollars. According to Jastrow:

No other organ in the history of life has been known to grow as fast as the human brain. The growth was explosive – and it was early man's tool-making industry that triggered it off. The possession of a good brain enabled *Homo* to make tools in the first place. But the use of tools became, in turn, a driving force toward the evolution of a better and better brain . . .

Mr. Jastrow was right. He was, unknown to himself, writing about the basic theory behind the Antarean processing room. It was not the external use of tools that brought the human brain to maximum; it was the use of the ultimate tool — the brain itself — that allowed the breakthrough. Once activated, the entire brain became a tool of infinite capacity and depth. It was as infinite as the Universe it reflected. It was a mini-Universe, containing all that any life form required to comprehend existence itself.

But in a relatively obscure structure, in a corner of Coral Gables, Florida, nine hundred forty-one human beings made a quantum leap into the full realization of their capacity that would take their own race several thousand years to accomplish.

The Geriatric Brigade was almost complete.

• **45** •

"I think it's going to be close . . . very close." A concerned Ben Green sat quietly with the Antarean commanders. Three weeks had passed since the processing had begun. Several events, some lucky, some disturbing, had occurred. Now all that remained was to move the occupants of the nursing home to the Antares complex and process them. They would complete the army. "Thirty-six to go, all from the home."

"Yes, Ben, you have done a wonderful job." Beam sat next to Ben and touched him as she spoke. Kindness flowed between them. The feeling was still fairly new to Ben. Its warmth still surprised him.

Amos spoke. "When will you bring them?"

"Tonight. I figured they won't be missed for at least two days. That should be enough time."

"Yes, that is enough, now that we have so much help. We will have to alter the commanders soon, also." Beam touched Ben again.

"We are ready. I will be the last — Joe and I, that is. We have to finish the business of the wills. Also the matter of Mr. Stranger."

"Have you seen him today?" asked All Light.

"Joe spent some time with him today. He is still being most unreasonable. That will be Jack's problem after we leave. I don't envy Jack."

"Jack has been most helpful to us all," Amos said. "I want to reward him in some way that will make his life easier after we have gone."

"Do you have any ideas?" asked Ben Green.

"Yes, I have arranged to meet with Mr. DePalmer at the bank tomorrow. I am going to sign the complex over to Jack, with the suggestion that Jack involve Mr. Stranger in some way to repay him for his detention here these past weeks."

"Good. What about the other loose ends?"

"They concern me," said Amos. "I only hope that we can hold them off for the few days we need. After that it really won't matter."

Poor Jack, thought Ben. *He's going to have a lot of explaining to do.*

They all agreed.

Tropical Storm Ellen had flirted with the Florida coast for almost a week before striking the peninsula near Boca Raton. It then swung north, went back out to sea, and, in a most unusual maneuver, did a turnabout and went south again, hitting the Florida Keys with hurricane force.

It was under cover of the storm that the Antareans brought their mother ship down and placed it underwater, near The Stones.

Madman Mazuski and Phil Doyle scouted the Antares complex once, but saw little. The storm kept them away for a week and a half after that.

The Miami International Airport tower, and the new radar-tracking station attached to the Strategic Forces Base in southern Florida, both picked up the large Antarean ship on their radar. Because of the size and speed of the image on their screens, they concluded it was an electrical disturbance caused by the storm. Also, since it was discovered moving through the most violent part of the storm, they concluded that it could not have been any kind of airship and survive the turbulence.

Had the airlines checked their passenger manifests, they would have observed a slight growth in passengers from St. Louis, Boston, and New York. Had they checked further, they might have found the average age of their passengers a bit older than usual for this time of year. But there was nothing strange about older people coming to Florida.

The records of the Miami police were a bit more disturbing. There had been a series of disappearances of older people from the lower Collins Avenue district. Fifteen complaints in three weeks was more than average. Had they checked carefully, they would have found more than one hundred people actually missing. But the detectives assigned to the area had little to go on. There were no signs of violence, robbery, or murder. There were no ransom demands. The people were from a variety of backgrounds, races, religions, and politics. The only common denominator was their age. None of them was under seventy. They couldn't even stake out the neighborhood. Everyone down there was old. Who would the police watch? What would they watch for?

Judy got the Florida Power and Light commercials. The shooting had been delayed because of the storm, but there were costume fittings and rehearsals to keep her busy. Jack spent some time with her for two weeks, but then the last week he began to shuttle people out to the mother ship. Judy was so excited about her job, and about the treasure that Jack would share, that she didn't bother him about his absence. On the last day Judy, Arnie, and Sandy would meet the Antareans to learn the truth. Until then, it was understood that Jack would say nothing to her.

Arnie and Sandy went about their business, keeping their word to remain silent about the treasure. Mr. Miner, Arnie's boss, did press him a bit about where he had taken the *Banshee,* and why. Arnie satisfied his curiosity.

Wally Parker was out of the hospital with a wired jaw, a lawyer, and the burning revenge that came from a bad beating.

Ralph Shields was out on bail, desperately trying to talk with Wally, who would have no part of him. He was also disturbed that Tony Stranger had mysteriously disappeared.

Tony was a guest of the Antareans'. He had visited Wally in the hospital, and the caretaker wrote down the events that led to his hospitalization. It immediately struck Tony that what had happened to Wally somehow had also happened to him. Amos Bright was behind it. The banker DePalmer, wasn't talking. So Tony had gone directly to Building B and when Harry and Hal caught him sneaking through the basement, he raised the roof, screaming and yelling and demanding that the police come. Now he sat in a locked room, a prisoner of his own curiosity. He was frightened even though one of the old men came to see him each day to reassure him that he would not be harmed.

With the weather clear, Jack, on the *Manta III*, and, Harry, on the *Terra Time*, began shuttling the processed humans out to the mother ship. The schedule meant four trips a day. Each boat could safely carry some fifteen passengers and their gear. At that rate they would fall short some two hundred fifty passengers, including the Antareans, by the scheduled liftoff time. So night deliveries for the last three days were discussed. Jack felt that the people at the gas dock were suspicious enough of his activities, and Phil Doyle had been asking about the *Manta III*.

"Do you think Mr. Doyle would like a charter himself?" asked Amos.

Jack was hesitant. "He's been nosing around and I guess he's a little mad at me for ignoring him when he came over on the chopper. I don't know. How would I approach him?"

Art Perlman spoke up. "Why not tell him the truth? You won't be able to lie when he sees our fellow soldiers go over the side and not come up."

"It sure would make it easier. With three boats we could even get a tank truck over here and save the time it takes to get over to the gas barge each morning. But I don't know how he would take the truth – I mean, the actual truth."

"We know he's been nosing around here and, frankly, I don't want to lock anyone else up like Mr. Stranger."

Bernie Lewis voiced his concern. Beam suggested that Jack call Mr. Doyle and ask him to come over to the dock. They would prepare a demonstration for him so that there would be no doubt that Jack was telling the truth. What they didn't count on was Madman Mazuski.

Jack sat on the bridge of the *Manta III* as the two men walked onto the Antares dock.

"So there really is a Jack Fischer!" Phil yelled.

Jack saw the two men and slid down the ladder onto the deck. He looked around wondering why the Antareans had let the Madman through. "Hi, guys . . . surprise. Mazuski, how've you been?"

They shook hands as they boarded the boat. Phil looked around to see if anyone else was on the *Manta III.* "You alone?"

"Sure. I didn't know you were bringing company."

"He's one of us. I was with him in the chopper a few weeks ago when we saw you over at The Stones. What the hell were you doing there?" A voice came from the dock. "He was working for us."

Hal, Harry, Amos, and No Light were on the dock, standing next to the *Manta III*.

"Where did you guys come from?" asked Mazuski. "No one was on the dock a second ago."

"We came from far, far away, Mr. Mazuski," Amos said as he boarded the *Manta III*.

"Very far away," said No Light as he, too, boarded Jack's boat. Hal and Harry remained on the dock.

"And gentlemen," said Amos Bright, "we would like to talk some business with you both. Shall we go below?"

An hour later there were two more helpers, and the Antareans had an unexpected bonus — one serviceable helicopter flown by a pilot who thought he had seen it all until, as the clincher, Jack brought an eighty-five-year-old woman onto the boat. She was Ruth Charnofsky, Rose Lewis' aunt, from Collins Avenue. The woman greeted the visitors and proceeded to jump over the side of the boat into the canal. She settled to the bottom, some ten feet below, and remained visible, waving from time to time at the astonished pilot. After ten minutes he gave up. "I believe . . . I believe. Get her up here. I'm losing my breath."

Mazuski arranged for the tank truck to park at the dock the next morning and the shuttle operation began.

• 46 •

Mr. DePalmer handled the arrangements for Arthur Perlman to buy the nursing home. The owners were given, as Arthur liked to joke, "an offer they couldn't refuse." The entire staff of the home was given two weeks' notice and was replaced by members of the Geriatric Brigade who had not yet been completely processed. Betty Franklin, Bess Perlman's sister, was removed the day the processing had begun. Now, after the original staff had departed, she returned to speak to the remaining tenants of the home. These were people who had been left by their families to end their days under the care of strangers. Their families had overlooked their complaints about harsh treatment and cruelty. Had Bess not seen it for herself, it would have been hard to believe that human beings could treat other human beings with so little dignity or care.

Yet Bess and Art were bothered. Their job

was to arrange to move the people from the home to Building B. Could they pluck these people up and send them on a journey of light-years? Could they take them without consent of some kind?

The answer, hard as it was, was yes. The files were examined and thirty-six of the fifty tenants of the home were found to be alone in the world. They had not had visitors for years. They had no family on record. Some were wards of the state. Some had turned their life's savings over to the home in return for care. Art and Bess knew that later, after the processing, these people would be grateful. But it was a responsibility that they took on seriously, after much thought and soul-searching.

The night approached for the departure of the nursing home contingency. Art chose a Sunday night, after visitors, few as they might be, were gone. At two in the morning a charter bus pulled up in front of the home and thirty-six octogenarians, confused and frightened, took the first step toward an adventure none could ever imagine. The bus driver was told that there was a gas leak in the building and the people had to be moved to safety. Art hoped the story would hold for as long as they needed. He was wrong.

Detective Sergeant Matthew Cummings of

the Dade County Sheriff's Office had been assigned to the Collins Avenue disappearances for two weeks. He was as baffled as the rest of the force. However, the matron, who had been fired by Art Perlman, returned to the home on Tuesday afternoon to pick up a few personal possessions she had left behind. The home was now staffed with members of the Brigade who were in the process of hiring new people to take care of the remaining tenants. The matron, Mrs. Blackwell, was a vindictive woman. She immediately realized that several occupants of the home were missing. She found the woman confronting her was somehow familiar, but she couldn't place the face right away.

"If you have your things I would appreciate your leaving the premises." Bess was firm.

"I asked you what happened to the rest of the patients here."

"They are out visiting . . . on an outing to the park."

"Baloney. I know those people. Some of them couldn't walk more than ten steps. You can't take them out like that."

"But we did, Mrs. Blackwell. Perhaps you and the former owners didn't try hard enough to make life pleasant for them."

"Something is fishy here and I intend to find out what. This isn't the last you'll hear from me." The woman turned and left, and Bess called Art to tell him about the problem.

Within an hour, Sergeant Cummings had the complaint about the nursing home on his desk. He called Mrs. Blackwell and sent a car to pick her up for questioning. Within another hour the sergeant and Mrs. Blackwell were at the home. Bess had gone, but the other members of the Brigade held to the story of an outing. The police were told that the group had gone to the Seaquarium and would return in a few hours. Cummings felt uneasy and decided to check out the Seaquarium himself. A call was made to Art Perlman, who, upon hearing the news, instructed his people to leave the home in the care of the few regular people whom they had hired.

"No such group was here today." The words kept ringing in Sergeant Cummings' ears. Back at the home, he was told that a bus had taken several people out a few nights ago. He put the home under police guard and radioed for his office to begin checking bus charters for the night before last. This was the break he had been looking for in the case. Even though it wasn't Collins Avenue, he was sure it tied in somehow.

By Thursday morning the last of the people from the nursing home had been processed at the condo. All that remained was for the human commanders to be transformed, the equipment packed up, and the final trip out to the mother ship could take place.

Amos Bright met with Mr. DePalmer at the bank. Jack Fischer sat with them, signing the papers that made the Antares condominium complex his property, free and clear.

"Of course, Mr. Fischer, our bank will be delighted to assist you in any matters that you deem necessary. We are at your service." DePalmer was trying to make sure that he kept the business.

"I'm sure we can work things out, Mr. De-Palmer, and I'll rely on your help."

"Good. Let us know whenever you need anything." He gathered all the papers and checked them again to be sure things were in order.

Ralph Shields watched the meeting from the corner of the bank. Then he approached. "Mr. Bright, could I speak to you for a moment?"

DePalmer stood up. "This is a private meeting, Mr. Shields."

Amos stood, offering Shields his hand. "It's okay, Mr. DePalmer. Mr. Shields has something to say and I think we should listen. Yes, Mr. Shields?'

"Well, I wanted to say that I'm not the crazy

man you all think I am. Something is going on that I don't understand. I thought maybe you could tell me."

"Perhaps we can, Mr. Shields . . . perhaps we can. Why don't you come back to the office with us and we can talk this out?"

Shields was relieved. "Great. I'd hoped you would say that. I'll follow you in my car."

"Good," said Amos. "If you will excuse us for a moment, we have some business to complete. We will meet you outside in the parking lot."

Shields agreed and left.

"Mr. DePalmer, I want to thank you for all that you have done for me and for the Antares project. I know you will help Mr. Fischer, and I know the relationship will be of benefit to all."

"Are you leaving town?" the banker asked.

"I'm going away for a while. Mr. Fischer will know where I am."

"Have a good trip." DePalmer truly did wish his benefactor well.

"Yes, Mr. DePalmer. I believe I will. Good-bye."

• 47 •

"We are aliens!" Ben Green spoke to his nine group commanders. Mary, the Perlmans, the Finleys, Bernie Lewis, Betty Franklin, Rose Charnofsky – still called Aunt Rose – and Frank Hankinson had all been programmed as the Antareans had promised. They were all commanders!

"*Alien* is a strange word to use," said Mary.

"*Alien* is an alien word," answered Alma Finley. "What was strange before is not strange now. I cannot conceive of a life form of any kind as alien."

"True. It's only life," Joe Finley added. "We're not of this planet anymore."

Frank Hankinson stood and walked to the center of the processing room. "I feel as though . . . " He searched for words.

"As though you didn't belong?" asked Betty.

"As though I never belonged."

Aunt Rose spoke. "We did belong once and

now we have changed, but I, for one, can never forget how it was, and what I was before. Now we are grown."

"And we will grow even more! Isn't it wonderful?" Bess touched Art on the neck, close to the place where Beam had made the final incision.

Ben stood and surveyed the empty room. "How long ago it began . . . or so it seems."

All the new commanders understood.

"It's time," said Ben. "Amos is ready. The boats are approaching."

The commanders left the room that had changed their lives . . . silently.

Only the last words of nine hundred forty-one lives, meticulously transcribed and recorded for the human race, remained. Feelings about life from an expanded perspective. Messages from a new race to the old. Individuals speaking as one . . . asking that which any human could ask of another. They had come from many parts of the country, each with his own final reason: that special thought that gave them all the courage to reach into the unknown.

Many wrote to those they loved about love. Extra words and thought were for the grand-children and great-grandchildren. With their new awareness they knew the potential of a child's mind. They tried to reach it . . . to touch a place that would grow that mind beyond the narrowing influence of adults.

Is it curious that they came so readily? If you have grown old in this world, you understand a great deal about potential . . . human potential. You know the value of life and the wonderful gift that it carries. You have patience, even as you are discarded from the more "beautiful" people. We are a race which finds aging too painful a reminder of what we will become.

If one voice could speak for all of them, it would say, simply: "We have done this to help our fellow beings, because they asked us, and because they needed us."

• **48** •

Jack kept the stern of the *Manta III* tight to the front of the dock. *Terra Time*, captained by Arnie Fischer, berthed on the left. The *Razzmatazz*, with Phil Doyle on the flying bridge, snuggled close on the right.

"My God!" said Judy Simmons. "Is that Mr. Green? What happened to his head?"

"He's a commander now," answered Jack. There was a hushed respect in his voice. "They are all commanders."

Amos and Beam met the group of ten commanders at the top of the path. They all touched and gathered for a moment. *It's good*, thought Amos Bright. *What we have done is good.*

All responded in agreement. Then they walked slowly toward the dock.

Tony Stranger stood next to Ralph Shields on the deck of the *Razzmatazz* watching the procession approach. "This was worth being locked up for weeks. What a story! Look at them."

Shields couldn't answer. He was trying to recognize the previous tenants of the Antares condominiums, and he was walking a delicate line between the real and dream world.

Sandy touched Arnie's arm. "Oh, look at them. Aren't they glorious?"

He answered softly, "Special . . . I feel very special, honey."

The tranquil moment was suddenly broken by the crackle of Phil Doyle's radio and the simultaneous sound of Madman's chopper as it swooped over the pool and hovered over the dock. "Hey, you guys, this place is crawling with cops. They're coming in from all sides. You'd better haul ass out of there. They're armed and look like they mean business."

All the pieces had finally come into place for Detective Sergeant Cummings. The bus went to the Antares complex. The owner of the home lived at the Antares complex. There had been mysterious assaults at the Antares complex. The owners of the Antares complex had just sold the place . . . or actually had given the place away to a charter-boat captain. It took two days for all the information to filter through to

Cummings . . . then three hours to get a judge to issue the court order . . . and now he was here in force to capture the largest kidnapping ring in the history of the state of Florida . . . or so he thought!

As he came over the hill running in the direction of the helicopter, he saw the three cruisers, in single file, with engines at full throttle, moving away, up Red Lake Canal toward the main channel.

"Betters . . . you in the canal yet?" he shouted into his hand radio. A voice crackled back from the police boat at the end of the canal. "Roger, Sarge. We have it covered."

"Okay, watch it. There are three boats coming out at high speed."

"Got it. I see them."

The radio crackled and then let out a high-pitched hum, so severe that the sergeant had to turn off his radio.

Farther up the canal, one very expensive police launch beached onto a beautifully manicured lawn, crossed it, and stopped in a swimming pool.

"You did that rather well," Amos complimented Ben Green.

"We all did it, Amos," Ben answered. "But I don't think that's the last we will see of the police."

Sergeant Cummings was back at his car, on the radio to the Coast Guard. He described the boats and the chopper. He then called for another police launch to meet him at the municipal dock in Coral Gables. Whatever happened to Betters's launch, he didn't know, but he suspected that it was out of action.

As they cleared the wall, Phil picked up the Madman again. "They're on to us, Phil. I can hear the Coast Guard on the radio. They'll be in the air in ten minutes. Two cutters, also."

Ben Green took charge. "With your permission, Commander Bright."

"By all means, Commander," the Antarean answered. "It's your planet." Ben spoke to Mazuski on the radio. "Mr. Mazuski, can you let us know when the helicopters from the Coast Guard are in sight?"

"Roger."

"Good. Once you see them, clear the area. Let them come."

"You gonna do to them what you did to me and Phil?"

"Something like that. Keep an eye on the cutters for us. Okay?"

"You got it . . . Commander."

It was a strange sight, indeed: three charter boats unloading what appeared to be elderly people into the water. Two of the newest and most sophisticated Coast Guard jet helicopters suspended in midair above. And a small Sikorsky was circling the scene.

Sergeant Cummings put down the binoculars. "I'll be damned. What the hell is happening?" His launch rode to the south of the Coast Guard cutters, which were making thirty knots toward the scene. They could not raise their helicopters on the radio.

The last of the old people went over the side and disappeared beneath the green sea. The Coast Guard helicopters suddenly rose, as though released from a slingshot. It took a minute for the pilots to regain control of their aircraft.

The cutters and the launch approached the three pleasure boats with horns blaring and sirens wailing. The helicopters hovered lower and lower.

Then the ocean turned white.

All sound disappeared.

And the ocean began to glow.

A quarter-mile to the north, a huge white needle broke the surface. For three minutes the Antarean mother ship, a craft not of this world, slid from Earth's ocean, pointing upward, and became a dot that quickly blended into the fair Florida sky.

All the humans below heard a single voice in

their minds as the travelers sent their final message back to the sleeping Antarean cocoons below The Stones:

We will serve the Master for you now.
We are joined with you forever.
Sleep.
We Love You.

THORNDIKE PRESS HOPES you have enjoyed this Large Print book. All our Large Print titles are designed for the easiest reading, and all our books are made to last. Other Thorndike Press Large Print books are available at your library, through selected bookstores, or directly from the publisher. For more information about current and upcoming titles, please call us, toll free, at 1-800-223-6121, or mail your name and address to:

THORNDIKE PRESS
P. O. BOX 159
THORNDIKE, MAINE 04986

There is no obligation, of course.